Cover Art and Design by Gerrin Tramis

www.thewanderersnotebook.com

Undying Curiosity
Copyright 2022. All rights reserved.

ISBN: 978-1-7357249-2-8

Contents

Homeland 1

Double Vision 61

Outer Wilds 78

Pale Love 131

Cade 157

Journey Beyond II 183

Wyrm 227

Desert Flames 287

Appendix I 334

The Wanderer's Notebook Volume II

I

Homeland
Niwltir, -78 ER

The cool waters of the western sea that surrounded Cyfeiriad were themselves surrounded by the smooth stone walls of the cave tunnel. Reaching out with both hands, the sea elf gripped the ridges in the stone and used them to propel himself forward. His long white hair flowed behind him, while his mist grey eyes with faint, whisp-like traces of pale blue moved back and forth continuously, taking in every detail. Around his neck hung an intricate crystalline object filled with several powerful bioluminescent insects that bathed the undersea cave in a bright yellow-green glow. He was returning from a branch that had led nowhere and was eager to see what lay beyond the next bend.

He reached the fork and turned right, his mind mapping out the tunnels as he went. The tunnel was long and the burning in his lungs from holding his breath began to tug on his concentration. The idea of turning back and heading to the last cavern with air flashed through his mind but was quickly dismissed by an almost obsessive desire to know where this path led.

Cyfeiriad propelled himself faster, twisting and turning his body in sync with the tunnel. He was beginning to question the wisdom of his decision when he saw the next cavern.

With a final surge of strength and will, Cyfeiriad shot into the underground pool and burst through the water's surface. His mouth gaped open immediately as he gulped in as much air as he could.

After several deep breaths, Cyfeiriad looked around. The chamber was small. If he stretched out his fingers and toes, he could just barely reach the cavern's opposite walls.

Cyfeiriad relaxed his body and floated on his back. The air was still and peaceful. He couldn't stay long, as there wouldn't be enough air to sustain him indefinitely, but he could at least enjoy a brief moment of peace and quiet. His mind's eye traveled through the twisting tunnels of his mental map. A smile crept across his face as he relived the pleasure of exploration with the thrill of the unknown.

Heaving a sigh, the sea elf ceased floating, took a deep breath, and dove under the water. The trip back to the start of the underwater cave system was far quicker and less exciting than its reverse, though still enjoyable in its own right. He stopped in a few caverns along the way to catch his breath and eventually made his way to the entrance.

Pausing at the cave opening, he looked back and forth, scanning the dark depths for any signs of movement. Everything seemed clear, so he began to make his way toward the surface, exhaling as he rose.

A sudden sensation in the back of his mind caused him to twist and look behind him. A large, scaled beast with rows of four-inch-long teeth was swimming toward him. It turned its head to more easily clamp its open jaws on either side of Cyfeiriad's torso and surged forward. Cyfeiriad held out his hands as if to repel the attack. The end of the beast's jaws made contact with his palms, and he pulled his body up and out of the way as the creature swam through the space where he had been.

Before the creature could get too far, Cyfeiriad gripped its back with his hands and pulled his body close, so he could wrap his legs around it. The beast twisted and turned, trying to find where its prey had gone. After a few moments, it seemed to discern that it now had an unwanted passenger and dove straight down.

As soon as the beast entered its dive, Cyfeiriad pushed off and shot straight up. He exhaled air as he went, willing himself to rise through the water faster. Something tickled the back of his mind, and his eyes glanced down. The creature was now rising too. He looked back up and could see that he was nearing the surface. He wasn't sure if he could get back onto the boat before the beast caught up to him.

His attention began to turn back towards the creature, preparing to turn and attempt to evade it again, when something pulled him toward the surface. Cyfeiriad shot into the open air and up toward the boat's edge. He reached out with both hands and swung himself aboard only moments before the creature snapped its jaws above the surface.

Heaving a sigh of relief and attempting to catch his breath, Cyfeiriad looked around the medium-sized ship. He blinked. This wasn't his boat. And how had he risen so forcefully out of the water? He was a good swimmer, but not that good.

He turned to see Hyfrydmor watching him.

Hyfrydmor was an older female sea elf, though this age difference was more intuitively sensed than visually determined.

He watched as she stared at him with an almost stern expression before breaking into a wide grin and greeting him with a hug. She was only a couple inches shorter than him, with similar eyes and hair, though her hair was pulled back in a tight braid, while his was loose about his shoulders.

"I took the liberty of retrieving your map and kit while you were down there," she said, handing him a scroll case and pouch filled with quills and ink. "And your boots over there," she said with a nod toward the mast.

Eager to make his notes, Cyfeiriad sat down suddenly on the ship's deck, pulled out the scroll from its case, and unrolled it. He used the case and the pouch to pin down its ends and retrieved his writing implements from the pouch. He talked as he drew out the newly discovered passages, enjoying the cool breeze moving gently over the boat.

"Did you pull me up?" he asked.

"I'm here to take you to a special council of the Elders. Something is coming, and we must prepare," she replied coldly.

"That's not really an answer," he said, looking up from his work.

Hyfrydmor strode away from him and moved toward the helm.

"I've already arranged for your boat to be brought back to the harbor. Alarch headed back to the harbor with it as soon as I found your spot."

With a sigh, he finished his final notes and packed up his kit. He could feel the wind picking up and the boat gaining speed.

*   *   *

The wood elf crouched in the branches of an ancient tree in a dense forest, carefully examining the ground far below. Upper tree branches blotted out much of the sunlight, yet she easily focused her vision and read the details of the tracks beneath her. Her eyes were mist grey with whisp-like traces of yellow-brown in them. She was dressed mostly in leather, dyed various shades of green and brown. A quiver and a bundle of rope were strapped to her back. Hanging from her belt was a long dagger, and a recurve bow was clutched tightly in her right hand. Hela closed her eyes briefly, feeling the gentle breeze across her skin as she listened to the distant, heavy stomps of the razorback stag.

Turning swiftly and silently on the large branch, she then ran along one of its offshoots and silently leaped to the next tree. She continued this pattern, stopping every so often to re-examine the tracks below, until the creature came into sight. Hela crouched quietly on the branch and examined her prey.

Aptly named, razorback stags sported three lines of sharp, jagged spurs down their back. The blades of the central line started small on the creature's forehead and grew as they went down its back. The other two lines started just behind the ears and followed a similar course toward the tail. The tail was not a short bushy tail, but long, reaching about half-way to the ground, with its own row of spikes. It ended in a dagger-like blade of bone.

Hela estimated that this one was probably almost six feet tall at the shoulders with the full expanse of its antlers being about four feet across. Razorback stags didn't get to be this size without being clever, tough, and aggressive. This one was bigger than most. Its most vulnerable spot would be the throat, under the chin, where she could stab up into the brain or slice through its windpipe. That was where the hide was thinnest, but it was also easily protected by a tilted head, large antlers, and pounding hooves. She carefully moved away from the creature until she found a spot where she could drop to the ground and take careful aim at its flank and pierce its heart.

Hela's toes touched the ground, her ankles and knees bending freely to absorb the impact of her silent landing. The stag leaned its head down, grazing on the foliage. Without a sound, she removed an arrow and nocked it. Her prey's ears twitched casually.

Slowly, she pulled back the bow and found her target. She released the arrow.

The stag's body dropped several inches in a crouch, and the arrow missed its mark. The creature turned its great head toward her, lowered its antlers, and charged, bellowing as it tore through the undergrowth to get to the elf.

At the last second, Hela rolled to her right. The stag's antlers crashed into the tree and embedded themselves in the wood. As soon as her feet came under her again, she launched back towards the stag's neck, drawing her weapon in the process. Grabbing its antler with her right hand for support, she rammed her long dagger up into the creature's soft spot, twisting her torso to drive the thrust home. The creature shuddered and fell.

Hela examined her prey as she walked around it. She would divide up the beast and make use of it in a variety of ways. Most of the hide would be used for leather to repair her clothing and help keep her nest warm. Some of the meat would be prepared and stored for later. The intestines would become spare bow strings, and some of the spikes would become weapons. The rest that she didn't plan on using for herself, she would take back to the citadel and give away as pleased any elf she met along the way.

A twig snapped above her. Without thought, she turned, drew an arrow, nocked it, and aimed for the source of the sound. To her surprise, a wood elf Elder stood stoically on a branch, holding the twig he'd just snapped in his hands. He was dressed similarly to herself. His eyes were like hers and his hair was black, tucked behind his pointed ears. She lowered her bow and opened her mouth to greet him.

Her voice cracked in her throat, and she realized she hadn't spoken aloud in in several decades. She switched tactics and signed her greeting through the silent wood elf language of hand gestures and facial expressions. The wood elf Elder signed a greeting in reply and jumped down to stand closer to her.

"I apologize for disturbing the rewards of your hunt, but we must return to the citadel for an urgent meeting of the Elder Council," he continued silently.

"Has something happened?" she signed in return.

"There is a wedded pair not far from here who recently gave birth. I suggest we give them the stag, so they can spend more time with their newborn child. Take your cut for the road, and let's move this up into the higher branches before we go inform them."

Hela tilted her head and looked at him quizzically, but the older wood elf just went about tying a length of rope to the creature and hauling its carcass into the trees. She deftly climbed after it and removed a fair-sized chunk of meat and one of the large spines.

Hela wrapped her cut in some large leaves as the two silently moved among the branches and disappeared into the forest.

* * *

A large mountain stood on the western coast of the elvish continent; its features carved to the designs of its inhabitants. Roads spiraled up its slopes, covered by stone awnings supported on their outermost edges by a series of pillars. The various dwellings were carved along the inner walls of these paths and delved to varying degrees into the mountain itself. The peak had a large bowl-shaped structure that collected rainwater, which was then spiraled down the slopes in numerous aqueducts to bring water to dwellings and to narrow, soil-filled containers that lined the outer edges of the paths between the pillars. These containers allowed for gardens from which small plants grew and provided food, such as fruits, vegetables, berries, spices, and herbs.

The stone structures were carved and decorated with designs inspired by nature. Pillars had been carved to resemble vine-wrapped trees, with their bases carved as roots and their tops carved as branches that faded into the arched awnings. The walls along the inner edge of the paths were carved with scenes of plants and animals, mostly terrestrial, but some aquatic. Small carvings of elvish script that served either artistic or practical significance appeared on the sides of the pathway gardens and sometimes along the walls or pillars.

Gwyddoniaeth sat hunched over a worktable, gently placing a gear into position, while the faint sounds of hammer blows drifted through the thick cloth hanging over the doorway. Her black hair was held back by an intricate metal clasp. Her eyes were mist grey with whisp-like traces of red-orange. The air was still in the room, much to her liking, as it provided less of a distraction or hindrance to her delicate work. Three of the four walls were covered with shelves filled with a variety of codices and scrolls. The worktable was on the same wall as the doorway leading to the greeting room. To her left, a breach in the bookshelves allowed entry from the cloth-covered doorway to the forge room.

Inside the forge room, Gwyddoniaeth's brother, Ymchwil, worked patiently as he shaped the steel before him with his hammer. When the steel in hand had cooled to the point that it was no longer malleable, he would place it back in the forge and pull out one of the other pieces that had been sitting on the hot coals, awaiting their turn. His eyes and hair were similar to his sister's in color, but his hair was cut short.

The forge itself was in the corner farthest away from the doorway to the study. Thick cloths hung along the entire wall that was shared with the study to better dampen the noise of the forge. Most of the rest of the walls were filled with either tools or finished projects. A venting tunnel rose above the forge and traveled unseen overhead to the world beyond.

Gwyddoniaeth finished placing the final gear and began attaching the cover plate. The device she was finishing was an intricate metal frame that would house a new blank book. The high elves each carried their own journals with similar clockwork frames. The construct around the book contained a time-keeping device, an inkwell, a quill, and a small knife. It also had a locking mechanism to hold it all together when traveling.

A slight knock on the exterior door of their dwelling broke Gwyddoniaeth's focus on her device, and she turned to look through the doorway of the study into the greeting room. She carefully placed her tools and the next piece of the mechanism down on the work bench before answering the door. In the greeting room, the exterior door was to her left, and a doorway to her right led back to the kitchen and bedrooms. She opened the exterior door.

A wood elf smiled at her from the path outside.

Recognizing Llwynog, she began to sign to him in the wood elf custom.

"Don't worry, we can speak out loud," he said. "I've brought you some new specimens that might interest you."

"Oh, we greatly appreciate your generosity. Please come in," she said as she stepped aside and gestured him into the study.

"Welcome back, Llwynog," said Ymchwil as he came out of the forging room to greet their guest.

The three elves gathered around a small table off to one side, and the wood elf began to empty his pack. He placed various bottles of leaves, seeds, liquids, and insects on the table. Each was labeled as best as possible so that any samples from the same general source or location could be easily associated later.

"We thank you greatly for this collection," said Ymchwil as he eagerly examined the glass bottles.

"We have something for you as well," said Gwyddoniaeth as she strode across the room to the work bench. She retrieved a small clockwork device, came back to the table, and handed it to the wood elf.

"What is it?" he asked as he turned it over in his fingers.

"It's an experimental device that we hope could be used as a firestarter," replied Gwyddoniaeth.

"Please, let us know how well it works in the field, how weather affects it, and any suggestions you may have after your trials," added Ymchwil.

The wood elf pressed a button on the side of the device. Inside, a pin attached to the button changed position. Without its presence, a fly wheel was free to spin, which allowed the mainspring to turn both it and the rest of the gears in the device. A series of gears led to a small magnet that began to spin rapidly next to small, tightly wound coils of wire. These wires lead to other coils of varying numbers of loops before eventually leading to two prongs at the top of the device. A small arc of electricity jumped across the gap between the prongs and remained there with a steady buzz.

"Amazing!" breathed the wood elf. "It's like stationary, consistent lightning. Thank you very much for this new device."

"We also have replacement specimen containers for your next trip," added Ymchwil, removing a tray of glass jars from a shelf and setting it on the table next to the wood elf's pack.

The trio continued to discuss the device, the samples, and their plans for the future for some time before the visiting wood elf made his farewell and departed.

After placing the specimens on the examination table, Gwyddoniaeth and Ymchwil returned to their previous tasks, eager to complete them so they could study the new specimens.

A short time later, their progress was interrupted by another guest.

Gwyddoniaeth eagerly welcomed the high elf Elder Cariadllyfr.

"Thank you, but I am not here to stay. Instead, I have come to summon you to a council of the elders," he said as he stepped inside.

Gwyddoniaeth turned to retrieve her brother, but Ymchwil was already exiting the forge room. He removed his protective leather apron and hung it on the wall next to the door to the forge room. He picked up a belt from which hung a knife, several pouches, a codex, and some scrolls.

Gwyddoniaeth, having not been working near fire, had a similar belt on already.

Both elves quickly and quietly fell into step behind Cariadllyfr, as he silently turned and left their rooms.

*   *   *

Hela sat on a stone chair in a hallway deep inside the mountain of the high elves. Despite the chair being carved of stone, it was reasonably comfortable to sit in due to its thick seat cushion.

Saethydd had led her here and told her to wait outside the council chamber, while he conferred with the other Elders. The Elders were the first-born elves, and as such, were actually the living ancestors of every elf alive. They were not rulers but acted as parents and grandparents to their descendants. As far as Hela knew, they did not all gather very often, and never had there been any sense of urgency or dread.

She never really liked visiting the mountain of the high elves. Though they carved trees and vines into their walls and columns, even in these deep tunnels, it wasn't the same as being in the actual forest. Even the trees, bushes, and vines that they grew along one side of the paths that spiraled up the mountain weren't enough. Also, she was not fond of there being so many elves in one place; it was too social and crowded for her taste. Even high elves tended to keep to themselves, but she could sense their presence too much and it annoyed her. She much preferred the solitude of the forest.

Hela decided to occupy herself by observing the three other elves waiting in the hall with her.

To her right, on the other side of the hall, sat a sea elf who seemed unable to be still. He was constantly shifting in his chair, and his eyes scanned the walls around them. At least he was quiet and trying to be observant, even though he seemed restless. His hair was roughly shoulder length and white, like many of the sea elves. When he glanced her way, she could see his eyes were those typical of the sea elves. His clothes were simple: shirt, trousers, boots, and belt. It was common for sea elves to dive and swim, so their clothes tended to be easy to remove or replace. His belt held a knife, a small pouch that most likely contained writing implements, and a scroll case. They were also fond of map making, preferring the thrill of exploring for themselves as opposed to learning what others had seen first.

Across the hall to her left sat two high elves. Their hair was black, their eyes typical of the high elves. They had been silent the entire time they were there. At first, they spent some time reading books they had brought, but once they finished, they folded their hands and stayed almost completely motionless, looking forward with backs straight. She appreciated their stillness, but the way they stared at the wall ahead of them seemed odd. It was almost as if they had become living statues. Their clothes were elaborately crafted with multiple layers and subtly embroidered designs. They wore tabards over tunics and trousers above boots that were far less scuffed and worn than hers or the sea elf's. A knife, several pouches, and a book hung from each of their belts.

Hela's mind drifted to her own posture, relaxed and leaning back into the chair with her arms draped over the arm rests. She noticed that her fingers curled in an almost claw-like fashion as they hung out over the stone. While her head and eyes moved to observe her comrades, the rest of her body was still. Her own clothes were mostly leather that she had harvested and fashioned from her kills, dyed in shades of green and brown. Her boots were well worn, but still in good condition. She had set her quiver, rope, and bow on the floor next to her and leaned them against the wall. Her own belt held many pouches, a knife, and a dagger.

After several hours, the doors to the council chamber finally opened and a high elf Elder stepped out to greet them.

"Thank you for waiting so patiently. Please join us in the council chamber," he said, turning to the side and gesturing for them to enter.

Hela was quickest to her feet, followed closely by the eager sea elf. The two younger high elves brought up the rear, heads bowed slightly.

She had never been in the council chamber before. It was a high, domed room with a series of pillars forming a sort of cloister around its outer perimeter. Three large tables were positioned inside, each forming roughly one third of the arc of a giant ring. Lamps filled with bright bioluminescent insects hung from the tops of the pillars, above the tables, and above the open space in the center of the circle.

She and the others walked between two of the tables to stand in the center of the circle.

"Thank you for joining us," said one of the Elders. "We have summoned you on the advice our guest."

Hela noticed another figure standing off to the side behind the seated Elders. It looked like an elf, but unlike any elf she had seen, this one had golden metallic eyes. Somewhere, deeper in the shadows, she saw the yellow-green glow of one of the insects reflected off cupped hands. A pair of eyes glanced up at her briefly. The eyes were completely black with metallic blue irises. She did not recognize either newcomer nor sense any hostility or danger about them.

Her thoughts were interrupted as the Elders began to speak.

"The four of you have been chosen for specific tasks based on your individual aptitudes," began Cariadllyfr. The Enemy has returned. As of yet, he is not at full strength. We do not know when or if he will choose to attack, but we must begin to prepare in case he does."

Hela noticed grave looks on the faces of the young high elves and their gazes shifted to the ground. The young sea elf blinked in surprise at the news. Hela attempted to remain impassive.

"Cyfeiriad and Hela are tasked with learning the secrets of the mist, so that our people may flee safely to new lands should the need arise," said Hyfrydmor.

"We don't know from whence the attack will come or when. We may need to escape by sea or through the forest. We must be prepared for both," added Saethydd.

"Gwyddoniaeth and Ymchwil, you are to be living vessels of the knowledge and wisdom of the Elders," stated Cariadllyfr.

"How do we know that he won't attack tomorrow?" asked Hela.

"He is currently in a weakened state and is lacking both his memories and a great portion of his power," replied Hyfrydmor. "This is his opportunity to return to The Narrow Path."

"What about everyone else?" asked the young sea elf.

"Messengers will be sent to the surrounding islands and deep into the forest. It will take time to reach everyone.

While you carry out your missions, we will organize everyone else to prepare for various contingencies."

"We know that this news may seem dire, but do not allow fear or anxiety to rule your minds as you go forth," counseled Saethydd.

Hela and the others nodded. The four of them left the council chamber pondering what might lie ahead.

*   *   *

Cyfeiriad stood in his boat, facing the mist wall, and feeling the gentle, cool breeze wash over him. He tied a rope around his waist that had its other end tied to the boat. The boat itself was anchored into its place in the sea. He had spent half the morning staring into the mist, trying to see through it to no avail. Now it was time to explore it directly.

The sea elf dove over the side of the boat and swam into the mist. As the view above the water quickly faded into the shifting grey, images of vaguely seen large underwater predators flashed through his mind. He pushed his head under the water and noticed that the normally darkening depths had been replaced by the same fog as above. Resurfacing, he continued deeper into the mist.

There were no visible clues as to the passage of time within the mist, and Cyfeiriad even found himself lacking any internal sense of its passing as well. He continued for an unknown amount of time and distance until he finally realized that he couldn't feel the water anymore.

Pausing, Cyfeiriad looked around. The same grey mist surrounded his legs as that which surrounded his arms and head. He moved his arms a few times, as if swimming through the mist. He sensed his own movement but with no reference points to verify the sensation. The interesting part was that even though he felt like he moved, he didn't feel like his arms or hands had pushed against anything for it to happen.

Looking down at the disappearing view of his legs and feet, he tried to take a step.

He sensed that he moved again but didn't feel resistance from anything. He lowered his arms to his sides and did not sink. No water rushed to surround or choke him. Cyfeiriad continued to stride forward into the mist.

Again, he had no idea how much time passed as he wandered back and forth in the limitless fog. He had attempted to travel in a straight line but found nothing. He then began to intentionally change directions, what he imagined would be a zigzag pattern, but still there was nothing.

Maybe there wasn't anything here, or perhaps there was nothing on the other side. What if the mists were endless? Would he be lost in here forever? A certain fear and dread began to creep in around the edges of his mind as he realized that he had no sense of his position or what direction he was facing. The absence of his usual sense of position and direction was concerning.

At least there's the rope, he thought, fingering it nervously with one hand.

A wood elf he had once met had mentioned that forest animals, if chased, would refuse to enter the mist. They would move back and forth away from it and closer again as their panic and anxiety mounted. The approaching predator that could be seen was somehow less terrifying than what lay beyond the borders of the mist, and the terrified creature then rushed headlong into the predator's jaws.

Visions of undefinable horrors flashed through his mind. His eyes began to dart, and his head began to snap back and forth as he looked for non-existent threats.

That was when he sensed it. There was something in the mist. He couldn't see where or what, but he could feel it.

Cyfeiriad grabbed the rope and ran, pulling himself along as fast as he could. He heard an annoyed snarl from behind and moved faster. Everything in him focused on reaching the sea.

Cyfeiriad fell into the water with a loud splash. He resurfaced and blinked, looking around. Although it was dark, he quickly located the boat-shaped hole in the stars and swam toward it. Grasping the edge, he heaved himself onto it and lay on his back, panting. He hadn't even realized he was breathing so hard until that moment.

He waited.

Nothing happened. No monsters reached out of the mists or the sea to devour him. Thankfulness washed over him, and he sat up to look at the mist in the night. Unsurprisingly, it was just as visually impenetrable now as it had been in the day. He sighed, lay down, and fell asleep.

The next morning Cyfeiriad drifted awake as the sun's rays began creeping over the edge of the boat and onto his face. He washed himself in the sea and pondered what had happened.

There was no time or space in the mist, at least not of the sort that he was used to. Something did live in there, but it was not all powerful. He had escaped it. Perhaps he could even fight it. He had made it out. The rope had worked as a guide back to the normal world.

But he had also been focused, very focused on reaching the sea. He also hadn't felt any ground under his feet or water against any of his limbs. There had only been the rope and his focus.

He looked up at the mist and realized that it was farther away from his boat than it had been the day before. He checked the anchor, and it was still secure. The boat had not moved. Had the mists receded?

Cyfeiriad pondered all these things, somewhat analyzing, while waiting for an idea to present itself.

After much thought, he stood up, untied the rope, and checked his belt. He still had his knife and map making kit. He fingered the knife with his left hand. If needed, he could retrieve it quickly.

Cyfeiriad pulled up the anchor and rowed his boat so that the tip was just inside the mist. He lowered the anchor and stood up.

He inhaled deeply and released, allowing all fear and doubt to drop out of his mind. His steps were calm and sure as he stepped from the boat and walked into the mist.

* * *

Hela's journey through the upper levels of the forest to the mist wall ended in the middle of the afternoon after many weeks of travel. She had brought along extra supplies, since she did not know how long her journey through the mist would take.

She stood on a thick, high branch that reached out into the mist and then examined what lay before her. A gentle breeze made its way through the branches and twisted the leaves. The mist wall stood as a solid wall of fog rising from the ground and reaching as far into the sky as she could see. Branches and roots extended and disappeared into the fog.

Tying a rope around her waist, she carefully proceeded along the branch and into the mist. Almost immediately, the forest became invisible, replaced by shifting greys and still air; so too was the branch beneath her. Not wanting to accidentally step into the air, she crouched and placed one hand out in front of her, so she would have three points of contact with her support.

Immediately she noticed that she did not feel the branch. There was no sensation of rough bark beneath her fingertips. She moved her hand to touch the area near her feet. Again, there was no sensation of bark, even though her fingers were flush with the edge of her boot. She crouched on nothing, yet she was not falling either. How could the branch simply cease to exist? When she had been outside the mist, there had been no signs that the branch was broken or cut.

Hela very carefully pivoted on her toes while maintaining her crouched position. Her mental map said that the rest of the branch should now be in front of her, and she did not want to accidentally step off it as she exited the mists. She slowly pulled on the rope until it was taut and made her way back.

The forest exploded into view and her foot slipped. She dropped the rope and grabbed the branch with both hands until she was certain that only one foot was dangling in open air. Closing her eyes, she breathed a sigh of relief.

A moment later, she was walking swiftly and confidently along the branch and back to the trunk of the tree. Tomorrow she would enter the mist from the ground. Now it was time for rest.

Hela's eyes snapped open at the sound of a muffled animal cry and breaking twigs only to be greeted by the darkness of the nighttime forest. She quietly placed her palms on the wide branch she had fallen asleep on face down. Her legs dangled on either side of the branch, and she gently pushed herself up, raising her head from the soft leather blanket she had used to protect her skin from the bark. She untied the rope at her waist that connected her to the tree and drew up her legs into a crouched position.

She alternated peering over either side of the branch as she moved forward silently. A dragging noise caught her attention, and she looked down to see a large, strange creature dragging a deer carcass backward toward the mists.

The creature was jet black and appeared to be covered in fur. The creature's body seemed to absorb all light, the fur only being distinguishable by the shape of the silhouette, as there were no reflections on the hairs from the moonlight. Its tail was thicker and more agile than a panther or wolf, switching and twitching back and forth, as if feeling for obstacles that the creature could not see while moving backward. The ears were large and pointed, vaguely resembling oversized bat ears more than anything else. It had four legs like most animals, but she noticed that when it grabbed the deer with its front paws, it could rotate its forelegs in the shoulder in a way that elves could, but wolves could not. The creature's claws were long and curved, seeming to flex in and out more like a cat. Its eyes glowed red and were not merely reflective in the moonlight.

As she watched it move past her vantage point and closer to the mist, she realized that the mist seemed farther away than it had the previous day. She took a quick look at the branch which had previously been her entry point and saw that there were indeed several more feet of it visible now.

She turned back and watched the beast as it reached the edge of the mist. The beast and its prey faded from sight as it moved backward beyond the edge of the wall. An image of a golden thread leading from the forest to the beast flashed through her mind.

Hela spent the next day hunting. The first deer she found, she killed and brought back to the mist wall. The wall had receded several more yards from her camp while she slept the previous night. She strung up the carcass and lifted it high off the forest floor.

The second deer she hunted, she chased into a net. This had not been easy, as the animal had changed its direction frequently, and it had taken a while to steer the deer into the trap. Once she had it, she tied a rope around its neck, freed it from the net, and led it back to the mist wall. She wasn't sure whether dead meat or live would make the best bait.

Hela made her preparations for the night to come. She laid nets and snares all over the ground, surrounding the carcass and the live deer. The wood elf made sure that both traps were far enough apart on either side of a great tree so that the living deer could not see the carcass. She readied an exceptionally thin rope with strands of metal in it. Hopefully the creature would not be able to chew through this.

As night approached, she gutted the dead deer and flung some of its entrails into the mist, leaving a small trail of blood and gore to where the carcass now hung closer to the ground.

Hela took her position in the trees and waited. Hours passed with nothing but the sounds of the living deer pacing or eating. She was almost considering that perhaps it might take several nights, when shadows moved below.

One of the creatures emerged from the mist. It sniffed at the trail of guts and made its way to the hanging carcass. The creature looked at it and walked around it in a circle. It sniffed the hanging deer a couple times and then stood up on hind legs. Its front paws grasped the deer and pulled down hard. As the carcass fell, Hela activated the trap, and the edges of the large net flew into the air.

The creature was quickly smashed up against the deer and began flailing about inside the dangling net. Hela nocked her poisoned arrow and drew back the bow only a fraction of its full capacity. She wanted to pierce its hide, but only into the muscle. She did not want to kill it. The arrow was released and thudded into the creature's well-muscled shoulder. A few moments later, it stopped moving and hung limp in the net.

Hela moved through the branches and gently lowered her prey to the ground. The creature was sleeping soundly, but she didn't know for how long. She quickly untangled the net and attached a harness around the beast's chest and shoulders. The harness was connected to the thin, partially metallic cord, which was in turn tied to one of the trees.

Leaving the beast to sleep off the tranquilizer, Hela made her way to the where the live deer was tied up. She patted its head gently and cut the rope. The deer immediately dashed off into the forest.

Returning to her perch in the trees, she waited patiently, watching the sleeping beast.

Roughly an hour passed before the creature stirred. It raised its head, looked around confusedly, and noticed the cord. It tried to bite through it but was unsuccessful. Giving up, it turned its attention to the deer carcass. A few sniffs and nibbles convinced it that the meat was safe, and it began to drag it back into the mist.

Hela waited several minutes after it had disappeared before dropping to the ground and touching the cord.

It was time to see if this beast would be her key through the mist. She took a length of rope and tied herself to the cord.

Hela stepped into the mist wall and vanished.

*   *   *

Gwyddoniaeth and Ymchwil followed Cariadllyfr through the forest near the base of the high elf mountain citadel. He moved quickly through the dense underbrush, leaping and climbing as necessary to make his way forward as directly as possible.

After some time, they arrived in a clearing, its outer border littered with stones, many of which were a foot or more in diameter. The stone scattering gave the impression of ruins, but there was only one destroyed stone structure with which she was familiar, and it was closer to the harbor. As Gwyddoniaeth looked around, she noticed that some of what she had originally thought were smaller stones were, in fact, the shattered remains of larger ones. None of them looked like they had once been part of a larger, more organized structure.

Inside the irregular ring of trees and rocks was a well-worn, partially overgrown, low, circular platform made of cut stone slabs. The surrounding trees were tall and thick enough that the air was relatively still in the clearing. Gwyddoniaeth followed Cariadllyfr onto the platform and patiently awaited his instructions.

"While your peers learn the secrets of the mist and my siblings seek out our children to prepare them, you two will learn what, so far, only the Elders have discovered."

You will learn, my young children, how to extend your mind past your physical form.

Gwyddoniaeth's eyes widened as she heard the words but realized Cariadllyfr's lips were not moving. She glanced at her brother and their eyes met in astonishment.

"How did you do that?" they both said in unison.

Cariadllyfr raised a hand and gestured slowly in an upward direction off to one side. They turned to follow his gaze.

Gwyddoniaeth was once again amazed, but this time by what she saw instead of heard. One of the large rocks was smoothly and slowly rising into the air in sync with Cariadllyfr's hand.

"That's amazing," she whispered.

"I can't wait to learn these things, but why haven't we been taught them already or why hasn't anyone else?" asked Ymchwil.

"My brothers and sisters and I slowly discovered these abilities by many means, and it has taken us centuries to master them. Some began to wonder what was possible when they pondered how they could sometimes sense an approaching elf or animal. Others noticed that when they lost their balance, they would thrust a hand forward to catch themselves but would not actually fall. And still others just wondered if extending the mind in such ways was possible, so they started trying. We didn't tell the younger elves, because we were still learning and reasoned you would one day learn it for yourselves. Our lives are peaceful, so we thought allowing you the joy of self-discovery would be acceptable. Unfortunately, events may transpire to limit or distract from that possibility. Your task is to master these skills and pass them on. I will explain and train you as best as I can, but you must also meditate on how you learned and which explanations worked best. No matter how intuitively the skills come, you must understand exactly how they work, so you can best teach them to the others."

The elf Elder paused, then continued in a more serious tone, "Never forget that no matter how far you come in wisdom or ability, if you stray from The Narrow Path, then it will all be for nothing."

Gwyddoniaeth looked down for a moment in thought.

"Sometimes, the way you speak sounds as if you and the other Elders might not be here to teach us or help us in the future. How could that be?"

Cariadllyfr sighed, a look of sadness quickly moving over his features and vanishing into a gentle smile. "Even though we were young, we could still see the violence and hatred in the Enemy all those centuries ago. If we have grown stronger, presumably he has as well. If we are wrong and he chooses The Narrow Path, then our children will live in peace with greater skill and knowledge, but if he does not and we do nothing, then we could all die."

Gwyddoniaeth stood silently pondering this. For the first time, she felt a real fear and dread about the future. It was deeper and darker than the anxiety of ruining a project or the fear of injury when near a predatory animal. If something so horrible that it could and would destroy the elves really existed, would they ever really be safe? They had no experience with such things, and if they lost their mentors, how could they hope to survive?

A loud crack shattered her thoughts, and her head snapped to see the now broken remains of the rock that Cariadllyfr had been holding in the air.

"Lesson number one: Do not let the fear and doubt consume you."

* * *

Hela had no way to know how long she had been following the shadowbeast through the mist. She had given it this name while seemingly wandering in circles.

The wood elf would follow the cord only for it to suddenly be pointing in the opposite direction, so she would turn to face it. Then her forward movement would be stopped by the pressure of the cord cutting straight across her thighs. Sometimes it wasn't a horizontal line, as the cord angled up or down. The strangest part was that if she stood still and waited, the cord didn't move to change direction; it would just suddenly be pointing in that new direction.

Perhaps it is incredibly fast or can teleport, she thought to herself.

Hela decided to wait and count. There was no other way to measure the passage of time. Every couple hundred counts, the rope would change direction. One time it remained stationary for almost one thousand counts but soon after returned to its more scattered behavior.

She waited. As soon as the rope was stationary for 300 counts, she took off along the cord. She simply had to reach it this time.

The shadowbeast stood before her. She saw its blue glowing eyes quickly switch to red as she appeared in front of it. The creature's fur bristled, and it growled at her.

Hela took a step back, holding out one hand in front of her and making what she hoped were soothing noises. The creature lunged.

The wood elf swiftly sidestepped the attack, drew her dagger, and slashed the shadowbeast across the shoulder.

Obviously unaccustomed to prey that was so willing to fight back, the creature turned and vanished.

Hela waited again. She realized that the patience she had learned on the hunt was proving useful in this situation.

The next time the cord was stationary, she caught up to it again. And again, it vanished. The shadowbeast was obviously more well-adjusted to the mist than she was, making her efforts futile. Gripping the rope, Hela made her way back to the forest.

As she followed the cord back to the tree, she had an idea. Instead of following the creature, she could bring it to her.

* * *

Cyfeiriad stepped out of the mist and fell into the ocean. He laughed in exaltation. He had successfully entered and exited the mist without a tether.

After a few moments of treading water, he looked around. He could feel a nice breeze, but he couldn't see land anywhere nearby. Deciding that it would be easier with his boat, he swam back into the mist and started walking.

Cyfeiriad fell into the water beside his boat. He climbed in and rowed it into the mist.

His boat exited the mist into what he hoped was an uncharted sea. He set aside the oars and sailed away from the mist wall. The wind was at his back, and he made good time, enjoying the breeze and the spray of water as he continued forward.

Eventually, land came into view. Several minutes later, he leaped out of his boat and dragged it up onto the sandy beach.

He did not recognize the beach or what he could see of the coastline in either direction. As he had approached the shore, he had noticed heavily forested mountain ranges off in the distance. The elvish homeland did not have such ranges. With eager excitement, he walked into the forest, his head swiveling back and forth at his new surroundings.

*   *   *

Naga lazily sunned herself on the rocky outcroppings on the shore of the draconian continent. The warmth of the sun on her back and partially outstretched wings was relaxing while the periodic spray from the waves provided her with a pleasant coolness.

The dragon was a large creature with four legs, a tail, and two large, batlike wings. Her body was covered in scales with a line of spikes running from just between her eyes down her back and along her tail. The colors of her scales shifted slightly to more closely match the dark rocks beneath and around her.

Naga awoke to the sounds of squawking and miniature roars. She opened her eyes, lifted her head slightly, and turned to see three young dragons approaching the shore farther down the coastline. They were accompanied by two adult dragons who alternated watching the young ones and surveying their surroundings. Very few things could realistically hope to threaten a dragon, but protective parental instincts ran strong. The young ones pounced on each other, leaped away, and pounced again as they moved closer and closer to the water. Eventually, they were rolling around in the shallows, playful noises mixing with the sounds of the waves.

It had been many years since Naga had last hatched her own children. She thought fondly of them as she watched the family play in the surf.

After some consideration, Naga rose onto all fours. She stretched her wings to their fullest a couple times to shake off some of the water. She stretched her back legs and then her front legs. Spreading her wings, she took to the sky.

She climbed until she reached a height where she could see much of the landscape, but she remained low enough that she could see what swam beneath the waves. The old dragon gently flew back and forth, gradually moving away from the shore until she spotted what she was seeking. Far below her was a large shark.

Naga dove into the water and came back up carrying the writhing shark. Angling her wings, she turned back toward the shore. As she approached the family, she released the shark and let it fall onto the beach before landing a few feet away.

The parents looked at her and turned their bodies to fully face her. She knew it was only a precautionary readiness in case of attack and ignored them. The young ones stopped playing and stared at the shark.

Naga bent down and bit off the shark's head. She swallowed her piece, then tossed the rest gently towards the young ones with her left front paw. She bowed her head low to them and then the parents before taking a few steps back. The adults tilted their heads slightly in acknowledgement.

Naga turned and flew off. She sailed high over the trees and toward the mountains. The landscape of the draconian continent was mostly dense forest broken by several large mountain ranges converging on an enormous, long-dormant volcano. Dragons of various sorts had their homes in caves, on rocky cliffs, in deep valleys, and in hollows both high in the mountains and deep in the forests.

As she approached the central volcano, she noticed a group of dragons circling in the sky. She flew closer to see what they were doing. They were all looking down, searching intently for something.

Naga looked in the same direction, unsure of what could be so interesting. Then she spotted it.

A small bipedal creature was walking through the forest toward the mountains.

She and the other dragons followed its approach and landed just above the tree line as the creature drew near.

Naga leaned her head down to peer at it, as it stood between the trees. It was being cautious, which was wise, considering the size and power of Naga and her companions.

From this position, she could see the creature's soft skin and pointy ears. She could see its shoulder-length hair and the strange things it wore on its body. Naga had once seen creatures like this, but she knew to avoid and not hunt them. The dragons left all the little squishy, un-furred bipeds alone, and generally didn't even hunt in those creatures' realms.

As a gesture of good will, she folded her wings and lay down flat on the ground. The other dragons did the same. After some time, the creature exited the forest. It slowly approached Naga and gently reached out a hand to touch her snout. Its eyes, metallic golden irises streaked with red and green, gazed up at her.

The bipedal creature was as soft and weak as it looked. She could barely feel the pressure of its touch. This creature was harmless. Her lips parted and she gently licked her new pet.

* * *

Ymchwil stared at the large stone ahead of him. His mind was holding it roughly ten feet in the air and about twenty feet away from him. On the stone floor of the training area, underneath the large rock, sat his sister, Gwyddoniaeth.

"Why do we have to do this? It seems unnecessarily dangerous," said Ymchwil.

A sharp pain interrupted his concentration, and the boulder dropped several inches before his mind returned to its proper target.

I don't remember giving you permission to speak, came the now harsh thoughts of Cariadllyfr. Ymchwil could feel the irritation rising in him. Years had passed, and Cariadllyfr's training had become noticeably harsher of late; if Ymchwil had been calm enough to realize it, this change was making him angry because he was so unused to it.

Why take such risks? Ymchwil corrected himself.

Your lives have been easy, and you have not faced the truly horrible things that exist in creation. Those things are likely to come crashing down on us in one form or another. On a practical level, you need to be able to maintain your skills regardless of the harshness of the situation, as many lives may depend on it. On a moral level, you must also learn to control yourself, regardless of the pain or anger you may experience.

But she is my sister. Isn't this taking it a bit too far?
I wish it was.

Something large and hard hit Ymchwil in the back. He fell to one knee and reached out a hand toward the boulder, stopping it after it had fallen another couple feet. He turned his head to face Cariadllyfr, relaxing and expanding his awareness both to his left with his sister and to his right with Cariadllyfr while maintaining awareness of everything he was doing. If his mind was exclusively in any one place or nowhere at all, then he would fail.

Ymchwil raised his right hand and pushed forward. Cariadllyfr only smiled as he shifted back almost imperceptibly. Several large rocks rose beside the Elder before beginning to move continuously around the perimeter of the clearing.

The first projectile came from slightly behind. Ymchwil twisted his torso without moving his feet and swung his hand through the air horizontally, sending the rock flying off to one side.

He still held the boulder over his sister.

Then another projectile shot forward, this one from slightly in front. Ymchwil immediately twisted back and thrust his palm forward, the force of his mind knocking it off course so that it landed harmlessly elsewhere.

His mind still held the boulder.

Not giving him time to breathe, Cariadllyfr sent several rocks toward him at once. Irritation at the excessive concentration test and the unfairness of this position shot through Ymchwil. His right hand shot out and his mind gripped all of the projectiles when they were only an arm's length away. The rocks then shattered into dust and debris.

A pity about your sister, mused Cariadllyfr.

Fear and horror washed over Ymchwil, and he whirled around, images of blood seeping out from under the boulder flooding his mind. That was when he saw the boulder begin to fall.

Both hands reached out and he stepped forward to catch it with his mind, his body moving in sync with his will. The boulder stopped inches over her head.

Rage filled Ymchwil; Cariadllyfr had distracted him intentionally. The elf Elder had almost caused Gwyddoniaeth's death.

In fury, Ymchwil spun around, lifting one hand and the boulder high overhead. Seeing Cariadllyfr's smirking face made him angrier, and he brought down his hand in an arc. The boulder hurtled toward Cariadllyfr.

Stop! Came the mental shout from Gwyddoniaeth.

Ymchwil moved his hand slightly, shifting the course of the boulder at the last second so that it landed to Cariadllyfr's left without harming him.

That, my students, is the hardest lesson to learn. Not the concentration to move things with your mind while also focusing in multiple directions, but the choice between The Narrow Path and destruction. Any of us can be tempted. As you go forth through the ages, those temptations will play on your natural emotions and reactions. Pain, anger, and fear are natural reactions, which have their place. Be careful not to let them control you or, worse yet, to fester inside, twisting themselves into hatred, disgust, or a lust for revenge or dominance. Beware of the widening of the path. Beware of the temptation to put your own desires for yourself alone above all else. This can take many forms, so you must be vigilant. Best of all, stay focused on The Narrow Path, striving for justice and mercy while seeking wisdom from The Creator to know when to use one or the other.

* * *

Hela roamed through the upper levels of the seemingly endless forest. The trees here were several times larger than anything she had seen previously. The biggest trees in her homeland were around six feet in diameter, but these were often 20–30 feet in diameter. The largeness of the trunks led to deep furrows in the bark which she was able to use to climb into the branches that formed irregular canopic tiers.

The air was usually still near the ground, but she could feel more of a breeze the higher she got. When she had climbed to the top of the upper canopy, she still could only see forest in all directions.

Strange animals also lived in this realm. When she had explored near the ground, Hela had come across a strange, segmented creature with two heads that seemed part snake, part centipede. The creature had lunged out of the water and attacked a large herbivore that had climbed down to drink from a pool between some large roots. The herbivore itself had rows of spikes all along its back and large, sharp claws on its feet for climbing. Hela had observed that the snake-centipede had bitten the herbivore with one head and followed it as it tried to run away. It had not taken long for the poor animal's muscles to seize up and for it to fall over. The snake-centipede had approached the carcass, bit into it with its other head, and then scurried under it to wait.

When Hela had returned later, she had noticed that the area around the second bite was dying, and the insides were beginning to liquify. She had also seen several more of these snake-centipedes feeding on the corpse.

Some animals were slightly more normal, though still different. The closest thing she had seen to a wolf was an exceptionally large solitary hunter with dark green and brown fur to blend in with the shadowy, moss-covered roots. By contrast, instead of solitary panthers, there seemed to be packs of medium-sized cats that hunted amid the branches. Their coloration resembled a perched bird when the cat sat upright and still.

The most mystifying creature was a type of fox, small by the standards of the other creatures, that seemed to appear and disappear randomly. Remarkably, these animals lived in the lowest levels of the forest, mostly moving in caves or under huge roots, mostly surrounded by darkness—yet the creatures had bright, luminescent, red fur. Even their eyes glowed blue in the dark. Hela was not sure how such creatures could survive while standing out so starkly from their environment.

Hela made her way back to her camp by the mist wall. This land would most definitely suit the wood elves. The high elves would have to learn to adapt, as their current home offered few, if any, opportunities to practice primordial survival skills. The sea elves might be the most disappointed: As far as she could tell, there were no rivers, lakes, seas, or oceans. Only random ponds and puddles formed between tree roots and sometimes in hollows where large branches diverged from the trunk of a massive tree. Perhaps they would at least enjoy exploring the forest.

Hela descended from a tree and found the spot where she had tied the rope that now stretched between her homeland camp and her new one. As she approached the mist wall, the shadowbeast walked out of the mist to greet her. She knelt, petted, and scratched the creature as it rubbed against her affectionately. It was now tethered to a cable that ran from the original tree in the elvish homeland to an anchor point in this endless forest. Hela smiled and leaned her forehead toward the creature; it mirrored the movement until their foreheads met. She was glad that she had taken the time to tame the beast.

Sighing, she stood and looked between the mist and the trees while keeping one hand gently scratching the shadowbeast's head. She had been thinking about it and had decided on a plan. She would create a series of rope bridges through the mist so that her people could travel freely between the two realms. Retrieving her pack, she and her shadowbeast disappeared into the mist.

*　　*　　*

Cariadllyfr hiked the coiling roads around the citadel as Ymchwil and Gwyddoniaeth followed him. Without turning, he could sense their somber mood. Many more years had passed, and the two young elves were now quieter. It was difficult to determine if this was a result of maturity or the weight of responsibility and things to come. When they reached the upper ring, just below the water collection bowl, he stood aside, watching them as they moved to the edge to look out at the harbor. Their movements were more precise and controlled. He could see the discipline that had been beaten into them. Even their bodies were slightly less soft. Without touching their minds, he could see their alertness and awareness of their surroundings in their subtle movements.

"I wanted to show you what the others have been building while you have been training," he said, gesturing down into the harbor.

A fleet of strange craft had displaced the usual boats. They were positioned on either side of long piers, all of which were angled directly out to sea. The craft themselves were built of more metal than wood, an oddity for the elves. Instead of floating on the surface of the water, most of their mass was submerged with a smaller portion rising above the surface.

What are they? asked Gwyddoniaeth.

"Submersible vessels."

Amazing, commented Ymchwil.

"Should the need arise, we can descend below the waves and avoid detection as we make our escape."

He led them around the edge of the ring until they faced the vast forest that stretched between the sea and the mist wall.

"Far beyond even our sight are waystations that Hela has helped build along the mist wall. The migration and evacuation has already begun. Most of the wood elves have evacuated through the mist as well as many of the high elves."

Did Cyfeiriad never return, asked Ymchwil.

"We have not seen him, so we started the evacuation through the forest."

Why is anyone still in the mountain or the harbor, queried Gwyddoniaeth.

"Many of the sea elves are confident that the submersibles will be sufficient, and they are not as inclined to travel to a land-locked realm. The high elves that remain are gathering books and tools so that they can be divided between both escape routes."

Shouldn't they all stay together and go through the forest?

"We may yet be attacked from the forest edge, meaning the sea is the only chance for survival and vice versa. A handful of wood elves have volunteered to stay with the fleet."

Why have we not sent replacements for Cyfeiriad?

"We have, but none have yet succeeded. Some have vanished, others just return to their tethers in confusion. We are well aware that the seaside mist wall may not be as passable as the forest side, but we will take the risk if it becomes the only means of escape. Inside the submersibles, with our people working together, we will have a better chance of overcoming whatever obstacles dwell in the mist."

The two young elves paused, looked down at their feet, then turned to face Cariadllyfr, as if sensing what came next.

"Ymchwil will go through the forest, and Gwyddoniaeth will go with the ships. The selection was chosen by lot. The way stations are far away, so it is best to be departed as soon as possible."

The siblings looked at each other, then back at their mentor.

Their lips parted, yet nothing came out. Finally, they spoke as one, "We understand our responsibility."

With a bow, they turned and headed back down the mountain. Cariadllyfr watched them leave, empathic sorrow tearing at his heart. He knew how hard it would be for them to separate, but he was also thankful that they had accepted their responsibilities without argument.

* * *

Cyfeiriad ran straight toward the beach. He dared not look back at the crashing footsteps behind him as he ducked under branches and leaped over fallen logs. This had been a mistake.

Light exploded in his eyes as he shot out of the forest. His steps were slowed by the shifting sands, and he felt a moment of panic. What if the sand slowed him down too much?

Pushing such thoughts aside, he focused on reaching his target. As soon as his hands could touch the boat, he began pushing it back into the water.

A roar bellowed out, and the elf turned as he jumped into the boat to face the tree line. Practiced hands reached for the oars without looking, and he began to pull away just in time to see the large, feathered quadruped burst out of the trees, its massive tusks battering through the underbrush, sending debris flying all around it.

The creature charged into the water and pulled back. It paced, stamped, and bellowed as the elf let out a sigh of relief.

The mist enveloped, then released the young elf.

It was as if the teeth were waiting for him. No sooner had his boat exited the mist than a massive set of jaws exploded from the water and smashed it to pieces. Cyfeiriad was barely able to jump out and into the mist. He lay on his back, panting in the never-ending grey. After a moment, he stood and walked on.

The sea elf stood on the edge of a barren crater, gazing down at what must have been the most complete opposite to the world in which he lived.

The wind blew hot and dry across the land. In the distance, a thin layer of dust swirled with the breeze. He shielded his eyes and gazed at the sky. There were no clouds, and he was convinced there were three suns in the sky barely visible beyond his fingers. The heat was so oppressive that he wondered if the suns were closer than normal.

It didn't take long for him to turn and leave the suns-blasted land behind, welcoming the cool moisture of the mist.

The elf could sense the threat that he had thus far avoided facing directly. He knew that he must learn everything about the mist, and, luckily, he had been able to avoid the creature up to this point. A smile crept across his face, and he waited.

Cyfeiriad sensed movement behind him. He stepped to the side and turned.

A large black furred creature with massive teeth and glowing red eyes landed where he had been standing. It turned to face him.

Before it could lunge again, the young elf smiled and stepped back.

Cold wind tore across his back and arms, shocking the delight from the elf. He turned and took a few steps away from the mist wall, clenching and unclenching his fingers as the bitter cold ate into him. Flakes of snow swirled in his face.

He stood on a ledge overlooking the downward slope of a snow- and ice-covered mountain. This mountain appeared to be one in a long chain that ran indefinitely to his right and left. Ahead of him, barely visible between the peaks of the next row of the range, he thought he could see an ocean.

The ledge beneath Cyfeiriad's feet abandoned him, but the several feet of snow that covered the steep slope below rose eagerly to greet him.

The elf was thankful that the snow was as thick as it was by the time he slid to a stop at the intersection between this peak and the next.

Looking up, he sighed. The ascent was too steep to climb in this snow. He turned left and right, looking for the best path back up to the mist wall.

Sometime later, wrapped in the white furs of the predators he had barely managed to survive, Cyfeiriad finally heaved himself over the stone ridge and crawled into the mist. He stood and walked back out.

Building a new boat was not easy. He had done it in the past, but that had been with actual metal tools. Here in this land of rolling hills of meadows and forests, he had to build his own tools.

As a child, his teachers had taught him how to build tools from stone, wood, and bone. It had been many years ago, but those lessons proved their worth now.

Eventually, he was able to drag his new boat back into the timeless fog.

*   *   *

Naga opened her eyes and looked around the cave without moving her head as the sun's rays began to creep inside. A small rustling sound could be heard from outside, and she uncoiled herself from her nest. She walked to the cave entrance to see what had caused it.

The strange little creature with the pointy ears and memorable eyes was climbing up over the ledge outside the cave. It stopped when it saw her.

Naga cooed gently in greeting, carefully scooped the creature up in one paw, and set it on the ledge beside her. Excited to show her little friend what was in the cave, she gently guided it inside. The little creature looked up at her hesitantly a few times, and each time Naga gestured for it to move forward with her snout.

Eventually they arrived at the dragon's nest. Naga reached inside and moved aside the branches and small tree trunks to reveal several eggs. Naga circled the nest and wrapped herself around her clutch, making excited noises as she did. The little creature approached cautiously to peer at the eggs more closely. It began to reach out its hand and stopped. Naga moved her paws aside, clearing a small path to the eggs. The creature stepped forward and gently caressed the nearest one. A smile lit up its face and it began to sing.

The song was unlike anything Naga had heard before. The melodic sounds summoned images of waves gently washing against the shore, the sounds of leaves rustling in the breeze, and the relaxing sense of peace that came from birds and insects that felt safe enough to fill the forests with their own music.

Naga found her mind wandering and her concentration draining. Soon she was fast asleep.

The sound of a rushed landing and hurried steps woke her. She rose instantly and moved to face the entrance of the cave. She felt a strange wave of heat roll through as her mate appeared and rushed past her. The worry in his eyes scared her and she turned. Her mate collapsed in front of the nest. It was then that she noticed the smell. Something was wrong.

Naga approached her nest fearfully, terrified of what she might find. A dreadful croak escaped her throat when she saw the crushed eggs.

At first, nothing came out, but then the cave was filled with the tortured cries from Naga and her mate. She turned and twisted, but nothing offered any comfort or end to her pain. The dragon staggered out onto the ledge.

All around her cave on the mountain, the air was filled with cries of pain and roars of anger. Fire raged over slopes and smoke billowed around the peaks. Streaks of molten rock could be seen beginning to flow to the valleys and forests.

Naga understood. What had happened to her had happened to everyone. All their eggs were crushed, all while they slept.

All while they slept to the little creature's song.

The sense of betrayal transformed her grief to anger. The anger gave her focus and took away her pain. Rage and fire poured out of her mouth, and her claws began to penetrate the softening rock beneath her.

She knew where the pointy-eared creatures lived. They all knew. And they would all make the little monsters pay.

Naga took to the sky, joining the smoking mass of wings and wrath. The swarm of angry dragons swirled around, growing to contain almost all of their kind. The living cloud of smoke rose, turned, and aimed itself at the mist wall.

* * *

Hela walked out of the mist wall, guided by her shadowbeast in one hand and the guide rope in the other. As much as she trusted the creatures, she needed to be sure she'd always reach her intended destination.

She had just come from the infinite forest where many elves had already setup camp. Here on the homeland side, many were still gathering and preparing to leave. The elves around her were mostly wood elves with some sea elves and high elves mixed in. The high elves came most encumbered with books, tools, and other equipment that would be useful for rebuilding on the other side. The wood elves traveled light yet prepared for whatever survival or hunting situation might await them. They carried hunting weapons, ropes, knives, blankets, and food. The sea elves seemed the least encumbered, or prepared, depending on one's perspective. Their usual habitat was on a boat or the harbor, where they kept whatever tools they needed for building or repairing their ships. Most only carried navigational equipment and knives on their person. Here, deep in the forest, there was no need for boats, and dragging them across the continent would have been highly impractical. The benefit of their lack of belongings was that they were free to help everyone else with what they were carrying.

Despite an overall sense of adventure and exploration, there was still hesitation to leave everything behind permanently.

Hela surveyed the group. Everyone was laden with heavy packs, with some pulling handcarts loaded with more equipment. A couple wood elves were going around securing everyone's tethers to the guide ropes. A couple more stood near the mist, waiting with their shadowbeasts.

Taming the creatures had proven quite helpful, though they were not fully domesticated by any means. The first elves Hela had tried to lead along the guide ropes had been forced to fight off shadowbeasts when they attempted the journey by themselves. Keeping a shadowbeast with oneself while traversing the mist had so far prevented any further attacks.

The wood elves finished their tasks and looked to her. She nodded for them to depart.

Something was off. She looked around but saw no strange movements. There was something different about the movement of the air, but she wasn't sure what it was. Focusing on the sounds around them, she could faintly make out a strange sound. A few moments later, it become clearer.

Several razorback stags burst from the undergrowth and ran past her. She turned in astonishment and watched as they launched themselves headlong into the mists. A few cries rang out, and she looked down the wall. Farther from the camp, she could see shadowbeasts emerging from the mist and picking off stags and other animals as they tried to run into the mist.

Hela gave the signal, and everyone began tethering themselves to guide ropes, leaving behind anything that was not immediately ready to go.

*   *   *

The dragons burst out of the mist wall. Naga could barely see the distant lands of the pointy-eared little monsters directly to the south. She and her kindred flew in fury straight for the great mountain where they had previously seen swarms of these creatures in the past.

They would pay.
They would suffer.
They would burn.

*   *   *

Gwyddoniaeth followed Hyfrydmor through the harbor. She was excited for the next stage of her mission but sad about her separation from Ymchwil. The two siblings had been close companions their whole lives, spending centuries learning and practicing together. She reached out with her mind but could only faintly sense him. The increasing distance would only make it worse.

It will be ok, Gwyddoniaeth, came the faintly whispered thoughts. *We'll meet again on the other side and have so much to teach each other.*

Gwyddoniaeth smiled; *I will eagerly await that day. Be safe, dear brother, and stay on The Narrow Path.*

You as well, my sister; may your feet never stray.

Gwyddoniaeth was brought back to her surroundings by Hyfrydmor grabbing her wrist and pulling her quickly down the pier.

"It's time!" she shouted. "Get on the ships and head south to the mist wall!"

The noise and commotion rose as Gwyddoniaeth hurried after Hyfrydmor. She looked up and to the north. Just barely visible in the distance, she could see a small pin prick of shimmering light against the grey of the mist wall.

*   *   *

Ymchwil was walking through the forest with Saethydd along the evacuation path when the elf Elder stopped short.

"It's happening," he said, turning to Ymchwil. "Go now; take as many with you as you can and flee into the forest."

"What are you going to do?"

"The other Elders and I will stay and cover your retreat."

"I can help," he said, stepping forward.

"Go. Protect those you can. Don't waste our sacrifice."

As he turned and ran. Ymchwil reached out with his mind for any nearby elves as he ran down the path, thankful that the tall trees would provide at least some cover.

He didn't know how long he was running before he found the first travelers.

"Quick! Cut your packs and run!"

The other elves turned and looked at him in surprise as he ran to meet them. They were pausing and unsure about his urgency. Ymchwil reached out and touched their minds with the image of the concern on Saethydd's face when he was told to flee.

Run! Whatever is happening is happening now! We must sneak through the forest and reach the mist wall as soon as possible.

The other elves' eyes went wide at the mental intrusion, but they only hesitated for a moment. They all dropped their packs and ran.

* * *

Cariadllyfr stood in one of the awning-covered paths on the north side of the mountain, watching the advancing horde of dragons. He did not turn or move when the other Elders began to assemble on the paths around him. He closed his eyes, took a deep breath, and let it out, mentally preparing for what was to come.

The Elders began to reach out mentally to each other to coordinate their efforts. Cariadllyfr could see the approaching doom from many eyes. He could also see the sea elf Elders urging on the last few boarders into the ships.

Eventually all the Elders were gathered, and they waited.

The dragons became more clearly visible.

The wind carried the heat of their fire to the waiting elves.

The dragons were almost within range.

Cariadllyfr could sense the wall of pain and rage.

As one the Elders raised their hands, and a wall of force pushed into the fire and flesh. Flame and smoke were pushed back, and the dragons found themselves knocked off course, crashing into their kin.

There were too many, and before long, the Elders found themselves holding back streams of fire from all sides. Cariadllyfr could feel the strain on his mind and concentration. While the majority of the flames were held at bay, the air around them was still heating. They could not hold them off indefinitely.

Dropping his efforts to hold back the fire, he reached out and grabbed one of the dragons. The creature let out a tortured cry as an invisible force gripped its head and neck, forcing its head upward. With a loud crack, the creature's skull shattered and caved in. Cariadllyfr winced and tears streamed down his face as the dragon's mental anguish at the possibility, then finality, of its own death washed over him. He gritted his teeth and stepped forward. If they didn't distract and slow the dragons, then all their children might die.

Around him, others were taking similar actions. Tears marred their faces as they replicated his thoughts and experiences.

*   *   *

Hela stood in the upper branches of a tree near the mist wall. Everyone at the gathering point had left. Only the guide ropes remained and her personal shadowbeast waited below, tethered to the tree. She had to see what was happening.

Far in the distance, she could see the high elves' mountain. It was awash with smoke and fire. From this distance, the mountain was small and whatever was causing the destruction existed as mere specs in the air. Hela sighed. She would wait as long as she could in case anyone else came, but she could not wait forever. The flying specks would likely travel faster through the air than her people could on foot. She only hoped that she could wait long enough.

*   *   *

Not all of the elf Elders had returned to the mountain. The submersible ships had been designed to be neutrally buoyant, or close to it when filled. Hyfrydmor and her fellow Elders raised their hands and with a downward gesture sunk the fleet beneath the waves. A moment later, they thrust forward their palms and sent the fleet surging out from the harbor, hopefully unnoticed by the approaching dragons.

Hyfrydmor turned to head back to the mountain to join the others. She did not make it far before she sensed that the battle had started. A few moments later, a small group of dragons left the mountain to see what was happening near the harbor. She watched in horror as one of the dragons seemed to notice something moving beneath the waves in the direction of the escaping fleet.

Hyfrydmor clenched her fists as she tore stones and boards from the piers around her and hurtled them at the dragons. The other Elders followed suit and soon after raised a great wall of water to smash into the creatures whose attention they had drawn.

Within moments, the dragons had descended on the sea elf Elders. Their fire poured down on them, becoming more powerful as they approached. The Elders in the harbor were spread out and had not been prepared for the fight the way their counterparts on the mountain had. They were quickly overwhelmed by flame and claw. The raging dragons tore into the structures and boats in the harbor, igniting, biting, and tearing as they went.

* * *

Cyfeiriad sailed out of the mist wall. The waters churned around him as sea life swam headlong into the mist. Strange creatures leaped out of the mist and grabbed some of the animals as they fled something he had not yet seen.

He looked ahead and saw the smoke and fire rising from the mountain.

He was too late.

It had started.

With all the skill he had, he sailed his small boat toward the mountain, trying to will himself to go faster. Maybe he could still help.

Fear that everyone was dead and guilt at his failure began to eat at his mind. He pushed these thoughts away, focusing on getting back to the harbor as quickly as he could.

Something strange passed over his mind. He blinked and shook his head at the sensation. A moment later, a large object burst from the water, and his boat crashed into it. His vessel tilted to one side, and he fell into the water. Coming back to the surface, he heard a shout and looked at the unknown object.

"Cyfeiriad! Take my hand. We have to get out of here." The female high elf that he had last seen when he was given his mission stood on the object next to a now open hatch, reaching out to him. He swam over and took her hand, joining her on the strange vessel.

She grabbed his shoulders and looked at him intently.

"What is—" he began before being cut off.

"You discovered the secret, right? You can travel through the mist and lead us out of here, right?"

"Yes. Wait, are there more of these ships?"

"Yes. Come below, so you can lead the fleet through the mist wall," she said, pulling him toward the hatch.

"Wait, I can't just lead someone through; I have to the be the one to steer the craft. If there are multiple ships, they can't just follow us," he said as he climbed into the ship ahead of her.

She sealed the hatch behind them and turned. "What if I linked your mind to the other pilots?"

Cyfeiriad blinked; "You can do that?"

"Yes."

"Then let's do it."

The high elf reached out and touched his head. A moment later he could sense the minds of the pilots.

Please, allow me to guide your minds, he thought. One by one they agreed, and he began to see the world through many sets of eyes.

Acting as one, Cyfeiriad and the pilots steered the fleet into the mist wall, each pilot guided by Cyfeiriad's singular will.

*   *   *

The heat was immense now, and Cariadllyfr could smell burnt hair and flesh all around him. Many of his brothers and sisters were already dead. The dragons had begun to spread out around the mountain, with sounds of shattering stone coming from all directions.

A loud sniffing alerted him to the presence of one of the beasts poking its head toward the doorway of the room in which he was hiding. He did not want to die, but more importantly, he did not want his children to die. Every dragon killed was one less threat to their survival. Even now, hundreds of their reptilian corpses littered the mountain side and the sea below.

Cariadllyfr closed his eyes and sighed. His exhaustion eased slightly but not entirely. Hopefully, he could at least destroy one more.

The elf Elder whirled into the doorway and reached out toward the creature, ready to crush its head or snap its neck. All he saw was a swirl of bright colors as the flames washed over him.

* * *

Ymchwil staggered to a halt. He had felt it only faintly, but it had still cut deeply. The Elders were dead.

The group of fleeing elves around him skidded to a halt when they realized that he had stopped. They had been running for most of the day and were exhausted.

"They're dead. I don't know how long the empty rooms in the mountain will distract the dragons. Even if we could run without stopping, it would still take several days to reach the mist wall. Is there any place we could hide that might be nearby?"

The gathered elves began to murmur and look about. The group had grown considerably since Ymchwil had first overtaken the evacuees.

"There's an entrance to a cave system nearby. If we walk, we can get there around midnight," offered a young wood elf.

"Lead the way."

The group left the trail and walked into the woods. Ymchwil reached out, but he felt no one else nearby to urge to join them. He was saddened to note that he could not sense any vertebrate animals in the vicinity either.

The group marched through the trees as dusk fell and continued on well into the night. Faintly, through the tops of the trees, a bright orange glow could be seen. One of the wood elves climbed a tree and reported back what Ymchwil and everyone else had already guessed: The mountain was on fire.

The young wood elf guide's estimate had been right. They reached the cave entrance around midnight. Everyone filed in, found a place on the stone floor, and collapsed into sleep.

Ymchwil awoke early the next morning to the smell of smoke. He crept toward the entrance and found one of the wood elves keeping watch. She gestured for him to keep quiet, then motioned for him to follow her outside.

Ash was falling from the sky. The smell of smoke stung his nostrils. The forest was burning. Not far off, the sound of crashing trees could be heard moving steadily nearer.

The wood elf signed to him, "I checked earlier. They are tearing down the forest and burning it as they go. We need to move everyone farther into the caves, in case they try to burn us out too."

Ymchwil nodded and turned back. They quietly woke their companions and ushered them farther back into the cave.

Ymchwil turned and stared at the entrance. It was not small, but he wasn't sure if was big enough for their pursuers. He turned to follow the evacuees when he sensed something.

The dragons had seen the cave. Ymchwil could feel a creature moving quickly toward them.

Run, he commanded the elves.

The sound of claws scraping stone and an overlarge head trying to fit into the gap caught his attention. Before rounding a bend in the tunnel, he spun in time to see sniffing nostrils replaced by the side of the creature's head and its eye peering in. Ymchwil whirled around the corner, out of sight. He heard it sniff a couple more times, then inhale greatly.

Fire poured into the tunnel. Ymchwil was barely able to raise his mental defenses in time to stop it flowing over and past him to the others. He held his hands palms out, the invisible wall of his mind holding back the flames. He carefully reached out behind him to see if the others were safe. They were only a short way down the tunnel, forced to crawl one at a time into the small passage to the next chamber. There were too many of them and too little room to maneuver.

Ymchwil sensed other minds joining the raging one above. The heat became more intense. He could faintly see through the flames that the walls of the cave in front of him were beginning to glow. A few moments later, he could feel the stone around him begin to heat as well. He reasoned that the creatures must be blasting the surrounding rocks and not just the entrance.

Ymchwil reached out with his mind, desperate to find any way to stop the flames and the heat. The presence of the other dragons must have only intensified their rage, as the fire before him began to shift from orange to yellow and then from yellow toward blue-white. He had to stop the flames. If he did not, the elves behind him would die.

Desperation drove his mind to reach out in every direction, grasping at reality itself to find a solution.

All Ymchwil saw was swirling colors.

*   *   *

Naga smashed the stone structures on the mountain. The pointy-eared monsters were no longer able to withstand their fire. Many were already dead, but some had fled.

She sniffed and probed the holes in the mountainside. Everything reeked of the beasts. Their very scent filled her with rage, and she blasted fire into every hole she found.

Eventually, the structures were either broken or slowly flowing down the mountainside as molten rock. It wasn't enough. She needed to destroy, they needed to suffer, and everything needed to burn.

Naga leaped from the slope and flew down to the forest. She joined her kin who were either flying over the forest and igniting it or tearing and burning it as they walked.

*   *   *

Hela stood in the upper branches near the mist wall. She had waited a few days, but the tiny specks had begun to take shape into dragons. Their fires as they destroyed the forest were fast approaching. No one had come to the rendezvous point.

She hesitated before climbing down to the ground. She didn't want to leave anyone behind, but staying much longer increased the risk that the dragons would find the guide ropes and follow them into the mist. That was not a risk she could take.

Hela retrieved her nervous shadowbeast and cut all but one of the guide ropes, tossing them into the mist wall as she went. She made sure to cut the loop that was around the tree trunk instead of the line between the tree and the mist. She didn't want to leave a fibrous arrow pointing in the direction in which they fled.

She cut the last loop and began winding the rope around her arm as she and her shadowbeast entered the mist wall.

* * *

The elvish fleet maneuvered between the rocks and into a cave partially hidden between rocky outcroppings along the shore.

We should be safe here, at least for now, Cyfeiriad thought to the other pilots before Gwyddoniaeth dropped her hand from his head and severed their link.

The elves slowly made their way out of the ships and onto the sandy beach inside the cave.

"There's a path farther back that eventually leads inland," Cyfeiriad said unenthusiastically with a gesture.

No longer focused on getting them to their destination, he began to look around at the other elves. Looks of sorrow and confusion were common, with some managing masks of stoicism. Many were weeping, either collapsed onto the sand or shuffling about listlessly. He had never seen anyone in this state before, and he felt like his heart was breaking.

But that wasn't all he felt. Empathy for their pain was only part of what swept over his mind. If he had arrived sooner, perhaps more could have been saved. If he hadn't wandered the realms for so long, maybe he could have spared them their pain. At the time, he'd been excited and eager to explore, telling himself that he needed to know where he was taking his people, but now it all seemed immature and foolish.

  Cyfeiriad's heart ached for those around him, and he wished nothing but death upon himself.

* * *

  Gwyddoniaeth wandered along the shore and sat down on a rock. She reached out with her mind but could not sense her brother. She knew it was probably too far to matter, that even if he was alive, she wouldn't be able to reach him. He had been closer to the mountain and had farther to go than she had. There was a strong possibility that he could have been killed by the dragons.

  "Excuse me."

  Gwyddoniaeth looked up and tried to blink away her tears. A young male high elf stood before her.

  "My name is Gwarchod. I apologize for intruding, but I wanted to know if you had any instructions as to what we should do next. I would prefer to keep busy at the moment."

  "I, um, why are you asking me?"

  "Well, you were the one who linked the pilots to get us to safety, and you're the one the Elders trained as their replacement, correct?"

  "I connected the pilots to Cyfeiriad. He is the one who guided us to safety. The Elders only trained me to pass along their knowledge. That is all. At best, I'm a teacher."

"Understood," the young elf paused. "When you're ready, I would like to learn what the Elders taught you. I think it would be very helpful for us in times to come." He turned and quietly walked away.

After some time, Gwyddoniaeth stood and looked around. The young elf had made her think. Most of the elves had started wandering up the path, so she followed them. When she finally reached the forest above, she found most milling about near the entrance while some were already beginning to wander off into the forest. Several clusters of sea elves could be seen talking to each other. Some of the high elves were doing the same, but they were in slightly larger groups. The wood elves were mostly dispersing or preparing to do so.

Gwyddoniaeth walked from group to group, asking what each intended. Most of the sea elves were going to split up individually or in small groups to explore the coast and start over. The wood elves were almost unanimously going to disappear into the forests, either individually or as families. Only the large clusters of high elves had any intention of working together and organizing to rebuild.

As she went, she began suggesting that all three groups work together, so they all would be well prepared in case the dragons found them again or something worse happened. The high elves were more open to the suggestion, but the wood elves were not tempted. The sea elves seemed ok with the idea, but not enthusiastic.

When those less inclined to work together were asked why, most said that they weren't ready and just needed to be alone for a while. The elves as a whole had not been a close-knit community, so she was not entirely surprised when the survivors mostly went their separate ways.

* * *

An elvish submersible moved quietly out of the mist wall, just above the surface of the water. Cyfeiriad opened the hatch and looked out. He used a spyglass he'd found inside to survey his homeland from what he hoped was a safe distance.

Even without the spyglass, he could see smoke on the horizon. With the spyglass, he could see the flames. Everything was on fire. Even the mountain looked like it had been partially melted.

Guilt and loathing washed over him again. It was all gone. Everything was destroyed.

Movement caught his eye, and he turned the spyglass to see a dragon wheeling back and forth through the air. He didn't want to be seen or to accidentally lead it to their new homeland, so he dropped into the ship and closed the hatch. The vessel sank just below the surface, turned, and re-entered the mist.

Cyfeiriad collapsed to the floor on his knees. Pain and guilt ate at his heart. His thoughts ceased in a vain effort to avoid exacerbating the torment. Perhaps he would never move again. Maybe something would do to him what had been done to those he failed.

II

Double Vision
Dynoltir, +2004 TR

A man of indeterminate age and stern eyes sat in the barren, cinderblock room across the table from a woman in her thirties. He was rather irritated to be here.

He set the recorder on the table and looked at the woman. She was dressed in casual business attire and seemed slightly nervous. He did his best to present a bland expression and even tone. An agitated witness would only make things worse.

"Thank you for coming in today. Please state your name for the record."

She leaned forward unnecessarily and spoke toward the recorder, "My name is Lenore Johnson."

Lenore straightened up slightly and looked at him expectantly.

"Please relate the recent series of events leading up to the incident that took place two Fridays ago."

"Well, it all started when we hired that freak, Scott…"

*   *   *

About four weeks ago, I arrived to work and set up at my cubicle. I was an hour into my daily routine and had just finished answering emails that had come in late the previous night, when my boss approached me followed by a man I'd never seen before.

I should have known then that there was something wrong with him. I won't make that mistake again.

"Lenore, this is Scott Trevor. He just started today. I would like you to show him how things work."

I stood up and shook Scott's hand; "Nice to meet you, Scott."

"Thank you."

Our boss left us alone, and we got started.

Everything went fine those first few days. He would watch while I explained the systems, then we would trade off and he would practice while I guided him. The office wasn't big, so I would take him to visit and meet everyone else on our breaks. He seemed to fit in well at first. After a few days, he was able to work on his own and took up the cubicle next to mine.

The next week started and when I came in, I noticed that everything on my desk was slightly out of place. Nothing was missing, but it was obvious that someone had been messing with my stuff.

"Hey, Scott, did you borrow something or look for something on my desk?"

"Huh? Oh, no," he said as if he was slightly distracted. His tone was a bit colder than usual, and he looked like he was upset about something.

"How was your weekend? Is everything ok?"

"It was fine. I'm ok," he said with a smile that I could tell was not genuine.

I took a couple steps toward him and softened my tone; "Well, if there's anything you want to talk about, you can talk to me."

"Thank you," he said with a slightly more genuine smile before returning to his work. I let it go.

Throughout the day, I asked around the office about my desk. No one knew who had messed with it, but some suggested that maybe it was the weekend cleaning crew.

The next day I came in and this time the drawers on my desk were still open and my computer was unplugged. The invasion of my privacy and personal space was irritating. The cleaning crew didn't come on Mondays, so it had to be someone in the building.

"Someone is messing with my stuff, including my computer," I said, walking into my boss's office.

"Will you review the security footage to see who it was? I don't want anything to get stolen or broken."

"Fine," sighed Esme. She tapped away at her computer for a few seconds then spun one of her monitors so I could see it better.

"See, nothing, there's no one there," she said, looking at me.

"Look! There!"

Esme looked back and we both watched in astonishment as drawers and objects began to move by themselves.

"This place is haunted?!"

"No, that's ridiculous. There has to be a logical explanation."

"You saw it with your own eyes."

Esme frowned, turned the monitor back to face her, and waved me away; "Get back to work."

I started to protest but left and went back to my cubicle.

Leaning around the edge, I whispered, "Scott, you'll never believe what I just saw."

He turned; "What was it?"

"Esme showed me the security footage, and the drawers on my desk opened on their own. Do you think this place could be haunted?"

A worried expression crossed his face as he looked around the office nervously. Even I wasn't fully convinced that it was real, so I felt guilty when I saw his reaction.

"Relax, I'm sure it's just some prank," I tried to reassure him.

"Yeah, I'm sure that's all it is," he muttered and turned back to his desk.

The following day, whenever I, or anyone else, tried to use the copier, it would jam.

"Why won't this stupid piece of junk work?!" The sound of Esme's voice drifted over the cubicle wall followed by the sound of doors and panels being slammed open and shut on the copier.

We called the tech, and when he came to work on it, he somehow managed to injure himself quite badly. The sight of the blood and the shard of plastic penetrating his hand was quite disgusting. It made me feel unwell, so I went to the restroom in case I got sick.

After a few minutes, I felt better but noticeably colder. I heard a noise, but when I left the stall, there was no one there. None of the other stalls were even closed.

Brushing it off, I turned to wash my hands. The air was so strangely frigid. Then I felt a light but definite touch of an icy object on the back of my neck.

I have never moved so fast in my life as when I spun around in that moment, but there was nothing there. I couldn't take it and bolted from the restroom and ran immediately into Esme.

"Watch where you're going," she said sternly.

"I'm sorry. I—I just felt something touch me in the restroom.

Esme's expression was a mix of irritation and skepticism.

"Ghosts aren't real," she said before storming into the restroom and coming back a moment later.

"There's nothing there. Get a grip. Last thing we need is you going crazy on us." She disappeared around the corner.

I went back to my cubicle. I sat there a moment before leaning over and whispering quietly.

"Scott..."

He barely glanced in my direction before turning away from me as if distracted or just not caring. I wasn't sure, but it almost seemed like he was whispering to himself.

It only got worse from there. Everyone became more irritable, and Scott barely spoke to me. Esme was constantly annoyed and acted like I was just another part of the problem.

A few days later, I was the last one in the office. I didn't realize anyone had left early until it was almost five o'clock. The office was freezing, and when I looked around, no one was there. Once I realized that I was the only one, I decided I wasn't going to stay.

I packed up my stuff and started the rounds to make sure things were shut off, lights were turned off, and all the entrances were locked. Every time I turned off a section of lights, I started moving faster, until I was almost running from one area to the next. The cold and the unseen dangers I kept imagining had me on edge with goosebumps all over. I was almost done when it happened.

That same icy touch gripped the back of my neck. I shivered, yelped, and started to run, but this time sharp, stabbing pain erupted on the sides of my neck. Instead of moving forward, I was thrown back into darkness. I tried to get up but felt something force me back down, and I blacked out.

*   *   *

Lenore's voice caught in her throat, and the man with the stern eyes watched her closely. He could tell that this part of the story troubled her. These sorts of events were commonplace for him, but he forced himself to show sympathy, nonetheless.
"Take your time. If you need a break, we can revisit this later," he offered.
She sniffed and cleared her throat; "No, it's ok."

*   *   *

When I woke up, all I saw was darkness. I had no idea where I was. The panic really set in when I tried to move but could not. I struggled and tried to scream, only to realize that my mouth was gagged. Realizing that no one could hear my muffled cries sent fear shooting through me.
Frantic, I began twisting and turning against my restraints, looking all around for anything. This must have attracted its attention. Slow, shuffling steps began to approach. I tried to move away, but they just kept coming. Eventually, they stopped just to my right, and I stared straight ahead at the nothingness, trying to see what was there.
It sounded like something soft and small hit the floor near my head, followed by the sounds of several sharp objects digging into the surface. I felt a cold breath on my

face. My heart began to race even faster, and I tried to pull my head away.

Something grabbed me by the hair and held me still. A cold, sharp talon began to gently trace along my face and neck. Tears stung my eyes. I tried not to scream, but the sudden stab of pain as the talon's point pierced my skin shocked me, even though I feared that it was coming. It didn't matter. The gag kept my sounds muted to the point of uselessness.

I could hear it sniffing my face, and I felt warm wetness on my cheek. My captor vanished, and there was silence.

I closed my eyes, and eventually, my breathing steadied as my pulse slowed. I told myself that maybe it was gone, maybe it was over.

And then it came back. This time it dragged me across the floor and held my left foot into the air. I tried to kick free, but the icy grip was like iron. My free leg kicked at where I thought it might be, but I felt nothing. Then came the talon, slowly raking down my calf toward my foot. It stabbed into the sole of my foot and raked through my flesh. My body thrashed about and then it dropped me, my foot hitting with a thud that did nothing to help the pain.

I don't know how long this lasted. My tormentor would grab me, drag me, or throw me around. It would then cut me somewhere; sometimes shallow, sometimes deep. I couldn't relax and I couldn't sleep. I cried, I screamed, I panted, I even tried to prepare myself, but in the end all I felt was fear, pain, and fatigue. Everything was empty all around, but I could almost feel it smiling at me after a while.

Eventually, I passed out. I don't know how long I was unconscious before the angry, pleading voice woke me up. At first, I wasn't sure what was going on or what was being said, but as I became more aware, I recognized the voice and understood the words. It was like I could only hear one side of a conversation.

"You can't do this! If he finds he out, he'll send you to the void. I don't want to lose you."

It was Scott's voice.

"She's just my coworker. There's nothing to between us."

"Give me the locket. Thank you."

"I'll take her to the hospital, and we can discuss this when we get home."

"We'll probably have to move again."

Footsteps approached, different than the ones I'd heard earlier. Scott leaned down next to me, and I could feel the gag being removed.

"It's ok, I'm going to take you to the hospital," he said with dishonest sympathy.

I kept my mouth shut and just nodded. I didn't trust him, but I wanted to get out of there. He took my hand and led me to a bright hole in the ground. The pace was slow as I limped along, wincing at the pain in my foot and elsewhere. The darkness had become too normal for me, and I was blinded. When my eyes finally adjusted, he led me down a ladder.

We were in the office. I swore under my breath and looked around. I still had no idea who had kept me there or who he had been talking to. It occurred to me that he was probably insane. Scott most likely was talking to himself and had been the one tormenting me this whole time.

As we walked through the office, I looked around until I spotted a paperweight on someone's desk. I quietly picked it up and hit Scott over the head. There was a slight crunch and a thud as he hit the floor.

A locket fell out beside him. I picked it up, wondering if it held some clue as to why this horrible experience had happened to me. I turned, took a step toward the door, and ran straight into a ghastly, emaciated woman.

"How dare you touch him," she roared as she grabbed me by the shoulders and lifted me off the ground. The corners of her mouth tore open so that she had an unnaturally wide expression that revealed her many sharp, pointed teeth whenever she opened her mouth. She screamed at me again, freezing air blasting across my face. I was thrown off to the side and into a wall. The drywall shattered around me, and I slumped to the floor.

I watched in horror as the paperweight flew into the crazy woman's hand, and she instantly went from standing next to Scott's body to crouching right in front of me. She grabbed me by the throat and lifted me up.

"I'm going to enjoy killing you this time," she hissed and raised the object to strike.

"Stop!" Scott was staring at us with an outstretched hand.

* * *

The man with the stern eyes ground his teeth together as he looked at Scott Trevor sitting across from him, refusing to make eye contact.

They should never have met twice.

A look of concern washed over Scott's face, and the man realized that the shadows in the corners of the barren room had grown unnaturally large, beginning to consume their surroundings. He forced himself to relax, and the shadows returned to normal.

"Tell me, why we are in this room again, and why should I let you leave?"

Scott swallowed and looked up; "Ok, let me explain."

*   *   *

"Do you like the new house?" I asked as I held the pendant, walking from room to room.

I wasn't sure how best to show her around. I finished the tour without any signs of her presence. It was a little disappointing, but it is important to be patient with those you love.

Time passed and I started doing interviews for new jobs. After a few weeks of no success, I started to get worried, but I couldn't weigh her down with my own concerns.

"I think this interview went well," I said from my chair while sitting at the kitchen table.

Irene sat in a chair to my left, facing the wall to my right. She didn't look at me as I ate, nor did she respond. When I finished eating, I looked over at her. Despite my insecurities about my job prospects, it still felt good to have her there with me. My eyes drifted over her face and the long, arcing scars of her mouth. I felt blessed to have such a beautiful companion.

Her eyes moved to look at me without her turning her head. A strange expression twisted the corners of her mouth and she vanished. It had almost looked like disgust, but I tried not to dwell on it. She was with me, and that's what mattered.

I looked around; "I'm sorry if I made you uncomfortable. It's just that I can't help but stare at your beauty."

Something crashed in another room. I sighed.

On the weekends, I didn't have much to do. Sometimes, I would take the pendant to the theater with me. Occasionally, I would see Irene sitting a few seats down or standing behind someone, looking down on their head. Whenever we went to a horror movie, there would be a slight smile to her expression as she stood between the last row of seats and the wall, tentatively reaching out toward the frightened viewers in front of her.

If there was nothing else to do, I would sometimes stay home, watch tv, do chores, and so on. Every now and then, I'd catch Irene standing in a corner, staring at me, but she would vanish when I turned to look at her. It felt nice knowing that she was there with me.

"You know, you can come lay down in the bed if you want," I said as I got ready to sleep.

There was no response. I pulled back a corner of the blanket as invitation and crawled into my side of the bed. Sleep came quickly, but the cold awakened me some time during the night.

I pulled the blanket around me tighter and rolled onto my back.

At the foot of the bed was Irene, just staring at me.

I smiled and patted the empty space beside me; "You can lay down too if you want. You don't have to stand all night."

That strange expression came over her again, and she vanished. I drifted back to sleep.

One day I was sitting silently, staring at my laptop. It had been several days, and no one had called me back. I was beginning to really stress that this was all going to fall apart. The worst possible scenarios of homelessness and Irene returning to her old ways kept flooding my thoughts.

"What troubles you?"

My head snapped up, and Irene was looking at me this time. I explained my fears, and she gave me this wide, fanged grin and lifted a clenched fist.

"Do not fear. If we wander the streets, I will easily devour any who attempt to harm you." She paused, as if pondering; "In fact, that might actually be preferable to you finding a job."

I was elated that she had said "we"; that meant she was starting to think of the two of us a single unit. But I was also worried about her hurting people.

Irene snorted and continued, "I'm sure self-defense would be a reasonable exception to the rules."

We spent the rest of the night in silence, though this time she was slightly closer, whether it was on the couch or in a room. She even started standing next to my side of the bed, looking down on me at night.

When I got the job offer, I was overjoyed. I told her all about it, and she even smiled slightly. Once I started the job, things changed.

"I started my new job today. It seems fairly straight forward. Lenore is helping to train me."

Irene sat slightly farther away that night.

"I think I'm going to able to start working independently now. Lenore said I've been catching on quickly. To celebrate, we ordered sushi for lunch today. I should get some for us here."

I didn't see Irene all night.

I didn't know what had happened. I would call out to her in every room of the house, but there was no response. I started to get depressed very quickly and didn't even notice the odd things happening at work. Lenore's questions about her desk, or the issues with the copier, none of it clicked in my head until she suggested that the place was haunted.

"Irene, are you here?" I whispered. "If you are, stop messing with Lenore's desk. We don't want any trouble."

I decided to look for the locket when I got home. That's when I realized that it wasn't where I usually kept it in the house. Dreadful realization washed over me. She was there. Somehow, I had taken the locket to work, and she was messing with people.

I knew that you'd probably show up if anything bad happened, so I rushed to the office over the weekend in the hope that I could find the locket and calm things down before they went too far. That's when I found Lenore in the attic with Irene.

I apologized to her for talking about my female coworkers so much. It had not been my intention to make her jealous, and I was not romantically interested in them. I tried to comfort her and reiterate that she can't torment people anymore. She gave me the locket, and I went to help Lenore.

In retrospect, I can see why she wouldn't trust me, but I still don't appreciate getting hit over the head. When I looked up, Irene was about to kill Lenore.

When I shouted for Irene to stop, she did. There was a look in her eyes that was like relief. She dropped the object and came back to me and helped me up.

"What is wrong with you?!"

I turned to look at Lenore, who was glaring at us. She was badly bruised and cut. Her face was a mixture of anger, confusion, and disgust. I saw the locket on the ground by her feet. I was worried she'd take it or do something to damage it, so I took a few steps toward her. She backed away toward the door, leaving the locket on the floor.

"I'm sorry about what happened. Irene is trying to be better, but it's hard to change old habits. Please, let me take you to the hospital, and you'll never have to see me again."

"You're not taking me anywhere. I'm leaving in my car, and I'm calling the police. You will rot in prison for this."

The anger and hate in her voice stung, but it was understandable. I held up my hands and stopped approaching. "I understand," was all I said and watched her back out of the building, never taking her eyes off me. When she was gone, I retrieved the locket.

* * *

"So, why should I spare Irene this time?" growled the man with the stern eyes.

"Well, she didn't actually kill anyone. Lenore will make a full recovery, at least physically." Scott paused, looking around the room for an answer. "And she stopped when I called out to her. She's not the cold-hearted monster she once was. She's not irredeemable, just more like a recovering addict. It was only a small relapse."

The man rolled his stern eyes at this analogy. "Her 'relapse' was the abduction and torture of a human being." He paused. "You know, my grandfather would have offered to beat and cut you for every bruise and laceration on your coworker, but I'm not sure that would be fair, since you didn't actually do anything."

"Please," begged Scott, "don't condemn her to the void. Don't destroy her. There is good in her, and if you destroy her now, she will end being less than what she could have been."

The man snorted and gestured for Scott to leave.

*   *   *

An old locket sat on the table in the cinderblock room between one occupied chair and an empty one. The man with the stern eyes stared at the empty air across the table.

"Show yourself," he said with audible irritation.

An emaciated, pale figure appeared before him. Her head hung slightly, and she did not make eye contact.

"Explain yourself."

"At first, Scott's affections were strange and somewhat sickening, but I slowly grew used to his presence and constant chatter. Sometimes I would sit or stand nearby, his attempts at kindness making me feel awkward. Other times I would stare, pondering whether to torment and kill him.

"One day, he expressed his fears and doubts, and instead of delight, I felt a sickening sense of sorrow at the thought of his suffering. Afterward, the feeling of sympathy made me feel contaminated in some way. In the moment, I found myself trying to encourage him and threatening whatever might attempt to harm him.

"I was still trying to accept this new psychological stain, when he started talking about his female coworker all the time. I felt jealous and betrayed. How could he focus on her so much, when I had so violated my nature by being kind to him? I hid the locket in his coat one day and began exploring his workplace.

"At first, I was just lashing out, but soon the frustration and fear of the employees began to taste good. I combined my jealousy and thirst and continued to antagonize them. Eventually, I started tormenting and feeding on Lenore, since she was the one that he spoke about the most."

"What do you think I should do with you?"

The unnaturally far corners of Irene's mouth twitched, and she looked up.

"I failed to live up to our bargain, and I harmed another human. Their pain will always be deliciously tempting to me, and the longer I'm around Scott, the more chances are that I will fall back into old habits. That will only cause him more pain and difficulty in life, so it will be better if I am removed now before it gets much worse. You should send me to the void."

The man with the stern eyes stared at her for a moment.

"I will take your statements into consideration and deliver my decision tonight."

The man stood up and left the room. The ghost just sat there, staring ahead at the now empty chair.

*　　*　　*

The man with the stern eyes walked down a nondescript hall and turned a corner. Once out of sight of the room, he sighed and rubbed his eyes. This was such an exhausting hassle.

He walked through the cinder block maze until he came to another room. Inside was a girl with unkempt hair next to a table. On the table was a backpack, a textbook, and a notebook. She was looking back and forth between the open book and her paper, writing as she went.

The girl looked up at him with a mischievous smile. He greeted her with his own tired smile and slumped into the chair opposite her.

"How did it go?" she asked.

The man whose eyes were now slightly less stern recounted the events.

"What do you think we should do?"

The girl paused, tilted her head slightly, and looked up and to the side, staring either into a middle or infinite distance.

"I think we should let them be."

"Why?"

"Because she took responsibility for her wrongdoings and requested punishment to protect the human. If she was inclined toward her old ways, she wouldn't have done that." The girl paused, then continued, "besides, she didn't actually kill anyone."

"Should we tell them now?"

She looked at him and smiled; "No. We should just leave and let them stew until they realize we're not coming back."

"Good," he said expressionlessly and stood.

The girl gathered her belongings, laughing quietly under her breath in a way that amused her but would have disconcerted any innocent passerby.

III

Outer Wilds
Niwltir, +1633 ER

The creature ran through the upper branches of the great forest, the cool night air washing over its head. The trees of the endless forest were several times wider than the creature itself, tapering slowly as they reached immense heights. Only in the upper branches did sun, moon, or starlight penetrate. The lower one went, the darker the forest became. The creature was not sure if it could survive in those lower levels. Sometimes, it could hear heavy footsteps or terrifyingly deep growls. None of that mattered at the moment. There was too much fun to be had in jumping between branches and enjoying the night air to care about testing its own limits or risking unnecessary death.

The scent of another animal made the creature's nose twitch, and it stopped on a branch, gripping on tightly with its claws. The creature turned its head until it found the direction from where the scent was strongest.

The creature silently and much more slowly stalked its way through the canopy until it could see the shapes of several birds perched in the branches. It watched for a while, and the birds remained still. Perhaps they slept, which would prove advantageous.

The creature lowered its body, so it was almost flat against the branch, ears flattened and tail still. Carefully, one padded paw extended. Quietly, claws gripped the wood. Slowly, weight was shifted. The process repeated through several minutes until the creature felt it was close enough to pounce.

It launched itself through the air, reaching out with its forepaws, claws extended, mouth agape. The bird twisted and became unrecognizable. Reflective yellow eyes with vertical pupils stared at the leaping predator. By the time it landed, the bird was gone. Confused, the creature looked about. Instead of seeing dozens of birds taking flight, it saw that it was now surrounded by several strange animals with reflective yellow eyes and vertical pupils. Mouths filled with tiny, sharply pointed teeth appeared below those eyes, and a single angry hiss issued from dozens of mouths at once.

Before the creature could fully comprehend what had happened, the pack of feral tree cats had swarmed it. Tiny claws tore into the creature's hide, while dagger-like teeth gripped its neck. The creature hunched its shoulders and lowered its head to protect its throat. It was several times larger than the tree cats, but instinct demanded caution. The creature twisted and turned, frequently missing the agile animals with its claws and teeth. Eventually, it managed to sink its teeth into one of them. Now that it had something to eat, it decided to flee rather than fight.

The creature bounded away through the canopy. The tree cats tried to follow but soon were unable to keep up. Once the sounds of pursuit were long gone, the creature stopped to enjoy its meal.

Despite the punctures and lacerations to its thick hide, the entire experience had been exhilarating. Even this meal came with a sense of enjoyment and satisfaction. Only once did it pause, sensing that it was being watched, but it could find nothing when it looked in every direction. The creature finished its meal and drifted off to sleep.

Thunder rumbling in the distance woke the creature. It stretched and leisurely began loping through the trees again.

Eventually, it came to a point where it could go no farther. Ahead of it, there was no forest, at least not for some great distance. Instead of more trees, a large expanse of stone lie ahead. Thin red cracks could be seen in the stone, and mist drifted gently around the edges as vines and roots stretched out, touching the red cracks before beginning to sizzle and burn.

Inside this landscape of cracked stone, well away from the trees, stood a tall stone ring. The ring had an irregular shape, rising and falling with the ground, as it encircled a mass of mostly rectangular stone structures. Toward the center of this mass, the uneven patches of stone blocks gave way to a sort of terraced mountain with its own structures that were arranged more sparsely. The creature only understood that these structures felt vaguely familiar.

Movement along the stone ring caught its attention. Soft, furless, bipedal animals adorned in strange materials were seen walking along the top of the stone ring.

The creature sat and watched them.

*   *   *

The city in the endless forest was comprised of three irregular areas separated by great stone walls that attempted to challenge the height of the trees. Despite being two hundred feet tall, the trees still towered over them.

The innermost wall surrounded a mountain on which had previously been built three massive, stepped pyramids. These structures were now only vestigial, overgrown by constructs from the last couple centuries. It was here that the rulers of the city worked and trained. Luscious parks dotted the landscape.

From the inner-most wall moving out to the middle wall was an area referred to as the inner ring. Here, large estates and farming facilities took up most of the space. The wealthiest council members, scholars, artisans, and merchants dwelled in the estates. The farming facilities were tall, towering structures where each level contained the necessary resources to grow the food needed to feed the city. The complex aether-infused technologies used to sustain their operations were maintained by the educated elite that lived in this inner ring.

The outer ring was the widest, but the streets were narrow as they wound between the cramped cluster of buildings. Most of the city's citizens lived here and traveled to the inner ring to work on the estates or in the farms.

Ba'eru slipped between the tightly packed people that moved about between the tall stone walls of the outer ring. His boots splashed through puddles that reflected the light of the aether lamps, the main source of illumination this far beneath the shadows of the buildings. The sounds of voices and feet above elicited little to no reaction from him or those around him. The infrequent catwalks that crisscrossed the space above were only slightly less crowded.

It was early morning, and most were moving from their homes to their jobs. The cool night air was warming quickly from the press of moving bodies, but at least it smelled slightly better than it would that afternoon, when the hot, sweaty masses returned home from work.

He turned sharply to his right and came to a halt. The viscous flow of humans had congealed into a solid mass near the south gate. He hadn't expected there to be anyone here, since passage in and out of the city was highly restricted. Slightly annoyed, he craned his neck to see over the onlookers. City guards formed a semi-circle perimeter, keeping the onlookers away from the gate where a platform with several people stood to one side. The amplified voice of someone at the top of the gate caught his attention and made his heart sink slightly. It was another banishment, essentially a slow and cruel execution.

"The following individuals have been convicted of crimes against the state, threatening our tenuous existence by creating a breach in the outer wall. For the safety and security of the people, we carry out justice against those who would put their own selfish desires above the common welfare."

Ba'eru ignored the list of names and looked at the chained people standing on the platform. There were several men and women, a handful of children, and one stooped, elderly man. Most of them wore tattered clothes below their gaunt faces. Life was hard in the outer ring, especially if one lived in the lower levels. People frequently attempted to breach the outer wall just to drain the rain and filth that continually washed down from above. There were sewers, but they did not catch everything and were sometimes clogged or damaged. Some snuck out to forage in the endless forest for food, their desperation driving them to risk the unknown dangers of the outer wilds. There were always some who had merely been foolish youth, eager to explore the forbidden forest and break society's rules. Very rarely, one would see smugglers up for banishment, most likely being the few who had failed to please their wealthy and powerful clients.

Ba'eru sighed. The severity of an infraction didn't matter. Any breach resulted in banishment or death. Since they were still alive, none of them must have been able to create a portal to the outside. If they had possessed such skills, they would have been executed on the spot and would have looked more well fed when they died. He had seen these punishments carried out before. The convicted would be pushed and prodded through the inner gate and out past the outer gate. Onlookers closer to the wall or on top might hear those banished scream once they reached the forest edge or darkness fell. Most would huddle near the walls, waiting in vain for a safe moment to exist.

Turning, he charted a new path through the maze of streets. Putting the plight of the condemned from his mind, he focused on his task. His mind plotted out the way to his target. An informant had provided the location of the drug lab run by Saraqu. The bounty on Saraqu was substantial and would provide him with enough resources to survive several months of unemployment, should such bad luck befall him.

Eventually, he reached a dead end and looked down. Beneath his feet was an iron grate that led to the sewers. At least the money would afford him a decent bath and new clothes after this. Ba'eru bent down and heaved the grate out of position. He sighed once before lowering himself into the dark.

Despite the stench and darkness, the bounty hunter already felt calmer than he had above ground. Ba'eru reached inside his coat and extracted a short cylinder approximately four inches in diameter with a large red crystal clutched tightly at the top with his right hand. Holding it in one hand, he thumbed the switch on the side. The small piece of metal shifted position and a slight click could be heard followed by the sounds turning gears. He moved the switch a hair farther, and a flame appeared over the crystal. He adjusted the position of the switch until the flame was large and bright enough to light his way.

Ba'eru pulled a scrap of parchment out of his coat with his left hand and unfolded a crudely scrawled map that the informant had given him. Apparently, Saraqu would have his associates meet him at a point indicated on the map, and he would portal them into the secret laboratory. Ba'eru had thought about trying to portal directly to the lab but had decided against it. While he knew the maze of streets well enough from working cases for the past five years, the sewers were another matter. As long as he had a general sense of a location's spatial relationship to his own, he could open a portal.

Portals were generally banned from being opened, except in designated safe zones for transportation purposes. This prohibition existed to prevent the accidental opening of a portal in a human. Those who could open portals also had an intuitive feel for their target location, but it was not fool proof, and the greater the distance, the greater the chance of mistakes. Some could mentally view locations without physical line of sight, but the ability tended to decrease the farther out one reached. This is why Ba'eru knew that he needed to follow the map to as close to the drop off point as possible, in hopes of being able to sense a nearby hidden chamber into which he could create the portal.

Several minutes of careful walking, turning, and walking some more led Ba'eru to what looked like just another patch of tunnel. The one distinguishing feature was a small carved glyph directly overhead.

Ba'eru reached out to the wall on his right and stretched his mind beyond its confines. Proximity made his remote viewing much clearer. He turned slowly, scanning in all directions until he found it. Approximately 50 feet ahead, past the curved wall, was a chamber. He could faintly sense the objects inside, but he didn't need to see the space perfectly, just enough to get there and not step out into a trap. There was only one person inside.

He put the map back into his coat and placed his left hand in the open air in front of him. He pushed, both with his mind and his hand. What started as a small pinprick of light in front of his palm expanded into an ellipse a few inches taller than himself. Whisps of multicolored energy shimmered around the edges. Inside the disc could be seen the interior of the lab. A lone figure stood with his back to Ba'eru, hunched over a table cluttered with flasks, bottles, and various instruments. Stacks of crates cluttered the perimeter and corners of the lab. Though the lighting was low, Ba'eru knew they most probably contained reclusive water widows. One of the long, segmented, two-headed carcasses lay on the table near the man.

Ba'eru gingerly extended a leg through the portal. As soon as he shifted his weight, he knew his mistake. He had not looked at the floor. A series of crunches announced his first step to his prey. The man spun around, saw him, and turned. He created his own portal and jumped through. Cursing under his breath, Ba'eru hurried through the portal, deactivating and pocketing his aether torch in the process. He glanced down and saw that the floor was littered with dried reclusive water widow legs, obviously there to inform the lab's owner should anyone try what Ba'eru was currently attempting. Through the collapsing portal ahead, he could see the deeply shaded trunks of trees.

He managed to reach the portal by the time it was about a foot tall. His hands and mind reached out and forced it open to its full size again, so he could jump through.

Ba'eru landed on the curved surface of a giant root and almost lost his footing. He reactivated his torch and looked up to see Saraqu running haphazardly through the forest. The trees surrounding them were 20–30 feet in diameter, and the branches overhead almost completely blotted out the sun.

Ba'eru looked around and began pursuing Saraqu. The illicit chemist was much less careful in his frantic flight, tripped, and fell into the deep crevice between two large roots. Ba'eru stood at the top, looking down on his prey.

"You can't take me back. I'll tell them you followed me into the outer wilds. They'll execute you too," he said, holding up a hand to ward off the perceived threat. "But, hear me out, I'll make you a deal. You let me go, and I'll make you rich. I can pay you ten thousand now and a cut of any future profits going forward. You'll have more money than you'll know what to do with."

Ba'eru crouched and rested his forearms on his knees. "That's an interesting proposition," he mused. "But the problem is that if I become your partner, not only will I have to worry about you stabbing me in the back one day, but I'll also have to worry about the city guards and your rivals. The thing is," Ba'eru paused, reached into his coat, and pulled out an aether pistol. He checked that the chambers were loaded.

"No, wait!"

He looked down at his quarry, now frantically trying to climb out of the crevice.

"I don't like feeling trapped. By anything."

With a slow, deliberate calm, he raised the weapon, aiming at the drug dealer. A gentle squeeze of the trigger began a series of clicks as the mechanisms spun. A moment later, a burst of fire shot from the end of the barrel. Saraqu's body slumped down into the crevice, leaving a smear of blood from the burnt hole in the wood down to where he lay.

Ba'eru put the weapon away and hopped down to retrieve his prize. As he stood there, he took a moment, his mind sensing the enveloping nature of the surrounding roots, trunks, and branches. Instead of feeling constrictive or oppressive like the many storied stone structures of the city, he felt comfort and peace. It was more like being wrapped in a soft blanket on a cold night. He closed his eyes and breathed in the scents of the forest, listened to the sounds of wind rustling leaves, distant birds, and insects. It felt natural, almost familiar, but he knew he had never been to the outer wilds before.

With an internal shrug, Ba'eru placed his hand before him, instinctively knowing where he was in relation to the city. Reality rippled and tore into an ellipse, as his mind mirrored the gesture of his hand. The familiar whisps of energy curled and wafted around the edges. Ba'eru bent down and heaved the corpse onto his shoulders. Dead weight was hard to move, but with an arm over one shoulder and a leg over the other, it was easier to balance the weight of the cadaver. He turned and walked back into the murky depths of civilization.

*   *   *

Ba'eru dropped the corpse on the city guard's office floor. The female officer stationed at the entrance raised an eyebrow as she looked at him.

The officer's desk was situated directly across from the doors to the office. It was a high desk, easily reaching the officer's midsection and positioned on a raised platform. The height of the desk provided unseen storage and a defensive position, should anyone attempt to cause harm. The raised platform gave the officer a more intimidating position, causing entrants to look up at her, and gave her a different angle from which to observe behaviors and attempts to smuggle things.

"I'm here for the reward on Saraqu," he said as way of explanation for the bloody mess he had just created.

The female officer flipped through the pages of a book until she found the one labeled "Saraqu" at the top. She looked closely at the sketch on the page, then looked up at Ba'eru.

"Turn his head so I can see his face."

He pushed the body onto its back with his foot, then gently repositioned the head to face the front desk with the tip of his boot. The officer looked back and forth between the sketch and the corpse a couple times before making some notes.

"Bounty deposit," she shouted back through a small window behind her into the deeper reaches of the office.

While her back was turned, Ba'eru took the opportunity to examine her features more closely. The woman's femininity was not hidden by her uniform, and he visually enjoyed her details, but he kept his face impassive so that he would not be caught.

She turned back to Ba'eru. "He's dead, so your fee will be slightly less."

Ba'eru shrugged. No one wanted extra work or hassles, so it was common practice not to ask any specifics about why a bounty was returned dead instead of alive. The only time it became an issue was if the bounty specified that the individual was wanted alive only. Most bounties were agnostic on the survival of their targets.

The officer made notes on a new piece of paper and handed it to Ba'eru. "Take this to the bank on the east side of the inner ring. The reward will then be transferred to your account."

"Thank you," he replied as he took the paper. Bank notes were not as directly usable as coin, but they were much safer to carry for both the outpost and the bounty hunter.

As he turned to leave, two guards exited one of the doors on either side of the main desk and reached down to carry the body to the back.

* * *

Ba'eru finished cleaning up in his apartment. He was freshly showered and wearing a cleaner version of his usual attire.

He sighed and opened a portal. It was not something he would usually do in his apartment, but he was expected, and a landing platform had been secured. Ba'eru stepped through.

The crisp night air greeted him as he stepped onto a stone disc approximately ten feet in diameter. Two guards stood on either side of the platform. Their duty was to ensure that only those scheduled to arrive stepped through. Had he been an unexpected face, they would have executed him immediately. If he had merely been late, he probably would have been beaten but allowed to live. The Tupsarru family did not take chances with their safety.

The platform itself stood in a well-manicured lawn in front of the Tupsarru family estate. The lawn only separated the manor from the twelve-foot-high stone wall that established the estate's perimeter by about twenty feet, but any estate with land to spare in the city was a sign of wealth.

This manor, like most, was located in the inner ring of the city along with other estates and government offices.

Ba'eru nodded to the guards and made his way along the small stone path to the front doors. He knew his way because the family here had helped raise him when he was little.

Perhaps "helped raise him" was a bit too strong. More accurately, it could be said that they fed him and allowed him to live there. While they weren't cruel, they definitely did not see him as a member of the family. The servants had been rather aloof, unsure of how to treat him, especially when the family was around. The only one who had seemed to show genuine kindness was the daughter, Iskurtu.

Iskurtu had been his closest friend, and when they were older, more than friends. There were times when she had been his only friend. She was the reason he was here, once every ten days; she wanted him to be included.

The doors were opened when he approached, and he was ushered inside. The servants bowed and gestured in the general direction of the dining hall, and he made his way there automatically.

The walls were covered in ornately carved wooden panels. Some bore carvings that depicted the history of the city, others contained the Tupsarru family crest, a bird carrying a broken reclusive water widow in its talons.

When he entered the dining hall, Eresu, the matriarch of the family, was already sitting in her usual place at the head of the table. Her advanced age was evident in her grey hair and wrinkled face, but it was hidden in her straight, stiff posture. The oldest son, Maliku, was sitting at the other end. He wore the typical robes of a council member. The fact that he did this while at home among his own family always struck Ba'eru as a sign of vanity. Iskurtu got up and greeted him at the doorway with a hug. She then retook her seat, and he took his usual place across from her. At least if he had to be here with the two individuals who did not like him, he could console himself by gazing at Iskurtu throughout the dinner. Since it was only a small gathering, table sections had been removed to make the table much shorter. Eresu sat on his right and Maliku on his left.

Ba'eru ate in silence. Eresu was her usual stoic self. Iskurtu would look up and smile at him randomly while she ate, and he would smile back. Maliku never let the silence reign for too long.

"Tell me, Ba'eru, any exciting cases lately?"

Ba'eru could see a sneer and a glance from Eresu cast in his direction. She did not like his chosen profession for a similar reason to why he liked it: It got him away from the uptight trappings, vanity, and illusions of the ruling class in the city.

"Just a drug dealer. He had a lab underground in the sewers," he replied, ignoring Eresu, and turning to address Maliku directly.

"Fascinating. That seems like a rather inhospitable environment for a lab."

"The lab was actually several feet behind one of the walls. It was only accessible via a portal. Most likely, a black market aethercrafter had hollowed it out for him. Also, we were only in the upper sewers, mostly just rainwater runoff, nothing too disgusting."

"Why don't you think he made it himself or just walled off a section of tunnel?"

"When I 'viewed' the area, there were no passages to the hidden room, and when I stepped in, he tried to flee instead of fight. Most of the aethercrafters I've met try to bury you, burn you, or drown you. They can pull the elements out of the aether faster and easier than they can force matter to be reabsorbed."

"You say he tried to flee?"

"Yes. He began to open a portal, so I had to shoot him."

"How unfortunate." Maliku paused.

"Any excitement on the council lately?" Ba'eru asked to politely continue the conversation.

Maliku's face lit up at the opportunity to discuss his activities and life.

"The council is doing quite well. Crime is down, tax collections are up, and soon they shall come to see the light of my reason. Several of the council members have already agreed to my city expansion plans. It's been more than 100 years since the last outward push. The opposition says we can use the aethercraft devices with air and water crystals specially calibrated to keep the heat from becoming oppressive and dangerous the higher we build. With access to the aether, we can pull earth out and shape it into stone to forever build upward.

"My allies and I argue rightly that we humans should not live our lives in fear. This perpetual avoidance of the outer wilds limits our access to unknown new resources and promotes an enfeebling mindset among our people. Nature should bow to us, not the other way around. What do you think?"

Ba'eru swallowed a piece of food. "I think that if the outer wilds were so immensely dangerous, the illegal portals used by the dealers to hunt and capture reclusive water widows would either lead to the extinction of the dealers or wreak much more havoc on the city than we currently see. The council is very strict with executing even the smallest breach, yet the only attack from a creature of the outer wilds that I've seen was more than ten years ago, and it escaped from a lab in the inner ring."

"I'm not sure I'm comfortable with the risks of the outer wilds. I have studied the diagrams from previous expeditions and the skeletal remains at the university. The beasts of the outer wilds are several times bigger than us. I'm not sure how well we could craft an aether weapon large and powerful enough to take one of those creatures down fast enough. Even the remains we have were either scavenged from a carcass or only barely defeated after more than half the expedition was killed. The risks really aren't worth it to me," Iskurtu explained.

"Perhaps, we need to find ways of harnessing the power of those creatures," suggested Maliku.

"And how do you propose we accomplish such a feat? Should we toss a collar around their necks and lead them in by a leash?" retorted Iskurtu.

Ba'eru kept his mouth shut.

"By any means necessary," replied Maliku with a cold look in his eyes.

* * *

Ba'eru's mind floated up from the depths of slumber, opening his eyes to be greeted by the darkness of his bedroom, yet he felt restless.

Quietly and gently, he uncovered himself and shifted his weight until he could sit, and then stand. The entire time he kept a close eye on Iskurtu's sleeping form. Her mother would not have been pleased to know that her daughter was sleeping in the outer ring. Despite their efforts, Ba'eru suspected that Eresu was probably well aware of the emptiness of Iskurtu's bedroom at night.

He dressed, picked up his boots, and tiptoed into the washroom. A device was affixed to the wall above a basin. Inside the device was a large blue crystal. Ba'eru turned the handle on the device, which in turn applied pressure to the crystal. Water began to pour out of it. He reached down and scooped water with his hands. The first scoop he drank, and the second he splashed on his face.

Even though he was alone in his apartment with Iskurtu, he could still feel the walls, buildings, and people all around. He knew that the apparent solitude that was visible from within the apartment would vanish the moment he stepped or even looked outside.

Ba'eru put on his boots carefully, stood, and opened a portal.

The restless bounty hunter stepped into the lair of Saraqu. Having been there once before, he had enough of a sense of its relative location to portal straight to it from his apartment this time. The crunch of arthropod shells beneath his feet brought back memories of the dealer's attempt to flee. He absent-mindedly wandered around the underground lab, looking at the various instruments and partial specimens. Underneath the clutter, he spotted a worn, leather-bound tome. He picked it up and leafed through pages of what appeared to be a ledger with lists of clients, quantities, and payments. He noticed upside-down writing on the back of each page. Flipping the book over, he opened it again to find notes on the reclusive water widows, their anatomy, and how to turn their two venoms into various profitable substances.

Thoughts of the two-headed creature drifted to its natural habitat in the outer wilds. He had never seen one in the wild, but he'd only been to the outer wilds that one time. It had been remarkably peaceful.

After a long pause, he reached out with his mind to the area outside the city walls. He had a sense of the distance and spatial relationship, but not of what he'd find there. Ba'eru opened another portal. Inside the multi-colored shimmering oval of energy, he could see the shadowed trunks and hear the rustling leaves. At least it had opened next to a tree and not inside it or one of the roots. The bottom edge of the portal was a couple feet over the surface of a large root, so he stepped carefully over the edge and into the outer wilds. He immediately closed the portal behind him and looked around.

The forest was dark, the multilayered canopy above blocking out whatever moon or starlight might otherwise have illuminated the night. Ba'eru took in a deep breath. The air was fresh, the scent of trees and wet vegetation greeted him. A cool breeze washed over his body, and he closed his eyes to enjoy it. Inside the city, the walls generally blocked most wind, so the air tended to be stagnant and still, except when artificial air currents were made to keep the air from becoming completely toxic in the lowest depths.

Ba'eru reached into an inner coat pocket and pulled out his aether torch. He pressed a button and the gears inside whirred. A small flame burst into existence over the exposed red crystal. He adjusted the button until the flame was large and bright enough for him to see his surroundings more clearly. He held the device over his head and looked around.

Mostly all he saw were large tree trunks and huge roots. Above, he could see a tangle of branches and leaves. He began to wander between the trees, mostly along the top edges of the large roots, using them as a tangled path to avoid the numerous pits of water in between. He knew from his days at the academy that these pits of water were where he was most likely to find the reclusive water widows. He had no interest in experiencing either their neurotoxic or necrotic venoms firsthand.

Much of his gaze became consumed by the roots beneath his feet so that he could maintain his balance and stay on safe ground. Despite such a limited view, he felt himself relaxing more the farther he walked. From time to time, he would stop and examine the trees and his surroundings. He knew that he was surrounded by plants, but the thought was peaceful and relaxing, not oppressive or trapping like the walls and buildings of the city.

Ba'eru wasn't sure how much time passed wandering around the forest. His mind relaxed and he felt at peace again. In some ways it seemed familiar, yet very distant. Fatigue in his legs and feet hinted at the passage of time, and he wondered how long he had been in the outer wilds. He realized he should probably head back. It would not be good for anyone to notice that he was breaching the city's security.

He opened a new portal and stepped into the underground lair of Saraqu again, quickly closing the portal behind him. Then he reached out and created a new portal back to his apartment. He removed his boots, undressed, and carefully slipped back into bed.

Iskurtu mumbled and opened her eyes. "Where were you just now?"

"I went for a walk."

"Is everything ok?"

"Yes. Everything is fine."

He rolled onto his side to face her and reached out to gently embrace her from the small distance. She reached out and lightly stroked the side of his head, brushing his hair with her fingers. She began to hum softly as he drifted off to sleep.

*   *   *

The creature dug its claws into the vertical stone surface. The maze of high stone walls connected by walkways and ledges far above the ground vaguely reminded the creature of insect hives. Chambers were visible through variously sized holes in the vertical stone, and soft bipedal creatures could be seen inside.

Silver light from the moon above and the shades of red, orange, and yellow from the chambers created a tapestry of light and shadow, a maze on the surface of the maze. The creature ignored the chambers as it made its way up the stone walls and along several twisting paths before it reached its goal.

A variety of floral scents wafted out of the heavily curtained openings. The creature had thought it knew exactly which opening to enter but was surprised by how unusual everything appeared. This was not the perspective on the world that had been recorded by the old memories and instincts. Instead, it began to sniff until it found the scent.

The creature scurried to one of the openings and quietly dropped down onto the balcony next to it. It gently slid its snout under the bottom of the curtains until it could see inside.

A soft bipedal female sat in front of a reflective vertical surface. She was dressed in a loose, open robe and brushing her hair while humming quietly to herself. Behind her and to the creature's left was a large, exquisitely decorated bed. The room was filled with the scents of various plants. The floral scents could not hide the stench of the room's frequent carnal activities from the creature's sensitive nostrils.

The woman set down the brush and gently rubbed her exposed belly. Her figure was toned, and the recognition of abdominal muscle elicited a swift sensation of hunger inside the creature. It was moving before it was even fully aware of its own decision, guided by instincts it knew and impulses it could only faintly remember.

By the time the woman saw the creature, it was too late. Its teeth clamped over her throat, cutting short her cry. The feeling of blood flowing into the creature's mouth and the taste of human flesh sparked a pleasure and desire it had not known before. This was somehow more exciting and thrilling than killing the tree cats. Even the flesh and blood were somehow sweeter. Before the creature was even aware of its actions, it was tearing out great chunks of flesh and devouring them with enthusiasm. It slowed only when it tore open the belly and saw its contents. Then the faint memory solidified into understood purpose.

*   *   *

Ba'eru awoke feeling refreshed and relaxed. He slipped out of bed, letting Iskurtu sleep in. He had the vague sense that something was wrong but couldn't figure out what it was. Perhaps there was a task he had neglected, or something in the room was so subtly out of place only his subconscious could recognize it. The suspicion faded away quickly in the presence of the restful calm he felt.

"How are you feeling this morning?" asked Iskurtu, walking up behind him while he prepared breakfast.

"Great, actually. I must have been exhausted last night. I barely remember getting in bed. I woke up this morning feeling like I'd slept for a hundred years."

"Good," she said and kissed his cheek before leaving him to wash up.

The morning was uneventful, and he parted ways with Iskurtu after they ate breakfast.

When he arrived at the guard house to look for new bounties, he found the place in an uproar. Guards were holding back angry and frightened civilians trying to push their way in with shouted demands and questions.

He pushed his way through the crowd and was allowed past the line of guards once they recognized him. He proceeded to the officer's desk at the front of the station.

"What's going on?"

"A prostitute was found torn to pieces and mostly eaten in the outer ring."

Ba'eru kept his face impassive as his mind mapped out the location of the nearest brothel in comparison to his most recent bounty's hideout. A worry and sense of guilt began to fester inside him. There was a difference between the average citizen and the bounties he hunted.

"Do we have a deranged killer or invasive species problem, or do we not know yet?"

"Pasultu was dispatched to handle the investigation. One of the other prostitutes found the corpse and was barely coherent when the madame found her." The officer leaned in and said more quietly, "We don't know for sure yet, but it would appear we may have a breach."

Ba'eru nodded, "Any bounties up for it yet?"

The officer snorted, "Not yet."

He turned and squeezed his way out of the station.

Saraqu had created a portal in the lab to escape. He'd followed the dealer through, but what if it hadn't closed properly? He hadn't paid close attention when he'd pursued his prey to the outer wilds. That had been reckless and careless. If it was an animal from the outer wilds, they might track it to the lab. If it was tracked back to the lab, even if it was merely an escaped specimen or some other, unobserved portal, he might be implicated. Or worse yet, they would find out that he had been to the outer wilds without permission

If he was banished, he might be able to survive the outer wilds, but they usually didn't banish those who could make portals. In those cases, the condemned were executed and left to rot in order to send a message.

He'd killed bounties before, but he had also known very few prostitutes who deserved to die. The idea that his carelessness could have gotten someone killed unnecessarily gnawed on the back of his mind, adding to the mental distraction caused by concern for his own future wellbeing.

His calm from the morning was gone. He needed to find out what had happened and deal with it before the whole mess came back on him. The bounty hunter pushed his way through the crowds, his mind racing through every detail of the lab, the portal, the kill. Inevitably, his thoughts collided into his sense of guilt about the dead prostitute. There was something missing. His worry seemed stronger than it should be. It didn't make sense. There had only been that one trip into the outer wilds.

There was no way he'd die for such a careless error.

*   *   *

Ba'eru stood in the sewers near the hidden lab. There were no signs that anything had broken through the stone walls or clawed its way out into the nearest tunnels. That was at least some consolation.

He portaled inside the lab and began to look around. The broken pieces of carapace strewn across the floor showed the marks of where Saraqu had fled and he had given chase, but nothing else of note.

He looked behind every crate and into every corner of the lab but found no signs of recent activity. The walls and ceiling were rough but unmarked. There were no signs of tunneling, digging, or clawing.

As his eyes scanned the ceiling, floor, and walls for the tenth time, he knew there was no way that he could be linked to any breach. Yet, something kept bothering him. He searched his memories but found no logical reason to be concerned anymore. Was there something he had forgotten or overlooked?

Could something have altered his memories?

Whatever the explanation, it did not matter. He was going to catch this killer, gather his reward, and protect himself all at once.

* * *

The steps leading up to the level where the killing took place were blocked by two city guards when Ba'eru arrived. They recognized him and allowed him to pass.

The room was on the fourth level, and Ba'eru climbed the steps. Most buildings in the outer ring had well-worn steps and dirty stone walls, but these were relatively fresh. The prostitutes weren't allowed to ply their trade in the finer districts closer to the center of the city, but they were well funded by those who did dwell there.

When he reached the fourth landing, he turned right and found a private guard standing in front of a heavy metal door. The guard was easily a head taller than Ba'eru and armed with an aether pistol in plain view.

"I'm here to examine the crime scene, so I can pursue the bounty."

The guard looked down at him. "Proof."

Ba'eru sighed and rummaged in his inner coat pockets for the bounty hunter token. He displayed it to the guard who grunted, stepped to one side, and rapped his knuckles on the door, all without taking his eyes off Ba'eru. The door opened to reveal another muscle-bound, well-armed guard. Ba'eru nodded and proceeded down the corridor.

Every doorway was covered by a thick tapestry that both helped absorb sounds and provide an air of luxury to the place.

The crime scene was in the sixth room on his right. It was easy to spot due to its lack of tapestry and the stench coming from it.

Ba'eru paused for a moment before stepping into the doorway, bracing himself for the combined onslaught of stench and gore.

The scene was worse than he had imagined. The stench combined with the sight instantly made him nauseous, and he grit his teeth in a garish grin to prevent things from getting worse. There was not much left of the woman, and what was left was mutilated. Blood was everywhere, and the flies were starting to gather. The corpse had obviously been chewed and bitten with the belly being torn open and spread out.

"Welcome to my crime scene."

Ba'eru spun around to find an inspector standing in the doorway. Her uniform was a little less worn and rumpled compared to most of the city guards that he'd met, and her long hair was pulled back in a braid. Her eyes were keen, and her expression was neutral.

"I'm here to survey the scene, so I can pursue the bounty." He held up the token as proof.

"I see," she said and looked him over. "I am Pasultu, the lead inspector assigned to this case." Her tone and expression were professional and inviting.

Ba'eru made sure to keep his distance as she entered the room. The inspectors of the city guard were usually trained telepaths. The closeness of the population within the city generally made long-range telepathy painful, so most were only trained to read minds by touch. Having her think that he was only here for the money would most likely give her the false impression that she knew everything she needed to about him. This in turn would dissuade her from even thinking she needed to scan his mind.

"Well, I don't care about the bounty, but I do care about protecting people's lives. I will give you full access to whatever information the guards discover, and you will keep me apprised of your progress and request back up when you need it."

"That sounds like a fair deal."

Ba'eru walked around the room, carefully stepping into the few bloodless patches on the floor. The chair in front of the table with the mirror lie overturned and broken. Most of the blood and gore was concentrated in that area. What could be seen elsewhere was only in small amounts, most likely splattered in the killing frenzy. The rest of the furniture was untouched.

If a person had done this for money, it would have been simpler to just kill the woman quickly rather than create this mess. If it was a contract hit, it would also have been easier to kill her quickly or make it look like any of a number of possible accidents. The streets could be violent, and food wasn't always safe. This meant it was most likely an animal.

There were no signs that it had gone past the woman. Perhaps she had been enough to satisfy its hunger. His experience with wild animal kills was almost non-existent, but he sensed this was excessively messy.

Scratches and cuts in the carpeting led from the kill site out to the balcony. He followed the claw marks out onto the balcony. He examined the outer surfaces of the building and traced the claw marks in the stone as far as he could see them.

"I'll keep you posted," he said before climbing out onto the rigging and beginning to follow the claw marks. Pasultu followed him, much to his surprise. Most of the city guards that he had met did the bare minimum, which usually worked in his favor.

"Well don't just stand there; let's see where this leads," she said.

Ba'eru turned with a slight smile and continued up the side of the building.

*   *   *

The creature scurried through the underground tunnels, eager to reach the surface. Last time it had hunted among the humans, it had a purpose, something to restrain it. Now, it could indulge in its newfound euphoria.

The creature pushed aside a grate and climbed onto the open ground above. The tall stone walls on either side leaked the delicious scents of soft, tasty meat into the stale night air. The creature turned and dashed through the first window it found.

The mother in the room screamed, and the entire family jumped from their table. The husband tried to block the creature while the others ran, but it was futile. It sank its teeth into the human's throat and began devouring everything it could as quickly as possible. The thrill of feeling the flesh give way to its teeth and claws, the rush of blood into its mouth, was intoxicating. Though it had intended to eat everyone, the creature found itself distracted, its focus consumed by the feast underneath it.

The creature flopped onto the ground, its belly quite full, its desires temporarily satiated. It started to drift off to sleep when a clattering noise came rushing through the streets and into the building. It looked up in time to see armored and armed humans charging into the room.

Self-preservation instincts shot adrenaline into the creature's system, allowing it to momentarily not feel the weight or pressure in its stomach. The creature growled at the first approaching guard and slashed his throat with its claws. The second managed to hit the creature's shoulder with his weapon before being tossed aside by an angry backhand. The creature barely dodged two simultaneous shots of fire. It turned, jumped through the window, and disappeared into the sewer before the guards could make it back outside.

*   *   *

The city guard grabbed Ba'eru by the upper arm and spun him so that they were facing each other. He did not recognize this guard and reasoned that he had been transferred to the area from another section of the city.

"What are you doing out right now? There's a curfew."

Ba'eru reached into his coat and pulled out his bounty hunter token; "Two things: One, the sun is still setting, so the curfew is not yet in effect."

The guard squeezed his arm and jerked him forward slightly. The other guards turned to watch.

"And two, I'm meeting Inspector Pasultu to help her hunt the animal that has been killing people."

The guard looked at the token, then glared at Ba'eru. "The city guard decides who is violating curfew," he said through gritted teeth. "Don't forget that." He shoved Ba'eru away and continued to glower as Ba'eru walked off.

The other city guards patrolling the unusually empty streets turned back to their respective duties now that the hope for excitement had been disappointed.

Ba'eru made his way through the winding streets before he came to the building where the last victim was killed. Five days had passed between the first killing and the second. It had now been three days since the second killing, and both extra guard patrols and a curfew had been instituted.

He entered the building and started up the stairs. As he passed the landings, he noticed people milling about in the hallways. They weren't used to having their movements restricted this much and were pseudo-rebelling by staying in the building, but not in their homes.

The final landing had a ladder leading to a hatch in the ceiling. He climbed up and through to the roof. This building was like most in the city, with two slanted surfaces meeting to form a ridge. Inside these slanted tiles was a small attic space that was mostly the realm of rodents and fowl. The roof extended in a flat walkway around the attic space. A low wall along the edge of the roof had small holes at the bottom to allow water to flow into the gutters. Ba'eru exited the hatch into the low attic and carefully made his way to one end, staying bent over to avoid hitting his head. At the end of the attic was a door that led out onto the walkway. He exited the door and straightened up with relief.

"Good evening, Ba'eru."

He turned to see Pasultu already patrolling the roof to his right. His eyes grazed over her sun-highlighted contours while she was turned away.

"Good evening."

They talked for a short while along the rooftops before taking up positions on opposites sides, so they could peer down into different streets. The plan was to try to catch the creature as soon as it emerged, before it could harm anyone.

Ba'eru's eyes wandered across the tops of the other buildings and eventually to the outer walls. Above the outer walls, he could see the immense trees of the outer wilds. Even from this distance, he could tell that even one tree would be big enough to house several families if it was hollowed out.

The wind swept gently over him, and he watched the leaves twist and turn in the distance. There was something fascinating about the never-ending forest. The trees always looked so calm and inviting. Perhaps he would find peace out there, away from the noise and press of humanity. He continued to stare at the trees as the sky grew darker, until he could no longer make out their shapes through the blaze of the fire crystals that illuminated the city at night.

He sighed and turned back only to discover that Pasultu was gone. Images of her partially devoured form flashed across his mind, and he looked around quickly. It was then he noticed the falling flares in the distance and the silhouette of her running across the rooftops.

Cursing himself for getting distracted, he reached out with his mind to make sure nothing was hiding in the darkness ahead. He opened a portal and stepped through only a few steps behind her. She turned and glanced in his direction, a strange smile and confused expression flashing across her face before she turned back.

Many of the roof tops were connected by narrow walkways that they used to quickly arrive at the source of the flares. Below them several city guards were huddled around the mostly devoured corpse of one of their own. Others were quickly climbing down into a sewer grate at the opposite end of the street.

Ba'eru closed his eyes and viewed an empty patch of the street with no traffic. He opened a portal, and they both stepped out onto the ground below. He closed the portal, and they followed the other guards down into the sewers.

"What happened?"

"A guard was attacked. His partner saw the creature, shot at it, and it went back down into the sewers."

"What did it look like?"

"It looked like a cross between a cat and a monkey with spikes on its back. I've never seen anything like it... fur, huge claws, and teeth. And this massive tail."

Ba'eru and Pasultu looked around. The rain sewer ran roughly north and south. Approximately ten yards from the grating in both directions, the sewer tunnels turned into four-way intersections. Ba'eru looked around for some clue as to which direction the creature had gone. He could see no claw marks in the stone, and a cursory attempt at remote viewing revealed only the city guards running haphazardly down any path they found.

They picked a random direction and joined the search. Hours passed with no success. A city guard had died, and the creature had not been found, but now they knew for sure how it was getting around the city.

"Can you view ahead into the tunnels?" asked Pasultu.

Ba'eru closed his eyes and reached out with his mind. He couldn't see far but still managed to catch glimpses of searching guards, empty tunnels, and water.

"Nothing in the immediate vicinity," he responded, opening his eyes.

"Where are the guards not looking?" she asked.

"This way"; he turned and headed down a nearby tunnel.

The bounty hunter tracked Pasultu's position behind him by the sound of her splashing steps. After several twists and turns, there was still no sign of the creature.

"We'll return to the main group," stated Pasultu.

Along the way, they collected the other guards.

Pasultu addressed the guards once they had returned to the surface. "Get maps of the sewer systems. I want two guards at every grate." Several guards took off to relay the orders. "Get me every blacksmith and aethercrafter you can find. We're going to seal off the grates and force the creature to only surface where we want it."

* * *

Ba'eru found himself sitting next to Pasultu at the weekly Tupsarru family dinner. Iskurtu sat directly opposite him, and he made a concerted effort to avoid looking at Pasultu any more than he had to. This was not an easy task, as she was dressed in much less utilitarian fashion than usual.

"Are there any updates on the progress of your investigation?" Iskurtu asked Pasultu.

Ba'eru turned to watch her response and noticed Maliku eyeing her. He flicked his eyes back over to Iskurtu and Eresu. Iskurtu seemed not to have noticed and was taking a bite while waiting for a response. Eresu had a slightly less pleasant expression than she normally did.

"At this time, we still do not have any leads on how the creature entered the city, but we have successfully established how it is moving around and where it is hiding. The creature is using the water drainage sewers. By tomorrow night, we should have all but one grating sealed. The creature will either starve or surface into our trap."

"Impressive," commented Iskurtu with a smile. She looked at Ba'eru and he looked her directly in the eyes. She turned back to their guest; "I suppose this will mean the end of the extra city guard patrols and the curfew?"

"Unfortunately, that is not my decision to make," Pasultu turned toward Maliku. "That lies with the council to decide."

Maliku swallowed his food and nodded. "The council has yet to make a final decision, but there are those who suggest that the increased guard patrols and curfew have made the city safer, and, thus, should stay."

"The people won't like that," said Ba'eru, turning to face Maliku. "They only barely stay inside the buildings at night as it is. Once this threat passes, they will be eager to return to their former freedom, even if it is a freedom restricted by the outer walls."

"This is true," replied Maliku. "However, should the council retain the current restrictions, it will build a desire for freedom and free movement within the people. This may lend itself to support for city expansion. I have several proposals in place for expansion, as something I push for frequently."

"If the pretense for keeping the restrictions is that if one creature can breach into the city, then others can as well, wouldn't that discourage expansion into the outer wilds?"

"Ah, but by then we will have triumphed over the creature and shown the people that we are capable of overcoming the outer wilds."

"And if they release the restriction?"

"Then I will argue once again that it is our destiny to subdue the wilds. I may even suggest that the creature's attacks are an afront to our rightful place as rulers of this world. Pride and ambition will win the day."

"So, no matter what happens, you win?"

"Always," Maliku smiled.

*   *   *

'The dinner progressed uneventfully, and they began to part ways. Ba'eru said his goodbyes and followed Pasultu out to the portal platform. In the darkness and distance from the manor, Ba'eru let his eyes drift over the inspector. He offered to portal her home, and she gave him the nearest coordinates to where she lived.

Pasultu disappeared into her portal, he closed it, and made his own. Ba'eru washed up and fell into bed. He was asleep moments after his head touched the pillow.

The dreamworld that formed before him was a pristine and peaceful version of the outer wilds. The world was etched in a silver outline from a moon more powerful than the real one, able to pierce the canopies to the roots. He walked along paths that could not have existed amid the huge, tangled roots of reality. The presence of the trees and the shades of green and brown brought a sense of peace to Ba'eru.

He could stay here forever.

Pasultu walked out from among the trees. She was dressed as she had been at the dinner. The unnatural lighting transformed her into shifting silver lines and curves as she moved between the shadows. Ba'eru's pulse quickened as he reached out toward her.

* * *

The creature ran through the tunnels. Several of the grates had been sealed shut and would not move. Irritation and frustration motivated him to move faster, his claws digging into the stone.

Eventually he slowed as the scent of several city guards wafted down through the grate ahead. This must be it. This must be the trap they had set for him. The creature snorted. They wouldn't be able to stop him.

He quietly moved into position to see where the guards were located. They appeared to be standing in a rough circle around the grate, mostly talking and looking in different directions. The artificial lights cast their shadows into the tunnels, preventing them from seeing what he did.

The creature positioned himself below the grate and shot upward. As soon as he landed, he swept his tail in a wide arc, knocking over the guards. He pounced on the first one, tearing into its throat, relishing the energetic flow of fresh blood. While still licking at his prey, he reached out and sank his claws deep into the chest of the next guard. With great effort, he tore himself away and leaped from one guard to the other, ripping and tearing at their throats and chests. The exhilaration of killing so many so quickly was overwhelming.

Perhaps these traps were really a gift in disguise?

A searing hot flame cut into his left shoulder, and he turned to see a man and a woman running toward him. He leaped back into the sewer and ran. Splashes and shouts could be heard only seconds later.

The creature turned right down the first branch he came to in an effort to lose his pursuers. Suddenly the sound of footsteps closed in behind him again. He turned to see the man and the woman running from what looked like an elliptical shimmering disk. This happened several more times; sometimes they were behind him, sometimes ahead. He only narrowly dodged several more shots as he endeavored to out maneuver them. Instinct began to kick in, and the creature sought desperately for its home.

The creature suddenly found itself in a dead end. It knew intuitively that this was home but was too frantic to remember why or how such an indefensible place would be considered a safe haven.

Unable to decipher the conflicting instincts and analysis, it turned and fled back the way it had come, following a couple twists and turns, hoping to reach the next intersection before its pursuers.

The two pursuers appeared again. With nowhere left to run, the creature spun around and attacked. Two searing balls of fire dug into its chest, and it fell to the ground. Its enemies stood over it as the creature held still, feigning death. Stillness helped calm him, and he remembered what he needed to do to get home. He heard a strange sound followed by a change in the air as if flowing through an opening. Voices from the city guard could be heard.

The creature's eyes opened the faintest crack, revealing a new shimmering ring with a view of the guards on the street above. He lashed out and knocked down the two humans. Then, he turned and ran back to the dead end. Glancing upward, he pressed a stone in the ceiling. A section of wall moved aside. He slipped into the opening, and the wall sealed shut behind him.

*   *   *

Ba'eru got back to his feet and rushed down the tunnel, but the creature had disappeared. He looked around in confusion. There was nowhere for the creature to have gone. The tunnel was a dead end. The bounty hunter turned to one side and began reaching out with his mind. Viewing straight through the side of the twisting passage, he could see Pasultu lying on the ground, unmoving, blood trickling down from the back of her head.

He ran through the few twists in the tunnels to where she had fallen and quickly dropped to examine her. He touched the side of her neck; she still had a pulse. Relief flooded through him, and he gently picked her up to examine the back of her head. The cut on the back of her head wasn't deep, but he wasn't sure about the blunt force damage to her brain or skull.

Ba'eru viewed the surface above them to make sure all was clear, raised an arm, and reopened his portal. He lifted her and walked through into the street above. He asked the nearest city guard what street they were on. He then turned and closed his eyes to concentrate on the much more distant target. Raising some of his fingers while still trying to hold Pasultu, he opened a new portal straight to the hospital. He walked through onto their emergency portal platform.

Medics quickly rushed to him and took Pasultu. He was pushed aside as he watched them take her away. His desire to follow clashed with the logic that he was not a medic. It was a strange sort of pain. Ba'eru entered the building and waited. Eventually, one of the staff returned and led him to her room.

He sat down next to her bed and held her left hand. The feel of her skin beneath his fingers eased the pain, satisfying a desire of which he had only been vaguely aware.

Time passed and his head drooped closer to her hand. As he stared at it, an impulse overcame his better judgment and he kissed the back of her hand.

Pasultu shook her head and muttered something. Her eyes opened and she sat up. Ba'eru dropped her hand and began to stand. She turned and gave him a strange expression.

"How are you feeling?" he asked, trying to hide his sudden awkwardness.

Her eyes looked down, then moved back and forth as if examining something he could not see.

"I will recover. I suggest you return home and get some rest."

As he turned to leave, he noticed that she held her left hand, rubbing it gently while staring at it intently.

*   *   *

Ba'eru's mind drifted back to reality as the sounds of quiet sobs penetrated his dream. It took him a second to realize what he was hearing and from where it was coming. He turned and saw Iskurtu sitting next to him in bed crying.

"What's wrong?" He tried to blink the sleep from his eyes.

She didn't answer, so he reached his hand out toward her, and she pulled away.

"Don't touch me."

"What? Now I'm confused. What's going on?" Confusion roused his mind to full wakefulness.

"I know, ok."

"Know what?"

She turned and glared at him through her tears. "You want her, don't you? It doesn't matter that I'm the one whose been with you this whole time. I'm the one who loved you and protected you."

"Her, who?"

"Don't play stupid: Pasultu!"

"What?"

"I saw it."

"Saw what?"

"I saw it in your head. I saw you kiss her; I saw what you dreamed about her."

Guilt and shame rushed through him. His desires had been real, but this pain in Iskurtu was never something he had wanted.

A moment later, irritation and anger began to sprout in his mind.

"Wait, were you reading my mind while I was asleep? I thought you said you'd never do that? Why did you do it? How long have you been doing this?"

"Don't try to change the subject. I was only trying to protect you. You're the one who was betraying me, not the other way around."

"Protect me, how?"

Iskurtu didn't respond. Her tears had stopped, and Ba'eru sensed that she hadn't intended to say as much as she had.

"How can you be protecting me by violating my mind while I'm asleep?"

"By keeping you out of the outer wilds, so you don't wander off and get yourself killed by wild animals or executed for breaching the city defenses."

"What are you talking about? I've only been there once, when I was hunting Saraqu."

Iskurtu's gaze shifted, and her hand movements betrayed her nervousness. The confusion began to evaporate as a possibility solidified before him.

"Have you been wiping my memory? Is that why it felt so familiar when I chased Saraqu?"

"You know what, go on, go die in the outer wilds with your pet whore for all I care."

She was angry again, but he wasn't sure he cared. His anger gave him focus, blocking out the sense of guilt and the cold voice of logic. He embraced its heat.

"Don't deceive yourself. I was just another plaything for a spoiled child."

Ba'eru grabbed his clothes and stormed out of the apartment.

* * *

Ba'eru was fuming as he stormed down random streets. He wasn't sure what memories were real and what was fake. How much of his life was missing? What had he done that he could not remember? How much of his relationship with Iskurtu was the product of her own meddling? It was bad enough that he was trapped in this cramped, crowded city, but now he was being constrained by the person he thought he could trust most.

The idea that Iskurtu would manipulate him so callously like this existed in such contrast with what he knew of her; that cool logic began to dampen the flames of his anger. Maybe he didn't really know her? Maybe she'd wiped those instances from his mind that would betray her true self?

Some part of him still did not believe that such deceitfulness and callous manipulations fit her, but the behaviors did remind him of the other members of her family. They had always shown much greater inclination toward controlling others.

The thought gave him pause. Perhaps Eresu had put Iskurtu up to this? Ba'eru turned down the first dark alley he could find. Making sure no one was around, he reached out with his mind and viewed the estate. He opened a portal to an out of the way corner on the second floor, not far from Eresu's rooms, and stepped through.

The manor was dark and silent. The servants would have gone to bed hours ago, and the guards only patrolled the perimeters of the manor and the grounds, not the interior halls. The aether lamps on the wall had been dialed back so that only a soft, faint glow barely illuminated the halls. It was just enough light to allow someone to see where they were going.

Ba'eru moved quietly until he reached Eresu's room and gently opened her door. There was no response, so he slipped inside, closed the door behind him, and moved to the foot of her bed. He was debating how best to wake and address her when he heard a click from the corner to his right. He spun in time to be blinded by the flaring of a fire crystal. A few seconds later, he was able to make out the vague shape of Eresu sitting in a chair pointing a weapon at him.

"I always knew that little brat would break, and you would come here to kill me in my sleep. Your kind cannot be trusted."

Confusion mixed with his anger and took on the greater portion. "Why would I want to kill you? I want answers. Why did you make Iskurtu erase my memories? How long has this been going on?"

His eyes began to grow more accustomed to the light, and he could see the suspicious, judgmental glare as Eresu lowered the weapon to her lap.

"Someone had to keep you in line. It was either that or the cage. Experiments can't be allowed to wander freely without any kind of leash."

"Experiments?"

"You're a half breed, and we couldn't risk you wandering back to your people just so you could rile them up against us. But at the same time, if we kept you locked in a cage or dissected you, we'd never know what you were truly capable of. My daughter is soft-hearted and weak, so it was easy to convince her that if she didn't do it, horrible things would happen to you."

Confusion, betrayal, and irritation swirled around inside Ba'eru. He wasn't sure what she was talking about, but it did seem to confirm what he had always sensed, that he was not like them, though he still didn't understand in what way.

Annoyed, he said, "Did I live up to your expectations?"

"Mine, yes. I expected nothing from you, and you proved to be as worthless as I'd surmised. My late husband was somewhat disappointed that you proved incapable of reproducing, as this meant your bloodline could not be used to strengthen our own for us to ascend to our rightful place on top of this world."

"What?"

"I guess it doesn't matter now. Your mother was gutter trash that was bred by one of the people of the forest. I assume it was some kind of sport for him; why else would he waste his time with such a useless creature? Your father was killed during capture and dissected. It provided some useful information, but we hoped a live specimen, even a half-breed, would prove more useful for study. If they can live in the outer wilds freely, then they must have some biological advantage that we might be able to acquire. Sadly, your mother's genes seem to have dominated, and you never amounted to much of anything."

Ba'eru wasn't sure what to say as he processed all this. It explained why he always felt out of place and looked down on at the estate. Maybe this was why he felt so much more at peace in the outer wilds? His gaze drifted off to one side as his mind shifted inward, analyzing what had been said along with his experiences.

A slight movement out of the corner of his eye caught his attention, and he narrowly dodged a shot from the old woman. He could hear her curse her age as he ran out the door. An alarm sounded within the manor, and he heard the guards rushing in through the main doors downstairs. Ba'eru opened a portal and quickly stepped out of the manor.

* * *

Irritation burned at the edges of his mind. The thought of being controlled and manipulated for so long was infuriating. The city felt like enough of a cage in its own right that these new revelations just pushed him over the edge. Ba'eru was done with this place. He would kill the rampaging creature, buy some supplies, and leave the city for the outer wilds.

Ba'eru portaled himself into the sewers near where they had lost the creature. He looked around for signs of claw marks or another passage near the dead end where it had disappeared. He'd been too distracted the last time to figure out what had happened, and now he was almost too angry to concentrate. He focused on his plan to leave the city and what he needed to do to get there.

He closed his eyes and reached out with his mind toward the dead end. There it was: another tunnel on the other side of the wall in front of him. He could see mechanisms in the walls and ceiling. Reaching up, he pushed on a piece of the ceiling, and the wall in front of him moved away. A new concern entered his mind. If the creature could use a secret door, then it was more intelligent than they'd realized. Worse yet, if there was such a door for it to use, then it most likely had human help.

Ba'eru proceeded cautiously down the new tunnel, weapon at the ready. Periodically, he'd reach out to look for other hidden chambers or passages but found none. Eventually, after several twists and turns most likely designed to disorient unwanted guests who might be tempted to portal out, the tunnel opened into a large room that was some sort of laboratory. It was much cleaner than the drug dealer's lab. Tables with dissected creatures, shelves full of jars containing bits of animals preserved in liquid, instruments, and books were everywhere.

He slowly made his way through the lab. When he reached what appeared to be the primary workspace, he examined the journal with its notes on the table. At first, he only skimmed the materials, but once he realized what he was reading, he picked up the book and began devouring its contents.

The author of the journal had been performing experiments on combining humans with animals from the outer wilds. Apparently, he had succeeded on giving himself the ability to transform into a mixture of several creatures. He had used this form to both kill the prostitute he'd impregnated and retrieve the fetus for examination to see if the animal-like attributes had been inherited. The researcher had not wanted anyone to know of his dalliances, and if the offspring had inhuman features, then his experiments would be exposed on a timetable not matching his own.

Unexpectedly, the researcher discovered that he loved killing humans in his animal form. It brought forth feelings he had not previously experienced. He even noted that the more he killed in creature form, the more alive and aware he felt in that form.

Ba'eru snorted and pocketed the book. This person had only discovered in transforming his body what the bounty hunter had witnessed in human killers already. He looked around the lab. There were no more tunnels or hidden doors. The killer must have regained human form in the lab and portaled out from there.

*   *   *

Ba'eru searched the room of the dead prostitute that had started this whole affair. He was looking for some clue as to who had impregnated her. There was nothing under the bed or in the mattress. None of the drawers held anything helpful.

"May I help you, or should I call the guards?"

He spun around and saw one of the other prostitutes standing in the doorway.

"Sorry, I'm Ba'eru, I've been helping Pasultu track the creature that killed the former occupant of this room."

"I recognize you, but why do you need to search her things, if she was killed by an animal?"

"I have reason to believe that there may be a human element to this. She was pregnant when she was killed. I need to figure out who the father was. Would she have kept anything from her clients?"

The other prostitute's face showed surprise, then anger before returning to a more impassive expression. She crossed the room to a corner and moved a small table with a potted plant. Bending down, she lifted the carpet and retrieved a small box from under the floor.

"Clients like their anonymity, but sometimes it helps to have something to keep them in check."

She handed him the box. Ba'eru thanked her and began to examine its contents. There were rings, buttons, medallions, and scraps of parchment with various insignias and notes. One of the rings looked familiar. The crest showed a bird holding a broken reclusive water widow in its talons, and a small scrap of parchment was tied to it with the note, "For my child," followed by a date from three weeks past.

"Thank you again," he said, taking the ring and the note. He opened a portal and left.

* * *

Anger pulled hard on its mental leash, eager to take control of Ba'eru as he stalked through the halls of the estate to Maliku's rooms. He found Iskurtu's brother in his study. The irritation he felt about how this family had treated him and his parents was compounded by visions of the torn, pregnant woman.

"Good morning," he said, looking up from a tome in which he was writing.

"Good morning," Ba'eru said, fighting to keep the irritation from his voice.

"What brings you to my study this fine morning?"

"I have some questions for you."

The councilman leaned back and gestured toward a chair opposite his desk; "Ask away."

Ba'eru sat down and pushed himself back in the chair so that he was sitting straight. He kept his feet apart and back enough so that he could stand quickly if needed.

"Where were you the night the prostitute was killed?"

Maliku looked around as if trying to remember; "Why, in my study, most likely."

"Can anyone confirm that?"

Maliku looked him in the eye and replied coolly, "I'm sure all the staff would be willing to attest to my presence. Why do you ask?"

"Were you a client of the prostitute that was killed recently?"

A slight smile flickered at the edges of his mouth. "That is hardly an appropriate question to ask one's future brother-in-law."

"I found the lair of the creature and its journal"; he held up the journal he had taken from the underground lab. "It details how the journal's owner first turned himself into a creature in order to kill a prostitute he'd accidentally gotten pregnant. That's when I found your signet ring with a note about a child in the prostitute's possessions."

Maliku laughed; "Such a fanciful tale. Any pickpocket could have stolen the ring, or it could be forged. It proves nothing."

"But hasn't your family been looking for ways to improve human capabilities? That's why you killed my father and kept me around, isn't it?"

Maliku's smile faded slightly.

"The council would believe me. The forest people are not common knowledge to the people in the streets, but surely the council is aware of their existence. Besides, I already summoned Pasultu on my way over. She'll be here soon to arrest you."

"No one will be arresting me," Maliku sneered.

"Why would they arrest you?"

Both men turned to see Iskurtu standing in the door. At the sight of Ba'eru, expressions of pain washed over her face.

Maliku stood and strode over to embrace his sister.

"See what you've done? You already betrayed my sister and the city by breaching the walls, and now you come to threaten me with false accusations of impropriety and murder? After our family showed you such kindness."

Anger got the better of him and Ba'eru stood quickly, spinning on the spot to face Maliku. He could see concern at his angry expression in Iskurtu's eyes.

"How dare you accuse my brother! We raised you. I protected you all these years."

She reached for her brother's hand as a sign of unity; "I will not have you slandering my family—"

Iskurtu's words cut off. Her eyes went wide, and she turned toward her brother. Ba'eru looked at Iskurtu's hand clutching Maliku's and realized her brother's memories must now be open to her. A pained and horrified expression spread across her face.

"How could..."

"It is unspeakably tragic that you chased my sister here to silence her," Maliku said, looking Ba'eru in the eyes.

Maliku spun Iskurtu to face Ba'eru and slit her throat with a partially clawed hand. Surprise filled her eyes, and she dropped to the floor.

Letting out a roar of pain and rage, Ba'eru drew his weapon and fired at Maliku. Maliku dodged and took the shot in the arm instead of the center of his chest. He ran from the room, and Ba'eru followed him out.

Ba'eru turned and watched Maliku run down the hall. He raised his weapon and fired, hitting Maliku in the back. The man fell to the ground. Ba'eru walked over and kicked him onto his back.

"You killed your own child and your own sister. You are the real scum of this world." He raised the weapon, preparing to fire it into Maliku's face.

"Stop!"

He turned to see Pasultu and several city guards. She was aiming her weapon at him.

"Drop the weapon!"

"He's the killer! I have proof!" Ba'eru choked back tears; "And he killed Iskurtu." He lowered the weapon but did not drop it.

A guard from the other end of the hall entered the study and returned. "She's dead."

"The gutter trash killed her to hide the fact that he breached the walls," shouted Maliku.

One of the guards asked, "Did you breach the walls?"

Ba'eru hesitated.

Pasultu's expression stiffened. "Yes, he did. I saw it when he touched my hand in the hospital."

Turning her attention completely on Ba'eru, she said, "Drop the weapon."

"Yes, I breached the walls, but I did not bring this creature into the city. Maliku figured out how to change himself into it."

Anger and disgust washed over Pasultu's face. Seeing this caused Ba'eru to feel a sharp stab of pain in his chest.

"The selfish monster broke into my room last night to threaten me into telling him where Iskurtu was. She had found out about his crimes."

Eresu stood behind the inspector and the guards. One of the house guards nearby said he could confirm that an alarm was raised the previous night.

Ba'eru closed his eyes. Fury surged through him at the thought of these people taking lives without consequence. He took a deep breath and started to relax his grip on the weapon. As he let it slip from his fingers, he dropped to the floor. His palms slammed into the ground, and a portal opened up beneath him and Maliku. The monster's eyes went wide as they both fell through.

* * *

Ba'eru and Maliku hit the stone floor of Saraqu's secret lab, the broken pieces of carapace crunching beneath them. Ba'eru crawled over to Maliku and grabbed him by the throat. The man grabbed his wrists and struggled for a moment before a smile crept over his face.

Fur began to sprout from Maliku's skin, and his neck grew thicker. The hands gripping Ba'eru's wrists grew claws. Realization hit Ba'eru, and he jumped back before Maliku's grip could get any stronger.

Maliku rolled onto his stomach as the transformation continued. Clawed hands tore away his clothes as muscles grew and bones shifted. A tail sprouted and grew. Toes lengthened, nails growing to claws. The once-human face mutated as bones restructured themselves, teeth extended and sharpened, and ears expanded. Even the eyes morphed from circular pupils to vertical ellipses. Short, sharp spines mixed with the fur along his back. The final result had a rather simian-feline appearance.

Ba'eru looked around and patted down his own body, looking for some kind of weapon. He found the aether torch, drew it from his coat, and began adjusting the dials.

The monster rose and turned toward Ba'eru. The bounty hunter looked up in time to see the beast leap toward him. He raised his hands palm out, and the claws disappeared into the portal between them.

Ba'eru leaped into his apartment. Spinning around, he saw the beast looking around in confusion. Before it could turn, he hurled himself onto its back. The sharp spines pierced the thinner material of his pants, but his jacket mostly protected his chest.

Using the pain-induced anger to his advantage, he wrapped his free arm around the monster's neck.

A long fur-covered appendage reached up and wrapped around the bounty hunter's throat. Sharp claws tore through his sleeve, while another set reached up and over to rake along his back.

With a painfilled roar, Ba'eru forced the device against the monster's chest and thumbed it on.

A blue-white flame shot from the device instantly, searing a hole through the creature's ribs and organs. Ba'eru could feel nothing, then a sudden spike of pain from the edge of the flame. He pulled the device across the creature's chest, tearing it open.

The monster's limbs went limp, the pressure released from Ba'eru's throat, and both fell to the floor. Ba'eru rolled off and lay there, panting.

After some time, he got up, created a portal on the floor that led inside the guard house, somewhere near the ceiling, and pushed the mutated corpse through.

Startled shouts erupted as the body collided with those nearby and hit the ground but remained still. He didn't wait or bother to look more; he just deactivated the portal.

*   *   *

Ba'eru stood on the outermost city wall in the dark. Images of Iskurtu's tears the previous night and the look of horror on her face when she was murdered haunted his mind. His thoughts were interrupted only by memories of the look of betrayal and condemnation on Pasultu's face. He tried to shift his thoughts to his one success, but it did not help. Maliku would no longer be able to terrorize the people of the city, but Eresu and her kind would not stop their manipulations. There was nothing he could do to change these facts, and there was nothing in the city left for him.

Even the outer wilds no longer seemed appealing; the pain of failure and loss made them seem as hollow as the city. He'd failed, and neither Maliku's death nor the once peaceful trees brought any comfort.

His gaze shifted up from the darkness below to stare at the portal hovering in the open air before him. Ba'eru lifted a foot and held it in the space between the portal and the wall, hesitating for a brief moment before making his decision and shifting his weight forward.

IV

Pale Love
Dynoltir, +2005 TR

The rain created a solid sheet over the windows as Naila gazed out into the darkness. She could vaguely hear the voices of her parents in the front two seats, but she wasn't paying attention.

Sounds of her parents' voices blended with the rhythmic beats of the windshield wipers and the irregular but constant pounding of the rain. Every now and then, lights would appear in front of them and then pass by. Naila stared out the window, strangely comforted by the mixture of sounds and the water-distorted darkness outside. Her eyes would widen in awe and excitement whenever she was lucky enough to see blue or purple lightning arcing through the sky, illuminating the clouds.

Another set of lights grew in the distance, but something seemed off to her budding subconscious observations. These lights were not steady and seemed to be shifting back and forth. Naila turned to watch as she heard the tones in her parents' voices change.

Suddenly, the lights were directly in front of them. Her father turned the wheel hard to avoid the oncoming car. As he tried to turn back, to return to the proper path, the car began to swerve. She saw his movements become quick and frantic. Her mother's arms reached out to grip the car for support.

Everything tilted. Naila could feel herself being pulled toward the side of the car, then toward roof, then toward the other side, and then back into her seat, over and over. The seatbelt cut into her body painfully. She was nearly too surprised and disoriented to fully realize what was happening.

The sounds of shattering glass and crunching and tearing metal filled her ears, mixing with her mother's screams.

Eventually the car came to a halt on its side. Naila unfastened her seatbelt and fell onto the shattered window that she'd been staring out of only moments before. She stood up carefully and then half climbed, half peeked over the back of her mother's seat.

"Mommy?"

Naila's mother lie motionless, and her father hung awkwardly above her. Her father began to move first.

With a groan, he looked down and saw Naila staring up at him with tears beginning to well up in her eyes.

"Daddy, why is Mommy sleeping?"

"Shhhh, it's ok, just move back a bit, and we'll take care of Mommy. She'll be ok."

Naila backed up and watched as her father slowly freed himself from his seatbelt and carefully positioned himself so that he could stand without stepping on her mother. He wriggled out of his jacket and used it to cover the broken bits of glass still sticking out of the door frame.

"Let's get you out of here first," he said while reaching down for her.

Naila held up her arms, and he grabbed below her shoulders and pulled her to him. He paused a moment to hug her, and she wrapped her arms around his neck. The feeling of her father was comforting and gave her a momentary distraction from worry about her mother.

"Ok, I'm going to lift you up through the window. I want you to sit still on the back door until I get up there with you, ok," he said, holding her away slightly, so he could look at her.

She wiped away tears and nodded. He lifted her up, and she climbed out the window toward the back door. Naila tried and failed to avoid looking over the edge. She moved cautiously to avoid falling as she turned around to watch and wait for her father on the slick surface. She watched his hands grip the window frame near the roof and side and heard him grunt slightly as he pulled himself up to sit on the edge with his feet dangling inside the car. He looked around and sighed before carefully bringing his feet up and out over the edge of the car.

Her father spun away from her, hopped down onto the ground next to the underside of the car, and winced. He seemed to take his weight off his right foot as he turned and held out his hands for her.

"Come here."

Naila gingerly reached out, and he lowered her to the ground. They walked hand in hand away from the car over to a large tree.

"Stay here. I need to go get Mommy from the car."

"Ok," she said.

Naila watched as he returned to the car and climbed back in. Several minutes later, she saw him crawling out of the trunk, dragging her mother. Tears began to fill Naila's eyes once more, and she started to sob. She took a step toward her parents, and her father turned to see her. He looked at something on the underside of the car and back to her.

"Stay back," he shouted.

The harshness in his tone hurt her feelings, but a moment later she saw liquid dripping from the car catch fire. Her father dropped her mother and ran toward her. As he knelt down in front of her, a bright light followed by a loud boom filled the space behind him. He shuddered and slumped to one side as the light faded.

Naila reached down and touched her father; "Daddy?"

Suddenly the rain seemed to stop in midair. Naila could see individual droplets suspended above her and her father. Silence surrounded her, and she looked around.

A black robed figure stood in the space between her mother and her father, the still flames of the mangled car visible behind him. She wasn't sure if she would have been able to see him without the light as contrast.

The figure moved toward her mother and knelt beside her. He reached out a thin hand and gently touched her face. A soft blue-white glow flowed out of her mother and into his finger.

The figure stood and slowly walked toward her father. Again, the figure knelt and reached out. Now that he was closer, she could see just how skeletal his finger was as it touched her father's face. The blue-white light welled up in his eyes and faintly outlined his features before flowing into the skeletal finger.

Naila looked up at the figure. He was looking down, and his hood obscured the side of his face, so she couldn't see it. Slowly, his head began to lift and turn toward her. A strange fear gripped Naila, and she stepped back as the impenetrable void inside his hood stared at her with two glowing blue-white eyes. Naila stared at the spheres of light, weirdly fascinated and almost comforted by them.

The skeletal hand rose slowly into view, fingers spreading out so that the palm faced her when it reached the level of her face. Her eyes shifted to the bony hand as it approached. She wanted to scream and opened her mouth.

But instead, everything turned black, and Naila fell asleep.

*   *   *

The little girl went through the motions of life. Adults came and went, each producing sounds that formed the background noise of her existence.

The interior walls of an ambulance were replaced by the wide, pale-colored walls of a hospital. These were replaced by quick flashes of the warm, inviting walls of her grandparents' home, intermixed with the artificially warm walls of the funeral home. There were many vertical stone slabs, many shifting black objects, but mostly, just endless fields of green grass.

Somewhere, deep inside her mind, she knew what was happening; acknowledging it was confusing and painful. She didn't want to cry. She didn't want to hurt.

So, her inner eye looked for something else, anything else that would provide solace. In the darkness, it found two things: two glowing blue-white orbs suspended in a void.

There had been something peaceful in those spheres. Their light had been soft and comforting, as if the hard edges had been worn away by untold millennia of shared pain, leaving only the smooth curves of compassion.

When her inner eye began to drift and tendrils of pain began to creep into her sinuses, throat, and heart, she would redirect it back to that last peaceful memory.

*   *   *

Naila sat on the bus, in a seat toward the back. She rested her head on the glass and stared out at the passing trees and fields. Her class had gone on a field trip to the state capital to hear about the legislative process. It had been incredibly boring, and now she was just zoning out, ignoring the other students' chatter.

Nothing went through her mind as the bus continued along the highway. The only thing that made her aware of the passage of time was the lengthening of shadows as the sun made its way west.

The sun was blazing almost directly through the windows on the opposite side of the bus, and Naila started to feel uncomfortable in the direct sunlight. She shifted and looked around, no longer distracted by the scenery.

A few minutes later, the bus came to a slow crawl. She could see the teacher talking to the bus driver near the front. A murmured wave swept back through the students until it reached her ears: There was a bad accident up ahead, and they were going to pass it.

Much to her annoyance, the other students began to crowd around her side of the bus. Something deep inside her was disgusted at their voyeuristic fascination with the tragic event.

The students grew quiet as the bus crept past the accident. Naila turned to look, the reactions of her classmates arousing instinctive curiosity.

Sympathy for the victims and shame that she even looked mixed with the curiosity. A car had gone off the road and hit a tree. As they passed, she could see paramedics working on one of the bodies that had been thrown from the vehicle. The movement of the bus slowed to a standstill.

Naila grew angry at the thought that even the bus driver was stopping just so they and these stupid kids could leer at someone else's pain. She turned to confront the other occupants of the bus and saw that no one was moving. Something deep in her memory stirred.

She turned quickly and looked out the window. A black robed figure walked slowly between the victims. He bent and touched the first, the soft blue-white light flowing into his finger. Then, he approached the second and repeated the process.

Naila's jaw dropped open in amazement. Memories so old and faint she had begun to doubt their veracity began flooding through her.

It was real and happening again. She opened the window as far as it would go and tried to shout to the figure.

The black robed figure turned slowly in her direction and raised his head. Two glowing blue-white orbs looked out of the darkness within the hood. A peace she had not directly experienced since she was a small child flashed through her. Those eyes had been her sole comfort for so long in this now distant world.

"Who are you?" she whispered.

The figure stood silent and still.

"Who are you?" she tried again, this time louder.

The figure vanished and time returned to normal.

Naila slumped down in her seat and looked around. No one seemed to realize that anything out of the ordinary had occurred.

She slouched down, staring straight ahead at the seat in front of her. That robed figure was real. She had seen him again. Looking into his eyes had brought back that sense of peace and comfort. In some way, her child's mind had grown attached to the memory of them, and experiencing this again made the difference between the experience and the memory stand out more sharply. It was like the difference between remembering a friend and actually spending time with them. In some strange way, she felt better having seen him again, but now there was a slight pain that he was gone.

Naila wanted to see him again.

*   *   *

The years passed by in a haze. The chatter of people around her shifted, rising and falling like waves as she moved through time. The rows of lockers lining the halls of her high school were replaced by the crowded, old halls of buildings on a college campus. Rows of chairs filled with bodies shifted to cold rooms with hard tables, sinks, and the smell of chemicals. Eventually, these were replaced by warmer, though still sterile environments where patients came and went. Eventually, even this faded into a dull routine through night shrouded halls and sleeping patients nearing the end of their lives.

There was a change in the background sounds that caught Naila's attention and dragged her back into full awareness of the world around her. She knew what it meant and felt a spike of worry that she might be too late.

Naila grabbed the door frame and swung into the room. The black robed figure was just beginning to straighten up. He turned slowly to look at her.

She held out a hand and panted, "Wait!"

He was gone and time returned to normal. Naila was irritated. She had waited so long and had been so close. Frustration at her own failure ate at her insides, and it took an effort of will to mask it from her colleagues.

The frustration had the positive effect of motivating her to find a better way. Charts and files burned themselves into her mind as the monitors on the computer wore away the patience of her eyes. She blinked away the strain, determined to know who would die soonest.

The old man in the bed before her stopped wheezing. His chest became still as the small clock in her hand audibly ticked away the seconds. Naila looked at the readouts and saw no heartbeat. A moment later, the ticking stopped.

The black robed figure stood over the patient, on the other side of the bed. He looked at Naila with his glowing blue-white orbs, then languidly turned and reached out toward the patient.

"Who are you? What are you? Are you actually Death? Are there more of you?" She blurted out her questions as quickly as possible, leaning forward in her excitement, not knowing how long he would remain.

The figure ignored her, continuing to reach out toward the patient. Naila had gone to great lengths to be there when he appeared. Years of planning and study, weeks of waiting, and now he was ignoring her.

She reached out in irritation and grabbed his wrist; "Please, just say something."

His wrist felt like cold bone beneath her fingers. She could feel no flesh or warmth, yet the arm continued to move. There was no pause, no hesitation, no slowing its inexorable path. She watched in frustration as his skeletal finger touched the patient's face. The soft blue-white glow lit up the eyes and faintly outlined the face before flowing into the finger.

Naila knew he would disappear soon.

"Please, I just want to know who you are. You were there when my parents died. You don't know it, but you helped me through that terrible time."

She released her grip and reached for his hood as he continued to straighten. Her arms weren't long enough to let her pull it back, but maybe she could touch his face.

Her fingertips disappeared into the void beneath the hood. At first, she was worried that something bad was happening, but then she felt a smooth cool surface beneath her fingertips. Naila didn't have time to explore or ponder what she was touching.

The figure was gone. The ticking in her hand resumed; the heart monitor continued its single, continuous tone.

*   *   *

Naila was vaguely aware that she was moving through the halls of the facility, but her mind was focused elsewhere. The conundrum that preoccupied her focus and exacerbated her frustration was the inconsistency with which people died. Some lasted days, others lasted months. Some died in the day, others at night.

While it was true that she had been patient these many years, she didn't want to keep waiting for some unpredictable chance to see the black robed figure again. His lack of response was offensive, given her years of dedication. Even after all she'd been through, he said nothing.

In short, she wanted answers, and she wanted them now.

A bony hand grabbed her wrist, and she looked down in shock.

An old woman whispered something Naila could not hear. She bent down, closer to the patient.

"Please, let me just die. I don't want to suffer anymore," came the strained whisper.

Naila was shocked and recoiled from the elderly woman.

"I—I can't do that," she stammered before recovering. "Do you need your meds adjusted?"

"It will never be enough. Please, just end it," the old woman begged.

Faced with the enormity of such a question, Naila turned and ran out of the room.

She walked hurriedly down the hall, not having any real destination in mind. Before she realized it, her palms were touching cold metal, and she was walking up cement steps in the cool side emergency stairwell.

When she reached the roof, she paced back and forth, her heart pounding. How could someone ask her that? Didn't they know she'd seen her parents die right in front of her? How could she watch that happen and be the cause of it? Even if she didn't have such an experience so young, murder was still morally and legally forbidden. She couldn't go to prison; why would someone ask her to throw away her life like that?

After a few deep breaths, a cool calm seeped into her mind. A thought came with it. A thought that made her pause her frantic pacing, made her heart race in excitement.

Granting the patient's request would be an act of mercy, but also an act that would solve her dilemma. If she did it, the black robed figure would come. He would be there when she wanted him there. It would give her another opportunity to ask her questions. It might even show him that she was in control. She could summon him at her whim. This would give her all the time and opportunity to understand him and to control him if he did not want to cooperate. She would no longer need to wait. Their meeting would be on her terms, not his.

Adrenaline surged through her. She would have to be careful. She didn't want to get caught, but she needed to make the most of this opportunity.

After a few minutes of thought, she made up her mind and returned to the patient's floor. She went first to a supply closet and got what she needed.

Naila walked back into the woman's room and closed the door behind her.

"Are you awake?"

The woman nodded.

She stood over the woman; "Were you serious? Do you really want to die now?"

The woman smiled faintly and nodded.

Naila turned and injected something into the IV line that was already attached to the patient. The woman's movements slowed until they were nothing. The heart monitor went flat.

Then it stopped moving.

The figure stood before her on the other side of the patient. It tilted its head slightly, looked at her, down at the patient, and then back up at her. He slowly shook his head, then began to bend and reach toward the patient.

Prepared for her less than advantageous position, she dashed around the bed and grabbed the back of his hood from behind. With a swift tug she pulled it down.

The figure paused and turned toward her. She stared in wonder at the smooth flawless surface of his head. The blue-white glowing orbs stared down into her eyes. She reached up to stroke his cheek with one hand. He began to raise a skeletal hand toward her wrist, while his other moved up and back toward his hood.

"Please, you were kind to me when I was a child. You sent me to sleep instead of allowing me to sit and stare at my dead parents. My memory of you helped me through that ordeal. Surely you must care. Please, I just want to know you. I want to know what I've been seeing this whole time and what it means."

The black robed figure pulled her hand away and returned his hood to cover his head, the shadows obliterating his face once again. He turned back and completed his task, before vanishing as usual.

Naila sighed and walked from the room. She had seen his face, though she could not remember if it was bone or gaunt skin. All she knew was that she had seen and touched what no one else had. His secret existence was hers alone, though she did not know why.

* * *

"I guess after my parents died, everything my classmates said seemed insignificant," Naila commented as the black robed figure straightened from his task.

The figure stood amid a tangle of physical obstacles that had been placed around the deceased patient's bed. Tables and chairs lay overturned as they were unable to stop his calm but inexorable movements.

The figure vanished, and the clock began to tick again. Naila quickly straightened the furniture before slipping out the door. Her mind began to recede inward as she contemplated her next move, when a sound behind her penetrated to her consciousness.

"Again," sighed a nurse. "It seems like they die so much faster these days."

A pang of worry erupted in her mind. She had been careless. Why hadn't she considered the natural death rate in the facility? She had unnecessarily exposed her activities.

Paranoia made her acutely aware of every subtle movement and sound throughout the facility for the remainder of her shift.

Was that nurse behind her watching her? Was she walking suspiciously? How should an innocent person walk?

"I think she's hiding something," whispered one nurse to another around the corner and to the left as Naila approached an intersection in the hallways.

"You should definitely confront—" the second voice cut off as she rounded the corner and headed in the opposite direction of their conversation.

Both coworkers had looked at Naila with startled expressions. Did they suspect her? Were they afraid that she knew of their suspicions?

No one said anything to her as they got ready to leave at the end of their shift. Were they avoiding her now? Did they fear that she might retaliate?

* * *

Naila walked away from the lights of the facility into the welcoming shadows of the surrounding neighborhood. Her eyes never fully adjusted to the darkness as the streetlights incessantly found ways to overcome the tree branches above.

Patches of light and dark alternated in irregular intervals, gradually forming a visual equivalent of white noise. Her mind mulled over recent events and possible future solutions, as no one had confronted her the past several days. Two thoughts kept emerging in her mind: She could not stop, and she needed to find a new source of subjects.

A shift in the lighting jarred her out of her reverie enough for her to look up and notice a bar across the street. Images of the people inside flashed through her mind. They weren't connected to the facility, and sometimes bad things happened to drunk people.

Naila crossed the street and entered the bar, unsure what she would do or if she could do it.

Scents of various types of alcohol drifted through the air. The sounds of conversations blended into an unintelligible wall of noise around her as she made her way to the bar.

Naila ordered a drink and stared at it, waiting for her subconscious mind to find the epiphany of how she should proceed.

She waited, but no epiphany struck her.

Her eyes began to scan the room, bringing her surroundings into focus.

A couple men in dust-covered t-shirts and jeans sat at one end of the bar, drinking and chatting pleasantly.

A woman dressed in business attire sat at another end. Her hair and clothes were disheveled, and she was downing shots at an alarming rate. There were obvious signs of fatigue and stress etched in her face.

Across the room, a group of girls sat around a table. Not far away was another table with a group of guys. Both sets were trying their best not to make it too obvious that they were sneaking peaks at the other.

A young woman walked up to the bar and was soon being chatted up by a young man. When they ordered drinks, she saw the man surreptitiously drop something into the woman's glass.

Naila's mind focused in on this pair. She watched closely as they sipped their drinks, the man always consuming much less than the girl. He was quick to order her a new one whenever her current drink was getting low. When they got up to leave, Naila followed.

The man led the woman around the corner of the bar, her steps already faltering. Naila's fingers curled around the spare poisoned syringe that she always kept in her pocket these days.

She followed them, sticking close to the shadows, until they reached the parking lot behind the bar. By the time the man reached his car, the woman was almost incoherent and could barely stand. As he struggled to get the almost dead weight into the back seat, Naila moved up behind him.

Naila rammed the syringe into the back of his neck and pressed the plunger. He screamed in surprise and pain, attempted to reach back for her hand and turn to see his attacker, but it was too late. His knees hit the pavement with the surprised look still on his face.

That face stopped mid fall.

The black robed figure stood before Naila on the other side of the man. He looked down at the woman in the car, then at the man on his knees, then at their surroundings, before finally looking at Naila and shaking his head.

"I'm sorry, but people at the facility are getting suspicious. We're going to have to find safer ways to meet," she said.

Again, the figure shook his head slowly.

"I know it's not what we're used to, but I can't let you slip away from me, not after everything we've been through so far," she explained.

He began to bend toward the man and slowly reached out as he always did.

"I wish there was a way for us to have more time," she mused, watching him. "These few seconds are so short. Even the barriers at the facility didn't grant us much extra time, but don't worry, nothing can keep us apart forever."

The figure finished straightening from his task and vanished.

The man fell over and hit the ground. Naila looked around to make sure no one was watching. She rolled his body under the car and made sure the woman was comfortable. Then, she quietly closed the car door and left.

* * *

Naila walked down the darkened sidewalk, hands in her thick coat pockets, arms stiff at her sides as she tensed against the chill night air. The wind whistled around her ears and mixed with the sounds of leaves periodically crunching under foot.

She kept her head angled down, watching the leaves skitter along the ground. It was pleasant to watch, but it wasn't her true focus. Her eyes frequently darted around, searching for anyone else on the street, especially if they were alone.

A car drove past and parked up the street. As she approached, she noticed no one else besides the driver through the windows. She pulled her hands out of her pockets.

A man got out and they collided as he stepped up onto the sidewalk. As they made contact, she stabbed him quickly with a small sharp object that she then deftly concealed in the flurry of apologies from both of them.

Naila backed away a few steps. The man's apologies stopped, and he slumped to the ground. The leaves stopped skittering along the sidewalk.

The black robed figure looked at her and then at the fallen man. She hopped up to sit on the hood of the car as he shook his head slowly at her again. Naila gave him a smile in response.

"I'm not sure I like this weather," she said, sandwiching her hands between her butt and the warm car as he began to bend toward the corpse. "Work has been quiet lately. I think things have settled down, so I should be relatively safe now." She paused and smiled at him; "I think I have something special planned for the holidays. We'll be able to spend more time together."

The figure vanished.

Naila sighed, hopped down, then disappeared into the shadows of a nearby ally.

*   *   *

The empty warehouse below was mostly dark despite the spotlights aimed at one end of the space. People moved and writhed in the darkness, their shouts and conversations mixing with the voices and instruments under the spotlights. Naila was excited, but not by the music, the dancing, or the crowds.

When the musical queue arrived, she activated the fog machines around the stage and perimeter of the building. Thick white mist descended on the revelers, spreading out through them.

As her excitement and anticipation mounted, a smile crept across her masked face.

The mist slowly spread through the room. When it reached the center, the music began to falter. The edges of the writhing mass began to disintegrate. The center became more frantic, but that only increased their consumption of the tainted air. None of them made it to an exit.

Naila watched and waited for a couple minutes to make sure no one remained conscious. When she was confident that it was safe, she activated the fans to vent the building and climbed down to walk among the slowly twitching bodies.

Some of the bodies along the edge stopped moving. A moment later, time stopped.

The black robed figure stood in the center of the room and turned in a circle, surveying the bodies around him. When he came to look at her again, he stopped.

A deep, menacing voice that reverberated through some ancient, invisible chasm spoke one word, "Stop."

Naila's eyes went wide, and she rushed to the figure and flung her arms around him.

"You spoke to me," she cried, exuberantly squeezing his cold, bony frame. "I knew this day would be special, but I didn't know that you'd actually speak to me. I'm so happy. Thank you!"

The black robed figure turned and moved toward the corpses at the outer edge. In a moment of fear and excited hope, Naila walked beside him and reached out to take his left hand. He did not pull away, the touch of his hand in hers filing her with elation.

"I've been planning this for a while," she began, moving with him as he began his rounds. "I know our time together is usually so brief, so I wanted a chance to really get to relax and spend time together.

"This was an expensive occasion to arrange. I had to find a venue with lots of people who would not want to attract legal attention, get a job helping out, then plan the logistics.

"The poison from the fog machine should act slowly enough that they will die sequentially, and we'll have plenty of time together. I was so excited about tonight that it was difficult being patient, waiting until no more guests were going to arrive, knocking out the bouncer, and locking the doors."

She squeezed his hand and hugged his arm; "But it was all worth it."

Naila chatted away as they moved around the room. When the last of the deceased at the perimeter were gathered, the figure vanished.

A few seconds later, he returned.

Naila stifled a squeal of excitement and skipped through the bodies back to hold his hand. Again, he made his rounds through the crowd, collecting those who had most recently died.

The pattern continued for what amounted to hours to Naila. Each time anyone died, time would stop, the figure would appear, collect them, vanish, and then time would resume. Once it did, another would die, restarting the process all over again.

Eventually, Naila ran out of things to talk about and just quietly clung to the figure's arm, head resting against his shoulder as he moved around the room, releasing him only to hold his hand whenever he knelt by a corpse.

When he knelt over the final corpse, Naila crouched down to hug him tight one last time. Tears welled up in her eyes knowing that he would vanish, and their hours spent together this night would end. The feel of his body was comforting, but the knowledge of his imminent departure was sorrowful.

When he vanished, his absence caused a great pain in her chest.

*   *   *

Plans formed, fell apart, and reformed relentlessly in Naila's mind as she arrived at work and clocked in. She was oblivious to the world around her, desperately seeking the perfect solution, whether by reason or epiphany.

Her deep meditations were interrupted when she found several of her coworkers huddled outside the manager's office. When they saw her, they stopped talking and scattered.

Naila looked around, now acutely aware of her surroundings. Something was wrong.

A door clicked open behind her, and she turned.

Her supervisor had opened the door to her office and was gesturing in Naila's direction as two police officers walked out.

"Good evening, ma'am. I'm Officer Newbury, and this is Officer Steel," said the first cop. "Are you Naila Jones?"

"Yes," she said tentatively, looking around for some clue as to what was happening. "Why do you ask?"

"We need to ask you a few questions about an incident that occurred over the weekend. Would you be willing to come down to the station and help us with our investigation?"

Naila kept her face impassive as fear and alarm swirled within her. Had she been caught? Did she make a mistake? How had they connected her to the concert?

"Sure, let me get my coat," she replied pleasantly.

"Certainly," he responded.

They followed her as she walked in the direction of the break room and the lockers beyond.

Adrenaline surged through her, and she fought to keep an even pace. If she went with them, she'd be at their mercy in the police station. She couldn't risk being in such a vulnerable position. A thousand escape plans collided together in her mind as she entered the break room. It was unlikely that she'd be able to outrun them on foot. If she managed to get to her car, then they would just start pursuing in their patrol cars, and their radios would allow them to coordinate with other officers to catch her. She needed time.

As she retrieved her coat, she felt one of the syringes she had prepared but had not used. Inspiration struck her.

She put on her coat, and they turned and headed back toward the front where the patrol car was parked. Everyone was keeping their distance as she passed with the two officers, but she could see several gathered near the entrance to watch. She suppressed her annoyance and prepared herself for what was about to happen. When they drew near one of her coworkers, she pretended to trip and fell toward the nurse. Before the nurse could step out of range, Naila stabbed her with the syringe. The woman screamed, drawing everyone's attention.

The officer behind Naila shouted. The lead officer lunged toward Naila, while the other moved to the nurse. Naila narrowly evaded the officer's grasping hands as she stumbled to her feet.

The officers froze.

The black robed figure stood next to her fallen coworker as time stood still.

"Do not do this," came the menacing, inhuman voice.

"I'm sorry to drag you into this, but thank you for helping me again," she said quickly.

A new thought appeared before her. She turned quickly and grabbed a gun and a knife from the closest officer. Calmly she walked from person to person in the entrance way and slit their throats. It would take him longer to collect ten dead than it would just one. This would give her even more time to escape and eliminate her pursuers.

Naila ran out the back of the facility, keeping the gun in case it could be useful. The falling snow was frozen in midair, creating a scene that would have been beautiful, if she had the time to stop and appreciate it.

Naila ran down the street, watching the falling snow flicker in and out of time. She reached a car, frozen in its path along the street. Naila opened the door, slit the driver's throat, dumped him on the pavement, and waited.

Several seconds later, the figure appeared.

She hugged him tight, kissed the side of his hood, and jumped into the car. When he vanished, she was ready. Time returned to normal, and she took control of the now moving vehicle.

Naila was careful to obey the traffic laws as she made her escape. She did not need any extra attention.

The beauty of the falling snow against the black sky and the pristine blanket it created on the ground began to lull her into relaxation.

A police car rocketed past her, and the adrenaline poured back into her system. She took the first turn she could off the main street and began winding through what she hoped would be obscure neighborhoods.

Several minutes passed, and another patrol car came into view. This time it turned sharply behind her and turned on its lights.

Naila pressed down on the accelerator and the patrol car followed suit. She turned down random streets and alleys, unable to lose her pursuer. Ahead of her she saw a gas station, and a thought occurred to her.

She took a hard turn and drove through the glass front of the gas station convenience store. The patrol car slid to a stop behind her. Naila jumped out of the car and shot the attendant as soon as he stood up from behind the counter to see what had happened.

The black robed figure stood in the midst of the shattered glass and broken displays. He looked from the attendant to her.

"Stop. Please…" there was a sorrow in his otherworldly voice that she did not have the time to process.

She scrambled over the car and ran to the police car. She threw open the door and slit the officer's throat. With some effort, she dragged him out of the car. She waited patiently for the black robed figure to collect the officer and vanish.

She drove away in the police car. The radio might prove useful in tracking her pursuers, while the vehicle lights and sirens would allow her to drive faster without arousing suspicion. She would still need to find a less conspicuous vehicle before this was over.

After a few seconds, dispatch began coming in over the car's radio. She wasn't sure what the signal codes and 10 codes meant, but after several minutes one was repeated a few times, and the radio went silent. Within minutes, she was being followed by several patrol cars, all with lights and sirens blazing.

Frantic, she tried her previous tactic and crashed into another gas station. This time the attendant was not behind the counter. Cursing, Naila ran to the back room and saw a door slam shut. She chased the fleeing attendant into the night.

Shouts could be heard behind her, and she knew they were close. Fear drove her forward, granting her speed she had not realized she possessed. She raised the gun and fired at the attendant ahead of her. The woman grabbed her shoulder and stumbled.

Naila closed the distance, and another shot rang out.

* * *

Naila rolled onto her back. She felt her heartbeat grow fainter and her limbs colder. Voices and movement existed in the periphery of her awareness. Eventually darkness consumed her sight.

A moment later, she felt a presence that seemed familiar. She felt herself moving, as if pulled along by a gentle current. As she passed into a void, she had the faintest sense of tears, as if she was passing by a great sorrow that she had never seen before. It was old and felt like something she had missed despite repeated opportunities to know it.

Then it was gone.

* * *

There was a brief sense of a reddish-orange glow in the midst of immeasurable and impenetrable darkness. Naila could no longer sense her physical form. She did not know where she was or what was happening. All she could feel was darkness and pain.

If she had eyes, they would have wept. If she had teeth, they would have gnashed.

V

Cade
Dynoltir, +2002 TR

Cade stood in the kitchen, next to the stove, watching his father cook dinner. He watched as the hamburger patties were dropped into the already hot skillet. As they cooked, tiny drops of grease popped and fizzled on the smooth material. Cade could feel heat from the fire on the gas top stove and watched as his father flipped the burgers. A slight worry crept into his mind as he thought about the potential pain of being hit by those tiny droplets of grease. He wasn't sure how his father could be so calm or put up with the discomfort.

Eventually, everything was cooked. Cade set the table as his mother instructed. When all the plates and silverware were in place, he took his seat and waited for his parents. His father brought over the burgers, and his mother dished out green beans onto his plate. Cade grinned at the smiley face his father drew on the hamburger bun with the ketchup and mustard.

Silence settled in as they began to devour their meal.

After a while, his mother asked, "How was school today?"

"It was ok."

"Are you looking forward to your friend's birthday party next weekend?" asked his dad.

Cade shrugged his shoulders as he ate.

Suddenly, the lights went out and the house went dark.

"Mom? Dad?"

"Just wait. Give your eyes time to adjust."

"But how, there's no light... I can't see anything." He could feel fear spreading into his mind, consuming him. How could they ask him to do the impossible?

"It's ok, just relax," a hand reached out and squeezed his reassuringly.

Suddenly, his thoughts were filled with the reassuring touch of his mother's hand, of thoughts of comfort and brighter moments. Cade momentarily forgot to be afraid.

"I'll check the breaker box," said his father.

Cade could hear him stand but could not yet see him.

"Won't Dad get hurt in the dark?"

"It's ok; I can picture the house in my head."

Cade considered this and imagined the table and the layout of their small home. He wasn't sure he could navigate it without light to see. What if something was out of place? What if he tripped or walked into something? What if he got hurt?

Slowly, after several minutes, Cade could start to make out details. They were dim at first, but eventually he could see the table and both of his parents. The more he could see, the more he realized that even in the dark house, there was still light. Moonlight crept in through the cracks in the blinds. Battery-powered devices glowed faintly, and his fear began to subside.

"The breakers don't appear to be the issue," said his father.

Creaking noises could be heard outside.

"What was that?" New images burst into Cade's head as he heard what sounded like claws tearing into the roof and the deck outside.

He could see his parents look at each other in the dim light.

"I'll check the doors and windows, then I'll check outside," his father said.

He checked the windows in the kitchen and then the back door before disappearing to check the rest of the house.

"Come here," his mother said, turning to Cade.

Holding Cade's hand, she led him to his parents' bedroom. He could hear scratching at the doors.

His mother knelt in front of him; "I want you to stay in our room and keep the door closed."

"What about dad?"

"He'll be fine."

"I'm scared to be in here alone."

"Ok, you can keep the door cracked to keep an eye on me while I keep any eye on Dad."

Cade watched as his father left through the front door. His mother quickly locked the door behind his father. She stood guard by the door, waiting.

*   *   *

As he listened to the claws scratching outside, the darkness of the house filled the landscape of his mind. His awareness became consumed by these internal shadows.

Unseen horrors began silently creeping in through the windows behind him and sliding out from the closet.

Gnarled hands with long, vicious claws reached out from under the bed. The shadows grew darker as they drew near.

Visions of the swarms of amorphous, terrible creatures swam before him, devouring and tearing his father or chasing him into the forest. The creatures materialized behind his mother and dragged her down beneath the floor.

There would be no one left. He would be alone, with the things in the darkness.

The monsters breathed and sighed in his ears. Their cold breath and sharp claws grazed the back of his neck.

Cade's focus snapped back to the real world, he spun around, and flattened his back against the wall. His eyes scanned the darkness of the bedroom, unable to determine fully if he was safe or merely not noticing threats that hid in the deep shadows. He periodically looked through the crack in the door to reassure himself that his mother was still at the front door and that nothing was beginning to sneak into the bedroom.

Long moments passed. The growling stopped. Then, he could hear claws running across the roof.

A blinding light flashed through the windows at the front of the house, bursting through the crack in the door. Cade closed his eyes at the pain. Instantly, his ears were assaulted by the loud, painful screeching of some otherworldly creatures.

The dark horrors in his mind were momentarily vanquished by the bright light and the distraction of such a strange event.

Cade was able to squint enough to see several more flashes and hear similarly pained screeches, but each time they grew weaker, until only silence and darkness remained.

A few moments later, there was a knock at the front door. His mother instantly reached for the door handle with one hand and raised the other as if to strike.

"It's done," came his father's voice.

His mother unlocked the door and lowered her fist. His father re-entered their home. He was unharmed.

*   *   *

Cade climbed into bed and looked up at his parents.

"What were those things outside?"

His parents looked at each other, then back at him.

"They don't really have a name. When I was little, I called them shriekers."

"What are they?"

"They are nocturnal creatures that like to swarm over and eat people. They only come out at night and do not like the light. That's why they killed the power to the house."

"How did you get rid of them?"

His father raised his hand, palm facing the ceiling; "With what they cannot stand."

A blindingly bright light erupted from his palm and lit the room as if the sun had suddenly come into being instead of a mere lightbulb. Cade squinted his eyes shut to block out the brightness. The light subsided and the room returned to normal.

"How did you do that?"

"It's a special talent in our family."
"Can I do that?"
"With practice."
"Will you teach me?"
"Later, now it's time for sleep."
"Ok."
Cade curled up under his blankets, and his parents turned off the light as they exited. He fell asleep imagining himself triumphing over living nightmares.

*   *   *

Cade sat in the car as his parents drove him down the sun-lit country road. He looked out the window, watching the alternating trees and fields as they passed.

"I'm not sure I want to go to this birthday party," he said.

"It will be ok. You will have fun. If anything happens, you have the backup cell phone in your backpack, so you can call us."

Cade wasn't convinced. He was annoyed at being told that he would have fun, as if that was a command or prophesy that his parents had any right or ability to make.

He was also worried about what would happen. The other boys were tougher, and he assumed they would be less scared of the dark than him. The night of the power outage had deepened and brought to awareness his own fears, and he was not eager to be placed in a position where others would discover them. The idea of being picked on was not appealing.

They arrived at his classmate's house. The front yard was small with an arcing gravel driveway that connected to the highway on both ends. Behind the house was an open, grassy space bordered by a tall fence. Trees and bushes lined the fence on the sides, and a wooded area was on the far end of the backyard from the house.

Cade got out of the car, and his parents were greeted by his classmate's parents.

"Go on inside and set down your stuff. Everyone is out back playing already," said the dad.

Cade walked in through the front door and looked around. He saw the pile of jackets, backpacks, and sleeping bags in the living room and set his stuff with the rest.

He continued through the house and out the back door onto the patio. Off to one side was a large tent and pile of wood for what would become a campfire once it got darker. The other boys were running around playing a rough version of tag or some other touch sport with which he was unfamiliar.

Tiburon and Jackson were chasing Zayn while he carried some kind of ball. This was Tiburon's birthday party.

Cade ran over to join them. It was not long before he was shoved by Zayn and fell over. Zayn was slightly bigger and a lot rougher than the others. The impacts of both the larger boy's shoulder and the ground hurt Cade.

"Weak," laughed Zayn looking down at him, obviously seeing the wetness at the corner of his eyes.

"Hey, don't be so rough," said Tiburon.

"Get up, it'll be fine," said Jackson looking down at him.

He did not feel that motivated to continue.

"I'm going to take a minute," he said. "I'll be back."

He got up and wandered back into the house. His classmate's mom was in the kitchen preparing something, and the dad was grilling something on the deck. He walked to the front door and confirmed that his parents were long gone.

Cade returned to the backyard. He watched the other kids play until the parents called everyone to eat. They quickly devoured their food and were soon ready to go play again.

"Let's go explore the woods," suggested Jackson.

Tiburon looked at his parents.

"Ok, but you have to come back as soon as it starts to get dark," said Tiburon's dad.

The kids took off. Cade's curiosity about the woods overshadowed any doubts he might have had, and he joined them.

The boys split up and spread out as they wandered through the trees, picking up sticks, looking under rocks, or gazing up at the branches.

"Let's play hide and seek," suggested Tiburon.

"Ok," replied Jackson.

"You're it," declared Zayn.

Everyone ran off in different directions to hide.

Cade ran off into the woods, not knowing where he was going. He stopped when he reached the barbed wire fence around the property and looked around. He saw a large bush off to one side, crawled under the branches, and curled up near the base. Excited by the chase, he looked between the leaves, watching for Tiburon.

Time went by and he could hear Tiburon calling out followed by the cries of those who were discovered. A thrilling fear crept into him as the excitement of the game mixed with the urge to not be found. Eventually, the other kids found him, and they split up to hide again.

They kept playing until the sun began to set. The shadows between the trees began to spread, and Cade felt increasingly anxious when he was separated from the others. He kept playing, keeping closer to the others as time passed, until Tiburon's dad could be heard calling for them to return. Cade was relieved when they turned around and headed back toward the house. As they exited the woods, he could see the campfire.

"I said to come back when it started to get dark," admonished Tiburon's dad. "I shouldn't have to come get you."

The boys muttered their apologies.

"Ok," he nodded toward the fire, "go make s'mores."

Cade and the others took off toward the fire with renewed excitement.

*   *   *

Cade sat near the campfire, listening to his friends talk. He absent-mindedly gazed into the fire, watching the flames twist and rise around the wood. The voices faded into the hum of the background.

Cade was having fun. The game of hide and seek in the woods had been exhilarating. The fire was fascinating, and just being around his friends, even though they weren't really doing anything, was enjoyable.

A slight crunch or scraping sound interrupted the white noise around him. Cade spun instinctively and was suddenly reminded that they were surrounded by darkness. It only slightly registered to his mind that he had been so focused on the fire and his friends that he had forgotten about the night. Now, as he gazed futilely into the shadows, he remembered the surrounding darkness. The constantly shifting mental images of what might be lurking in the woods or fields began to flit across his mind again. The boy got up and moved to a seat between the deck and the fire. This way the fire was in front of him, the house behind him, the tent off to his left. Only his right side would be fully exposed to the night.

Cade's eyes darted right every so often, keeping watch.

*   *   *

"Ok, boys, time to sleep," came the sound of Tiburon's dad behind him.

Cade turned to see the dad walking across the deck toward them.

"Ok," said Tiburon.

The other boys did not argue.

Cade got up and walked to the tent. He stood outside and watched the dad pour a bucket of water over the fire.

Instantly, a huge cloud of steam billowed up. The darkness rushed in, and only the light from above the deck illuminated the yard.

Cade climbed into the tent and found his sleeping bag.

"If you need anything during the night, just come inside and get us. Get some rest and talk to you in the morning." The dad zipped up the tent and left.

The other boys began to whisper.

"Go to sleep," came the stern command from the direction of the deck.

The boys got quiet and laid down. Within seconds, Cade was asleep.

* * *

A quick series of sharp sounds cut into Cade's consciousness, and he opened his eyes.

The tent was dark, and he could hear the others breathing gently. Cade lay there, listening for the sound.

A slight sniffing sound momentarily preceded the sound of something rubbing against the tent.

Cade's eyes went wide, and he jerked away from the tent wall. Not really thinking about what he was doing, he collided into the closest sleeping form.

"What are you doing?" Zayn asked irritably.

"Huh?" asked Tiburon.

"Why is it so dark?" asked Jackson.

Cade hadn't realized how dark it was until then. The light from the deck must be off.

"I heard a scratching sound, and then something started sniffing and poking at the tent," explained Cade.

"Stop being such a baby," grunted Zayn.

"I wonder if it was my dad messing with us," suggested Tiburon. Tiburon quietly stood and walked to the tent entrance. He carefully took hold of the zipper, then yanked it down quickly.

"Gotcha!" he called into the open air.

Tiburon looked around. There was no one outside the tent. "Dad? Are you out there?"

Jackson got up and joined Tiburon. Jackson turned on his flashlight. They both exited the tent, looking around. Cade got up and followed them. Zayn grunted irritably, threw off his sleeping bag and joined them. They circled the tent but found nothing.

"If your power went out, we should let your parents know," recommended Jackson.

"Ok," Tiburon led them up the steps and across the deck. "The light switch doesn't work," observed Jackson.

They walked through the house to Tiburon's parents' bedroom. The other boys stood in the hall as Tiburon entered and woke up his parents.

"Pst. Hey, Dad," whispered Tiburon loudly. "The power's out."

"Hmm?" The dad grunted and reached for the lamp next to the bed. It did not turn on.

"Ok, I'll check the breaker box," he said, sitting up and looking around.

"What's going on?" asked his friend's mom.

"Breakers must have flipped. I'll check it." He grabbed a flashlight from his nightstand.

"Ok," she said, sitting up as well.

Cade followed Tiburon's dad back downstairs and into the garage to look at the breaker box. Cade looked around the dark interior, partly from curiosity and partly from concern. The dad flipped the breakers back and forth, but nothing happened. Cade followed the dad back through the house and out the deck door.

They walked around the house, the dad moving the flashlight up and down, looking for any signs of damage.

"Stop."

Cade stopped and watched the dad shine the light on the ground. Several feet away was a long black cable running off into the night.

"Be careful not to touch the cable," the dad cautioned. "Let's head back, and I'll call the power company. Somehow the power line got torn down."

They walked around the back of the house toward the deck.

"I'm going to grab my backpack real quick," said Cade, dashing off into the tent.

He looked around, but his backpack was gone.

Fear of being left out in the dark alone combined with his panic at the missing backpack, which signaled the absence of his cell phone and ability to call his parents. He quickly rushed out to join the dad.

"Where's your backpack?"

"It's gone."

A rustling in the bushes between the tress along the fence caught their attention. The dad shined the light over to the fence, and Cade could see the tall plants swaying slightly as if something had recently run through them. Cade inched toward the back door. The dad took a few steps closer toward the edge of the yard, but nothing appeared. He turned back toward the house, and a scratching sound drew their attention upward.

Cade was too close to see over the edge of the roof's overhang, but he heard the sharp intake of breath from the dad as he angled his flashlight up.

"Get inside."

Cade opened the sliding door. An inhuman shriek, followed by a cry of pain and the sound of a large object hitting the wooden deck, sounded behind him.

"Run!"

Cade slammed the door shut and took off. He raced through the house and leaped up the steps two at a time, adrenaline surging through his veins. He skidded to a halt at the parents' room.

"What's going on?" asked Tiburon.

"Something attacked your dad," Cade blurted.

"What was it?" asked the mom as she hurried past him.

"I didn't see it. He told me to run," he said between breaths.

Tiburon ran down the stairs after his mother.

Zayn snorted and rolled his eyes at Cade, then walked downstairs.

Jackson followed without saying anything.

Cade took a deep breath and followed them.

When he reached the bottom of the steps, he heard a scream. He ran to the back door in time to see the mother running into the back yard, shouting and carrying the dad's dropped flashlight. Cade heard more noises and looked out as a flashlight briefly illuminated the dad being pulled into the bushes.

"Mom! Dad!" Tiburon shouted at his parents.

The dad's feet were yanked out of sight, and the mom started for the bushes. When she came within a few inches, something small and pale shot out and cut her across the legs. She screamed and jumped back. She shined the light into the undergrowth, and angry, pained screams erupted from them. The branches swayed violently, and then pale shapes shot out from farther along the bushes and attacked her from the sides. The mom screamed in pain and tried to run back to the house. She dropped the flashlight, there was a loud crack, and it went out.

Cade's eyes tried to adjust to the sudden decrease in light, but he could only just barely make out the small shapes chasing the mom toward the house.

"Get back inside. Run!"

Tiburon hesitated. "Mom?"

Jackson grabbed him by the arm to pull him inside. Zayn just stood there, shocked.

The mom reached the deck, and a loud hiss caused her to skid to a halt. She looked up over the roof overhang and screamed.

"Run!"

"Go," yelled Zayn, and the boys started to run into the house.

Cade heard a scream cut short and then the sound of something being dragged across the deck. Cade ran, though he wasn't sure where he was going. He dashed into the first room he found, jumped into the closet, closed it behind him, and tried to bury himself under a pile of coats. His breathing was ragged and fast as adrenaline surged through him. Tiburon's parents might easily be dead, and he might be next. The creatures might even get his friends too.

Cade sat panting in the darkness, hoping that the pile of coats might save him from discovery.

* * *

In the landscape of his mind, darkness was all around. He was alone in the land of shadows. There were no friends, no parents, nothing that could defend him.

Soon the whispers and images started to flow into him. Despite the darkness, he could see countless shapeless horrors: creatures with baleful eyes, sharp teeth, and ragged claws. He could feel the points of those claws on his skin. He could see teeth and claws tearing into the parents and his friends.

The whispers surrounded him and coaxed him toward the inevitable; "You will die here. You are weak. Nothing matters. We will enjoy your suffering."

Cade looked around for any escape, but nothing existed in the void.

He almost missed the tiny pin prick of light directly ahead, as he turned and looked everywhere around him for the enemies he could never see coming but were certain to destroy him.

In the tiny pin prick, he saw something else. It wasn't a monster. It wasn't someone's demise. There was a calm, a peace in the tiny dot of light. He saw his parents; he saw his friends. In the tiniest light, he remembered how safe he felt with his parents and how fun it was to be around them and his friends. Inside the light, the fear and doubt were forgotten as he focused on other things.

In this cool, calm space, a new thought came to mind: What did he need to do?

Plans formed and shaped, leading in a thousand directions. Instead of seeing the horrors that might befall him, he saw the myriad ways that the monsters could be dealt with.

Cade's mind took a step toward the light.

*   *   *

A sound caught his attention. There were tiny claws scraping on surfaces in the room outside the closet.

Cade took a deep breath and let it out slowly. He kept his mind focused away from thoughts of what might go wrong, refusing to gaze into the surrounding darkness in his mind. If he kept running and hiding, then he and the others would die. There was at least a chance they'd survive if he fought back.

Cade stood up, and the coats fell around him in the closet. He could hear the sounds of the creatures outside pause and shift. They had heard him. The door in front of him was faintly visible.

Cade burst from the closet with a cry and a raised fist. There was a creature in front of him. It was about three feet tall and standing on all fours. Its pale, thin body, covered in sparse hairs, stood like a barely covered skeleton. Its eyes were wide, it's pupils rapidly shrinking before him. The creature's ears were large and pointed, pulled back tight across its skull. The lips curled in a sneer away from sharp, needle-like teeth.

Cade thrust his fist into the face of the creature. It shrieked, and there was the sound and smell of burning flesh. He saw whisps of smoke rise from the creature.

Then he realized what was happening.

Light streamed from the gaps between his fingers. He looked down in astonishment and opened his hands.

The room was flooded as if exposed to the noonday sun. He felt a strange sensation over his eyes, and the pain diminished instantly. He could see the creatures fleeing the room with angry hisses and shrieks.

Cade stood staring at the light coming from his palms. He had no idea how he was doing this, but he was filled with an exhilaration he had never known before.

He looked around. The room was empty. The creatures were gone, and he was still alive.

Now it was time to find his friends.

*   *   *

"Where did you get such a bright flashlight?" asked Tiburon, stepping out of a closet.

"That's not a flashlight," whispered Jackson as he came back down the stairs.

Zayn just grunted.

"Where did the creatures go?" asked Tiburon.

"They are hurt by the light," said Cade, holding his right hand over his head, palm up like a lamp to illuminate the living room. He kept his left fist closed, though light could still be seen in the cracks between his fingers.

"Should we call the cops?" asked Tiburon.

"There's no time. We need to go after them, now," answered Cade.

"Psh, what can you do?" asked Zayn dismissively.

Cade lowered his arm until his palm pointed directly at Zayn. Zayn yelled and covered his eyes.

"Fine. I get it."

"Come on."

Cade closed his right fist and headed outside. It was interesting how quickly his eyes adjusted now between the brightness and the darkness. He could even see quite clearly without a substantial source of light, though the colors seemed off slightly. As he stepped outside, he slightly opened his fist so that it resembled a curled claw to allow some of the light, but not all of it, to illuminate his path. He didn't want to flood the night too much and scare the creatures away too quickly. There was no way to know if he'd be able to follow their trail long after they returned to their dwelling.

Cade ran to the bushes between the trees near the fence and shined his light on the area where he'd seen Tiburon's dad disappear. The plants were smashed where the adult had been dragged along the ground. He climbed between the barbed wires of the fence and began following the trail. The sounds of the others following and rushing to keep up let him know that he wasn't alone. He was surprised to realize that he felt quite calm walking into the night, intentionally looking for strange monsters.

They walked for quite some time, crossing the field, and approaching the tree line on the other side. The path led to a large, gnarled old tree with huge roots that protruded from the ground. The closer they got, the more Cade could hear the movement of creatures fleeing into the shadows.

When they reached the tree, they found a large opening between two of the roots. Cade knelt and extended his left palm in the direction of the opening. There was a hiss, and something darted out of view. The opening led down at an angle into some kind of tunnel that soon took a sharp turn beyond which he could not see.

"Ok, this is it," declared Cade.

"I don't know about this," said Zayn, taking a step back.

"We have to find my parents," said Tiburon, stepping up next to Cade.

"They won't mess with Cade," reassured Jackson.

"Fine," said Zayn reluctantly and joined them.

Cade crawled into the tunnel, palms down, causing the light to shift constantly. The tunnel became well-lit each time he raised a hand, only to darken momentarily when he set it down and had not yet raised the other.

The tunnel twisted back and forth, sometimes rising slightly, but inevitably moving downward. Every so often, there would be a branching tunnel, and Cade would feel a slight trepidation as to what might try to jump out at him when he reached the corner.

After a while, he began to worry that they might never find the parents. For all he knew, they might get trapped underground. The creatures would take them out, one by one: First, they would take the person who came last, farthest from the flickering light; then they would take the next. Eventually, he would be alone. There would be nothing he could do then.

The light began to fade, even with his hand raised off the floor. Panic rushed in to fill the void as swiftly as the darkness.

"Hey, what's happening?" came the calls from behind him.

Cade closed his eyes and concentrated away from his fears.

"No," he whispered, shifting his inner focus.

He felt himself grow calmer. Cade opened his eyes and raised his head.

A pale, twisted face shrieked its maw of needle-like teeth in his face and leaped at him.

Without thinking, Cade raised his right hand to defend himself and light exploded into the tunnel. The creature shrieked in pain and tried to flee.

Cade began to crawl faster after the creature. The scent of burnt flesh filled his nostrils as he moved through the space that the creature had occupied only moments before.

Cade fell into a large open space that had walls filled with tunnels. He raised his right hand over his head, illuminating the space while keeping his left fist closed, ready for whatever might attack.

"Mom! Dad!"

"Over there!"

Cade turned in time to see the pale claws of the creatures disappear into the darkened tunnels off to his right as Tiburon's parents were dragged inside.

"Grab their legs," Cade shouted as he ran toward them. He reached the tunnel with the mother first and knelt down. He thrust his left fist into the tunnel and opened his hand. The bright light slammed into the creature, and it shrieked in rage and pain. Smoke began pour from its body. The creature let go of the body, and Zayn began dragging the mother out of the of the tunnel.

"Help, they've almost got my dad!"

Cade ran over to the other tunnel. The dad's feet were barely sticking out, and Tiburon and Jackson were losing the fight. Cade knelt down and illuminated the tunnel. Two pained howls erupted from the just beyond the dad's head. They released him and retreated. The boys were able to pull him out.

Cade kept one hand raised to illuminate the room while the others tried to wake the parents.

"Dad, wake up."

"Come on, wake up."

The parents opened their eyes slowly and looked around.

"Where are we?"

"Underground, in their lair."

"How did you find us?"

"Cade did it."

The parents looked at Cade.

"How are you…"

"Not now. We need to get out of here."

"Ok, come on boys." The dad paused. "How do we get of here?"

"Follow me, I remember the path," said Jackson.

"Go ahead. I'll keep them back, so you can escape."

"I'm not comfortable leaving a child behind."

"Can you produce your own light?"

"No."

"Then go. It'll be ok."

Jackson entered the tunnel first. The dad went next, followed by Tiburon, and then his mother. Zayn looked at Cade, then crawled in after them.

Cade waited a few minutes for them to gain some distance. He wasn't sure if the creatures would attack right away or if they would wait. He just hoped they were mostly down here with him still and not waiting to ambush the others on their way up.

As Cade backed into the tunnel, his lighting of the chamber diminished. He could see the faint hints of malicious pale faces appearing in each tunnel. They growled menacingly. Perhaps their rage was now focused on him. He could see burn marks on at least four faces.

Cade turned quickly and began to crawl through the tunnel as fast as he could. The sounds of countless skittering claws rushed into the room behind him and became focused on the tunnel opening. Sharp claws and thin fingers grasped his ankles and began to pull him backward. Cade rolled onto his back and opened his palms to try to burn them away. The creatures roared in pain, but the nearest one ground its needle-like teeth together and lunged at Cade's hands. It opened its mouth as if to bite them, and Cade retracted his hands instinctively.

Darkness rushed in to fill the void, and the creatures yanked him out of the tunnel. Cade started to raise his hands to blast them with light, but creatures from either side attacked the back of his hands with their sharp claws. He winced and pulled back. Cade stumbled around, alternating between trying to attack them with the light and recoiling from attacks to his hands and back. He would hit them with the light, and they would scurry around or attack from behind. The scent of their singed flesh filled the room, but their shrieks became increasingly enraged and bitter.

If they damaged his hands, then he would lose the light. If he lost the light, then he would die. There were so many of them. He couldn't maintain the light on them long enough to make them stop or to kill one. Once they defeated him, then they would go for the others. Everyone would be dragged back into the darkness below never to return.

The light began to flicker and dim. The shrieks became more joyous.

Pain and fear began to overwhelm his mind. He was doomed. Soon they would have no reason to retreat before attacking again. He began to back away.

A loud yell echoed through the chamber, and something barreled into the creatures, knocking some of them over. The others scattered momentarily in surprise.

"Get it together, loser."

Cade blinked. Zayn was getting up from where he'd slammed into a couple of the creatures.

Cade closed his eyes and concentrated.

He opened his eyes, and the light burst from his hands. He rushed to the nearest creature, grabbed it with his right hand, and pushed his open left palm against its head. The creature let out a pained and terrified shriek as smoke billowed from its head. The others shrunk back at the sound. Cade did not relent. He ignored the clawing at his arms and body. The room was only dimly lit by the light slipping out from the sides of his hands that were pressed firmly against the creature's flesh. He could feel the flesh change consistency under each hand. He focused on his left. The hardness of the skull began to soften. Suddenly it gave way. A moment later, the creature's body went limp.

Cade dropped the dead creature.

"Whoa," said Zayn.

Cade looked around, fists clenched at his side. The other creatures were hesitating near the tunnels. Before they had been hurt and irritated by his light, but now they had seen one of their own die. The realization of what might happen must have given them all pause to reconsider.

One of the creatures took a step forward and bared its teeth. Cade stepped toward it decisively and raised both hands in its direction. The light washed over it, and it shrieked in pain but still leaped at him. Cade rushed to meet it and caught it by the throat, but its momentum knocked him on his back. The creature roared in pain and strained to bite him. Cade squeezed his eyes shut to avoid the claws that raked across his face. He concentrated on his hands while smelling the burning and feeling the changing flesh; within moments, the creature went limp.

Cade opened his eyes and pushed the creature off him. He stood quickly and looked around.

The creatures were gone. Most likely, they had decided that death was too great a risk for staying around to be worth it.

Cade and Zayn crawled uneventfully through the tunnels and back to the surface. They were greeted by the others. Tiburon's mother fussed over the scratches on Cade's face, arms, and hands and hurried him back across the field to get cleaned up.

VI

Journey Beyond II
Dynoltir, +3052 TR

Captain Yana sat in the captain's chair on the bridge of the seed ship, Daedalus. Continuing the mission to erect jump gates in the Castor galaxy, the seed ship sat before a set of large rings between two warship vessels newly added to the mission.

The warships, more maneuverable and smaller than the elongated seed ship carrying the pre-made gate segments, were designed with more powerful engines, armor, and weapons. Space Fleet High Command had decided to deploy the two warships, since the events of the first jump revealed that Castor was inhabited not only by sentient but also monstrously large life.

"Gate is activated," said Professor Grimm from one side of the bridge.

"Proceeding through the gate," announced the pilot of the first warship as it started to move.

"Take us through, Mr. Cheng," said Yana to the pilot once the first ship had vanished.

Cheng worked the controls, and the ship passed safely through the gate's swirling teal and violet etched silver vortex. The last warship quickly followed suit.

"Thank you, Cheng, Grimm," Yana said in turn to the only two people on the bridge.

There had been a slight delay after the first jump as High Command debated and finally decided on a course of action, but now they were back on schedule. Most of the crew had been present on the bridge for the first jump due to its significance, but their duties kept them busy afterward. Yana, the pilot, and the professor were the only ones that needed to be present for these jumps.

"Initiating star chart scan and recalculation," announced Cheng.

"Deploying gate modules and activating self-assembly protocols," informed Grimm.

"Thank you, gentlemen. Once things are in place, feel free to take a rest as we wait for the next jump."

Affirmative comments came from both crew members. Yana looked down at a console on her chair and pulled up the current surveillance footage inside the ship. She moved through the camera views until she found what she sought.

Booth was carrying a tray of food and walking down a hall. She followed him until he entered his quarters. If she was quick, she could get supper in the mess hall and be back in her own quarters before he finished.

"If there is nothing else, I will see you all again tomorrow."

"Good night, captain," replied Cheng.

Yana looked at Grimm and smiled. He was mostly distracted and vaguely waved his hand up by his shoulder without looking or turning in her direction.

The captain left the bridge and moved through the ship to the mess hall. No one was there when she arrived, so she quickly grabbed a couple packets of freeze-dried food and left. She made it to her quarters unaccosted and sat down to enjoy her meal.

The food was ok, neither amazing nor terrible. When she was finished, she put on her headphones and laid down to listen to music. Her mind relaxed, as she was able to forget the stresses of her position and even the boring routines while she drifted along with the sounds.

* * *

Cheng sat back in the pilot's chair, picking at the food from the packet in his lap as he stared out at the stars. The lights on the bridge were shut off and only his dimmed consoles were active.

The mission had become routine after the excitement of the first jump, and the pilot found the peaceful silence of the nighttime hours on the ship to be quite pleasant. He loved staring out at the stars. Even the super gates slowly assembling themselves were awe inspiring. He understood the basics of how they functioned, but it was still amazing to see them in real life. It was like coming across a huge artifact from some ancient civilization that dwarfed the gates he was used to in Praxis.

The pilot yawned and leaned the chair back. He set an alarm on his watch, so he could wake up later and shower before the rest of the crew arrived on the bridge. The low hum of the ship lulled him to sleep.

* * *

James Nix finished his inspection of the 3D printing lab and checked his data pad. There were no usage logs or any record of schematics having been uploaded to the system, but the resource wells were below their initial levels.

He moved to a different panel in the lab and checked the security logs. There were no records of entry into the lab either. The engineer frowned to himself. He knew from memory and had confirmed in the logs that the resource wells had been full when the mission started. If they were not full now, and there were no records of the lab being used, then that implied a security breach. Someone had used the lab without authorization and hacked the system to hide their tracks.

James left the lab and headed to Commander Tal's quarters. He pressed the comm buttons next to the door when he arrived.

The door opened and the commander looked at him. "Yes?"

"I was inspecting the 3D printing lab and discovered a discrepancy in the resource wells. Someone has used the lab without authorization and deleted all digital record of their activities."

"Are you sure that the resource wells were full when the mission started?"

"Yes, I checked them myself and verified in the logs before I came here. Someone has violated protocol, putting our ability to affect repairs at risk. The only question is whether the occurrence is sabotage or self-centered irresponsibility."

The commander paused, looking at the engineer with a stern expression that bordered on disdain.

"Send me your reports, and I will look into it. For now, do not mention it to anyone."

"Yes, sir," the engineer replied and looked down at his data pad. He selected his reports and sent them to the commander. When he looked up, the door was closed.

Slightly unsure how to respond to this abrupt dismissal, James looked around for a moment, then turned and left. It was not the reaction he had expected. Any violation of protocol was cause for concern, but this level of interference in security measures should have elicited a stronger response. The more he thought about it, the more annoyed he became. It was the commander's responsibility to help make sure that the ship was secure and the personnel were in order.

A vibrating alarm went off and he checked his wrist device. It was time for his scheduled meal. He made his way to the mess and saw the ship's doctor and the pilot sitting at a table eating. He ignored them and retrieved his meal packs from the storage area.

"James, why don't you join us," offered Dr. Edwards.

He looked down at his wrist device, then back at the other crew members.

"I still have inspections to finish; perhaps some other time."

The engineer turned and left without waiting for a response.

*   *   *

Grimm sat in the lab staring at the monitor as the data from the latest scans scrolled past. Since their encounter at the first jump point in Castor, they had not encountered anything of interest. There had been no more satellites, planet-sized life forms, or even signs of the people who built the warning satellite.

The professor sighed and spun his chair around to look at the rest of the lab.

Dr. Miranda Everett turned at the sound of his movement and watched him.

"I'm bored. Nothing interesting has happened since we found the creature on the first jump."

"It's only been a few days since we found the hatchling," said Miranda.

The professor's blue metallic eyes shifted around the room, searching for some unseen thing. "I need to find something interesting," he muttered. "You know, there are at least two other people on this ship hiding secrets"; he looked up at Miranda with a smile.

"I would advise against doing anything that would draw unnecessary attention. At this time, patience may be the best option."

He stood and gave her an annoyed glance. "I've been patient enough."

Miranda opened her mouth to argue, but Grimm was gone.

*   *   *

Tal moved silently through the darkened corridors of the ship while the crew slept. Most of the crew were in their quarters, but the pilot had fallen asleep in his chair, as usual. When Tal was finished with his rounds, he headed to the galley. He retrieved several packets of freeze-dried meat and returned to his quarters.

Tal set the food aside and ran through a series of exercises and meditation to help pass the time. After that, he completed what few reports were required of him and turned to his meal. It wasn't the best meal, but meat was meat and he preferred it to the other options available.

When he was done, he sat back and enjoyed the silence of his room. In here he could mentally block out the rest of the ship and, for a brief moment, bask in the illusion that no humans were nearby.

Eventually, he prepared for bed and fell asleep.

Tal wandered through the dense forest of his dreams. The tree trunks were several feet wide, with branches and leaves towering overhead that blotted out the night sky. In some places, vines wrapped themselves around the trunks and climbed their way to the upper canopy.

On the ground, large, gnarled roots created miniature cliffs and valleys filled with soil and moss. A gentle breeze moved through the forest, cool and moist.

Tal briefly closed his eyes to take in the scents of the wet vegetation that surrounded him comfortingly. He could hear birds and insects all around. Occasionally there would be the crunch of a hoof or the skittering of small claws on branches.

The commander opened his eyes and wandered around through the darkened forest. Despite the lack of light, he could see quite clearly and never missed a step. In this place he felt at home.

Something was not right. He could sense movement in the shadows. There was a creature here with him. It did not make a sound and moved from one patch of impenetrable darkness to another.

Slowly the deepness of the darkest shadows grew. More and more there appeared places into which he could not see. His knees bent and his senses sharpened. He turned around slowly, looking for the creature with his physical and mental senses.

Tal stopped.

There, ahead of him, a pair of glowing metallic blue eyes appeared in the darkness. Gleaming teeth were revealed in a ravenous grin.

Anger surged through him at the sight of this intruder.

Tal's eyes snapped open in his darkened quarters aboard the ship as he sat up straight.

*   *   *

The ship's doctor, Kira Edwards, sat down in the mess hall with the pilot, the professor, and Miranda.

"Enjoying the trip so far?" she asked.

"I actually enjoy this mission. The things we've seen so far are amazing. Back in Praxis, exploration missions were never this exciting," replied the pilot before taking another bite of his meal.

She turned to Miranda to see what she would say.

"I don't have much of an opinion at this point."

The researcher looked down and politely ate her food.

Kira looked at the professor, who was toying with his food absent mindedly while staring through the table at whatever he was pondering in his head.

"I have definitely found some interesting data to study," he said, turning to face her.

Kira smiled; "I'm glad to hear that. Any new discoveries that you can share with us?"

"Not yet," Grimm replied. "What were your previous missions like?"

"I've been on a lot of deep space exploration missions in Praxis. The more boring the mission is for me, the better it is for everyone else," she said with a laugh.

"Anything interesting ever happen in the deep exploration missions?" asked the pilot.

"Nothing as exciting as a planet-sized creature. Usually, the only hazards are debris in space or electromagnetic storms near planets, but we're able to avoid the worst of it by use of the probes. Accidents in deep exploration can be quite severe, and survival is dependent on a quick retrieval of the injured person."

*   *   *

An alert flashed on the monitor in front of Booth. It was time for his daily report from the captains of the three ships. He looked forward to these reports, especially since Yana was obviously irritated that she was required to make them to him.

While he was pleased to see the reports on his display, there was always a little disappointment that Yana's was there. If she failed enough in her duties, then he would have reason to relieve her of command. He read through the reports. They were routine, confirming the steady, uneventful march toward their objective.

There was a minor note about the resource wells in the 3D printing lab being low. Commander Tal was supposed to be investigating, but there was no comment as to a conclusion.

Booth got up, made sure his hair was perfectly aligned, straightened his uniform, and left his quarters. When he arrived on the bridge, the pilot and the captain were the only ones present. He walked over and stood behind and to the pilot's left.

"Status report, Cheng," he said, looking straight ahead at the main monitor at the mostly assembled super gate.

The pilot looked up at him, then twisted in his seat to look at the captain. Booth faintly caught the extra movement out of the corner of his eye.

"As you can see, the gate is almost completed. The computers need approximately four more hours to finish recalculating the star charts and plotting the next jump," replied the captain from behind him.

Booth frowned slightly, then returned to his outwardly pleasant expression.

Turning back toward Yana, he asked, "Any progress on the investigation into the missing resources from the 3D lab?"

Yana looked him directly in the eye; "You would have to ask Commander Tal. He is responsible for the investigation, and I have not spoken to him since yesterday."

Booth held her gaze for a moment.

"Thank you, captain," he said before leaving.

Annoyance fueled Booth's steps through the corridors of the ship to Tal's quarters, but he suppressed any outward signs by the time he reached his destination. He stopped abruptly in front of the door and raised his hand to activate the call buttons.

The door opened and Tal stood before him with the same slightly unpleasant expression he seemed to always wear.

"The resource wells in the lab are low because Dr. Everett performed an experiment without logging it. The importance of following protocol on board a ship has been reiterated. This will not recur. The details of the investigation have been sent to Captain Yana for inclusion in tomorrow's report."

Booth's jaw dropped slightly, but he quickly recovered his composure.

"Thank you for your prompt report."
"Anything else I can do for you?"
"No, that will be all."

The door slid shut and Tal disappeared.

Booth walked back to his quarters somewhat disappointed that the situation had been handled so quickly.

*   *   *

Miranda sat in her room and stared at a wall. She had completed all assigned tasks and several more that she had chosen for herself. Data had been recorded and analyzed. Several layers of contingencies plans had been formed and recorded for future use. The professor was safely asleep in his own quarters.

A bittersweet smiled twitched the corner of her lips at the thought. Yes, The Professor was safe.

She hoped it stayed that way.

Miranda laid down on top of the bed sheets and stared at the ceiling. Her eyes closed, but her mind remained active. After running through every scenario, she concluded that there was nothing constructive to be accomplished at the moment. Her mind's activity decreased to minimal levels as she waited.

*   *   *

The bridge was full. Even the engineer and the doctor were present for the final jump. They stood off to one side, near the doors to the bridge. Booth stood slightly to Yana's left, between her and the pilot. Professor Grimm and Dr. Everett were at their stations, and Commander Tal was at his.

"The probes show no immediate threats," relayed Grimm.

"Proceeding through the gate," announced the lead warship.

"Take us through," commanded Captain Yana once the other ship had vanished.

Cheng piloted the seed ship through the gate's swirling vortex.

As they exited the gate and the stars reappeared, Yana realized with some disappointment that everything looked relatively the same as it had before.

"Initiating scans to recalibrate the star charts," informed Cheng.

The ship continued to drift forward so that the second warship would have space to exit the wormhole. Once they were through, it collapsed.

"Launching the gate modules," stated Grimm.

"Thank you, everyone," Yana replied. "Deploy the probes to scan the area for the target."

"Yes, ma'am," confirmed Miranda.

"Do you know what the alien weapon looks like?" Yana asked Booth.

He barely turned his head back to look at her; "I do not. The intelligence report does not include a description."

"Captain, there is a planet to our port side," notified Cheng.

"Send the probes to investigate and move us closer."

Grimm and Cheng both gave their acknowledgement.

Long minutes passed before the ship reached orbit and the probes were deployed. Miranda brought the images from the probes up on the main display.

From a distance, the planet was a sphere of mottled patches of blue and shades of brown. The view from the probes moved closer and soared high over the planet's surface. The atmosphere was fairly clear, with few clouds. Faint hints of movement could be seen below on the surface.

Storm clouds loomed on the horizon, and the probes rose to avoid them. As they passed over the dark clouds, lightning could be seen flashing between and beneath them. The clouds gave way to clear air and what looked like a desert plain.

"Move the probes up and zoom out. I want a better view of this area," said Yana.

The world shrunk away from the flying probes, and the desert plain gained a more circular appearance. Dark storm clouds formed a solid border around the plain.

"Let's see what's in the middle," said Grimm.

The camera view zoomed in, and the probes descended in a spiraling pattern. Eventually, a small circular object could be seen in the center of the plain.

Then the view went dark.

"Professor Grimm? Dr. Everett?" The captain questioned them.

"Switching to a different set," came Miranda's reply.

The monitor was filled by the scene of distant probes shorting out and falling to the ground as they reached an apparent invisible barrier high over the plain.

"Professor Grimm, what is that?" asked Booth.

Yana glanced at Booth, then turned to see the professor eagerly hunched over his screen. She nodded when Miranda looked at her.

"There's some sort of barrier that disrupts the functioning of the probes like an EMP. Dispersing the probes now to test its boundaries."

Several minutes passed before Miranda addressed the captain, "We've determined the radius of the protective dome."

An image appeared on the main monitor of the desert plain and its storm ring. Overlaid on the image was a translucent graphic representing the electromagnetic dome, which covered the entire space inside the storm ring.

"Can we determine the source of the shield?" asked Booth.

Yana glanced at him again, then looked back toward Grimm and Miranda.

"The probes either are destroyed by the storm or lose contact with the ship," replied Miranda, looking at her directly.

Grimm spun around in his chair to face them with a smile; "I guess that leaves us no choice but to go down in person and walk through the storm and across that desert."

"Excellent idea. I will lead the landing party to examine the artifact," stated Booth.

Yana raised an eyebrow at him and turned toward her crew. "First, send the probes to scout the area surrounding the storm ring. We need to know what the terrain is like, as well as if there are any life forms. As best as possible, see if you can program the probes to scout under the cloud layer, closer to the ground, so we can gain as much intelligence as possible before we set foot on the planet."

Booth looked over at Yana but she ignored him; "I agree with the captain's suggestion."

Grimm and Miranda looked directly at Yana, and she nodded. Miranda turned back to her station, as Grimm spun his chair around again.

"Scouting the surrounding terrain now," said Miranda.

Yana could see Grimm stopping the probes and directing them in different directions to get a closer look at something.

Turning back to the main monitor, she addressed the rest of the crew, "Tal, inform the warships that we may have discovered the artifact but will need to land to approach on foot. We will meet again in 24 hours to review the data retrieved by Professor Grimm and Dr. Everett. At that time, we will formulate a plan. Most likely, Booth, Everett, Grimm, Edwards, and I will form the landing party. Tal, Nix, and Cheng will continue assembling the gates and report back to High Command as needed. I suggest everyone prepare. Dismissed."

The engineer and doctor left the bridge. Cheng took over monitoring the gate assembly, while Grimm and Miranda poured over the incoming data from the probes.

Yana watched Booth stare at the image of the planet below, then turn abruptly and leave.

* * *

Grimm and Miranda stood at the front of the room next to three large monitors. The outer two monitors showed the captains and crew of the two warships. The center monitor displayed images of the planet. The ring of clouds around the desert plain was in the center of the aerial view. Patches of blue spread out from the ring, becoming more irregular and smaller the farther out from the storms. Here the land seemed to dominate for several miles before more regular pools and streams began to emerge again.

"Our survey of the planet below has yielded valuable data," began Miranda. "The storm ring is approximately seven kilometers thick around a desert plain approximately ten kilometers in diameter. The constant downpour and lightning inside made it difficult for the probes to gather data. Outside of the ring, we were able to make some significant discoveries."

She nodded to the professor, and he activated the display. Video of a lake zoomed in to focus on large, slow-moving creatures. The creatures had bulbous bodies supported by six long limbs each that disappeared below the surface of the water through which they walked. The creatures were covered in a dark green, flat, shaggy material that hung off their bodies and upper limbs. Four long appendages dangled from each underbelly into the water below.

The view shifted as a probe dove beneath the water. It followed the limbs and appendages until it reached the bottom of the lake. The supporting limbs widened out into large, flat feet. The dangling appendages could be seen moving about, apparently sucking up bits of soil and water.

"This first specimen has been labeled CL002, as it is the second lifeform we have encountered in the Castor galaxy. All observations made so far indicate that it is docile and feeds on either something living on the bottom of the lake or the soil and water itself."

Miranda nodded again and the view changed. This time it was replaced by a nighttime image of a wide, almost flat dome made of a dark brownish-purple material. The dome had several ridges running from a central point at one end to another point at the opposite end. The central ridge was thicker and more prominent. The video moved forward and as the sunlight began to wash over the dome, the two halves of it rose into the air, the central ridge acting as a hinge point. Beneath the brownish-purple shell halves were several thin, dark-green membranes that feathered out and extended beyond the original boundaries of the shell.

The entire thing raised up off the ground and began to move. The probe moved around, and a head could be seen emerging from the soil as the creature rose out of the mud. It began to walk forward on eight stout legs. When it reached a shallow pool of water, the creature's head bent down, and it began to swallow large amounts of soil and water.

"This specimen has been designated CL003. Like the first, it appears to subsist on something that lives in the pools of water or on the water and soil itself. We will not know for sure without further examination and testing," Miranda continued. "No aggressive behavior has been observed in either lifeform."

"During the past twenty-four hours, these were the only lifeforms observed near what we propose as the landing site."

The view on the monitor shifted to an arial view of the planet's surface that was dotted by patches of brown and blue.

"As you can see, most of the planet is covered in pools of water, ranging from the size of a Terran pond to a lake. There do not appear to be any oceans or seas on the planet. This area," a dotted line appeared on the monitor around a space that was mostly soil, with fewer ponds, "is the proposed landing site. We cannot guarantee the state of the terrain inside the storm ring, but this gives us the closest place to land with the most direct path into the storm ring."

"Thank you," said Yana as she stood and replaced Miranda and Grimm at the front of the room.

The two scientists took their seats, and Yana continued the presentation.

"Because we cannot guarantee the passivity of the native wildlife, Captain Noire of the Tiberius has agreed to send down a squad of soldiers to assist in the mission.

Everett, Grimm, Edwards, Booth, and I will travel to the planet's surface tomorrow at 0800. We will land at the suggested location and proceed as far as we can via armored rovers into the storm ring. Due to the unknown nature of the microorganisms on the planet, everyone will be required to wear environmental suits. Any breach of a suit will mandate a quarantine before returning to the ship. Are there any questions?"

"If the probes can't survive inside the storm ring, why do you think it will be any safer for people?" asked the engineer.

Grimm turned in his seat; "The probes can survive the storm ring as long as they stay close to the ground. However, we cannot communicate with them through the storm, and the closer they get to the base of the energy dome, the greater the chance they will be rendered inoperable by the energy field surrounding the plain. That's also why we plan to land the drop ships outside the storm ring; we don't want to risk damaging our way off planet. Humans are not likely to be affected by the field in the same way, and we may be able to deactivate it once we can examine what is creating it."

"Did you not use the probes to zoom in and visually search for the source of the field?" asked Booth.

Miranda turned to look at him as she gestured with a remote towards a screen; "Yes, there appears to be rectangular, slightly curved objects just inside the storm ring."

The monitor displayed a blurry image of such an object obscured by heavy rain.

"There is a limit to the magnification capabilities of the probes, and they are not able to decrease their distance to the objects."

* * *

Grimm's knee bounced energetically with the ball of his foot still on the floor as the drop ship plunged through the planet's atmosphere. They were about to set foot on the surface of a strange new world with previously undiscovered lifeforms!

The ship's descent slowed until it jerked on impact with the planet's surface. Grimm sprang to his feet and a moment later reflexively flexed the joints in his hips and legs as the ship sank slightly into the soft ground.

"Final safety check," called out Captain Yana over the earpiece inside the sealed environmental suit.

Grimm glanced at the connections around the wrists, feet, and neck. He didn't want anyone complaining and slowing him down. Out of the corner of his eye, he saw Miranda staring at him with a slightly worried expression.

"Don't worry, it'll be ok; I'm not like the others," he signed to her with his hands. There was no private audio with the environmental suits' communication systems.

"Remember, this is an alien planet. We do not yet know what microorganisms live here or how they will affect humans. If anyone's suit is breached, it is imperative that you alert your squad leader or me immediately. This is for your safety as well as the rest of the crew's," Dr. Edwards reminded the team.

A moment later, the doors of the ship opened, and Grimm jumped out onto the alien planet. His boots sank slightly into the soft soil, but only a few centimeters. Looking down, he examined the ground beneath him and then looked out at their intended path. Even from this distance, the varying levels of water saturation could be seen. The transport vehicles they brought should be sufficient, but they wouldn't know for certain until they tried.

Grimm's head began to turn in a great arc to take in the entire world around him. The closest pools of water were devoid of the creatures they had seen earlier, but some could be seen off in the distance. Looking up, Grimm gazed at the clear blue sky, then back at the strange aquatic life forms. Absentmindedly, he began to wander in the direction of the nearest creatures as his eyes focused on them.

A hand grabbed his shoulder and he spun around.

Miranda gave him a stern look and gestured at the teams from the Tiberius and the Daedalus piling into their respective transports. The transport vehicles had solid, metal shells and large, wide tires that would help with both the lightning and the excess water on this planet.

"Fine," muttered Grimm, as he turned and trudged over to the vehicles.

*   *   *

Booth sat in the front passenger seat of the lead vehicle. Captain Yana sat to his left in the driver's seat, though he avoided looking at her, instead preferring to stare ahead at their destination.

"Proceed, Captain," he commanded.

"Not yet. Grimm wandered off and Everett went to fetch him," came the calm reply.

He turned and watched as Miranda trudged almost knee deep in the soft dirt as she made her way back. Booth smirked to himself. He wasn't sure how she was managing to make walking so much harder for herself than it was for everyone else.

The bureaucrat's eyes shifted to Grimm, who was looking around at everything even on his way back. Booth's brow furrowed and his eyes narrowed at the undisciplined, wayward professor.

When the stragglers finally reached the vehicle, it jerked sharply as they entered.

"I see you're having trouble; would you two like to remain with the ship?" Booth commented with a smile.

Grimm's pleasant smile and Miranda's stoic expression denied him the joy of a reaction from either of them.

"Everyone is accounted for on Transport One. Transport Two, are you good to go?" asked Yana.

"We are good to go," came the reply from the second vehicle.

Transport One shot forward and Booth was thrown back in his seat. He narrowed his eyes at Yana, but hers were focused ahead, and he was sure he saw a slight smile on her lips.

The landing site was the closest reasonably solid ground, but they still had a few kilometers to go before reaching the storm ring. The vehicles followed a winding path between ponds, pools, and lakes. The terrain was bumpy, but they kept moving to avoid sinking into the softer patches of ground.

Eventually, Booth began to gaze out the side window at the strange creatures that moved in and between the bodies of water. None of them seemed to really care about the alien metal objects invading their planet.

* * *

Yana steered the vehicle along the winding, bumpy path to the storm ring. She had been concerned that their presence would arouse the ire of the strange water creatures, but so far, they seemed oblivious to the landing crew.

"Captain Yana, there appear be objects approaching from the north, moving through the air in our general direction," came a warning from the military vehicle behind them.

Yana glanced roughly to her left and saw a few dark shapes in the sky.

"Grimm, Miranda, get some drones in the air. Find out what those things are and if they could be a threat," she ordered.

"On it," came Grimm's reply.

A compartment on the back of the lead vehicle opened up, and several small drones rose into the air. They flew in the direction of the incoming objects.

"They appear to be flying animals of some sort," stated Miranda.

"The creatures appear to be approximately two meters in length with a set of wings and three sets of legs," observed Grimm.

"In general, they appear mammalian,' commented Miranda.

"There are approximately two hundred of them," Grimm paused. "One of the creatures attacked a drone, but it bit into it and threw it aside."

"The creatures are diving," warned Miranda.

Yana glanced to her left and saw the dark cloud of winged animals descend. She looked back to the path ahead, glancing to the side every few seconds to know what happened next.

The swarm of flyers began to land on the aquatic creatures. Several flew in front of the vehicle, and Yana slowed to avoid hitting them. She watched in surprise as they landed on one of the tall aquatics and began tearing into the long, flat, shaggy masses that hung off of them. The tall aquatic did not seem to mind the attack. Somewhere to her right, she saw others land on one of the wide flat aquatics. They immediately began to tear into the thin green membranes, eating as much as possible before the hard shell halves descended. The aquatic then began to burrow into the mud to shield itself from the long claws of the flying creatures.

One of the flyers landed on the front of the vehicle, and Yana slowed to a halt. It looked at the machine quizzically then scratched at it a few times. It leaned down and tentatively tried to bite the metal surface. Shaking its head in frustration, it took off.

"Proceed with caution. Do not engage the flyers unless absolutely necessary. They appear to be more interested in the aquatics," commanded Yana through the communication system.

She continued to drive toward the storm ring, though at a slightly reduced speed. The flyers continued to move around, feeding on the thin membranes and long flat masses, moving from one aquatic to another.

The storm ring rose to fill the sky above as they approached their destination. Yana estimated they would arrive at the edge in approximately ten minutes. Some of the flyers flew past and landed on more of the tall aquatics ahead of them and to the right of the vehicle's path.

Dirt and water exploded into the air, and something surged up. All Yana could see were huge, sharp teeth sinking into a flyer, pulling it off of its perch.

Yana slammed on the breaks and the vehicle skidded to a halt in the mud.

What could best be described as a large, six-legged reptile with two great scaled wings now perched itself on top of the aquatic. It gripped the aquatic with its front and back feet while holding the half-devoured flyer in two thinner arms that reached up to feed its gaping maw from just below the front legs.

* * *

Dr. Edwards looked through the front windshield from the back seat at the strange new creature ahead. The large reptile ate the smaller mammalian flyer.

"Transport Two, prepare your weapons but do not engage unless absolutely necessary," ordered the captain from the driver's seat.

"Confirmed," came the reply.

Kira looked down at her feet and made sure her med kit was within reach. She didn't know what lay ahead, but she wanted to be prepared.

Slowly the vehicle started moving again. Everyone watched the new predator as they crept past it. Kira twisted in her seat to look past Miranda and Grimm as they made it to the other side of the creature.

Yana began to speed up gradually the farther they got from the predator.

Kira leaned back in her seat and began to relax. She watched the pools of water grow larger as streams from the storm ring fed into them.

"Captain Yana to seed ship," Yana said over the comms.

"This is the seed ship," came Commander Tal's voice.

"We are about to enter the storm ring. Be advised that there are at least two more species on this planet. Both seem predatory in nature. Grimm will send the details."

"Acknowledged," replied Tal.

"Done," reported Grimm.

Kira watched the wall of rain draw near. The first few drops began to splatter the windshield when they saw the predator fly past them into the darkness.

"Transport Two, be prepared; one of the large predators just flew into the storm. There may be more inside."

"Acknowledged."

Kira looked around at the other crew. Miranda was focused on her data pad. Grimm was staring out the windows, trying to see everything. Booth sat stiffly in his chair. She could see Yana's fingers twitch around the steering wheel as she drove them into the storm ring.

* * *

Yana activated the headlights as the darkness and downpour enveloped them. Visibility was limited, so she was forced to slow down, but she could tell that the ground was getting muddier and less stable as she proceeded.

The vehicle began to rock side to side and bounce up and down as she hit dips in the terrain that were obscured by the falling rain and accumulating water.

"Would you prefer that someone else drive?" asked Booth to her right.

Yana glanced in his direction and stifled a response. She did not appreciate his insinuation or his presence, but she could not openly defy High Command.

"Grimm, any way to tell how close we are?" she asked.

"As long as we continue in roughly the same direction, we will eventually reach the clearing on the other side. The storms block out communication with probes and the ships in orbit."

The front of the vehicle dipped sharply, and the crew lurched forward in their seats as they hit the bottom of the pool of water in front of them.

"Ma'am, is everyone ok in there?" asked the driver of Transport Two.

"Is everyone ok"; Yana looked around at the crew.

Booth was repositioning himself so that he could stand on the part of the vehicle in front of him. Part of Yana was slightly disappointed that he appeared to be OK. Everett had grabbed a hand hold on the ceiling and was holding onto the back of Grimm's suit with a vice like grip, while the professor was bracing himself against the seat in front of him. Yana mostly stood up and looked behind her to see Edwards holding herself up against the back of the driver's seat.

"Everyone appears to uninjured," Yana reported. "Check your suits, especially your helmets. Sound off if there is damage."

Everyone indicated that there were no breaches.

"We're going to attach a cable to the back of your vehicle and drag you out."

"Acknowledged."

Yana looked ahead at the murky water in which they were partially submerged.

"Proceed with caution outside the vehicles. I just saw something moving in the water," announced Grimm.

Yana turned in time to see large ripples greater than those created by the rain drops.

"We can attach the cable," offered Grimm.

"If you open the door, you'll flood the vehicle, and I don't think Transport Two will be able to pull the extra weight in this muddy terrain," countered Yana.

"Oh, I don't have—"

Grimm was cut off by a sharp squeeze of his arm by Everett.

Yana looked at them for a few more seconds, but they didn't respond.

"Transport Two, proceed," Yana confirmed.

She wasn't sure what Grimm had been referencing or why Miranda would stop him. They were sometimes odd, but they accomplished their tasks with great proficiency.

"Nothing on the thermal scopes," reported a soldier.

Clanking sounded at the back of the vehicle.

"Cable attached."

"Hold on; we're pulling you out."

The vehicle lurched slightly then slowly inched back but stopped before any meaningful progress could be made.

"Pull us out," ordered Booth.

"The ground is too muddy. We can't get enough traction."

"Understood," Yana looked around at the crew. "Everyone grab your gear; we're going to open the rear doors and climb out. Try to stay on the vehicle and use it to get to the ground."

The rest of the crew gave their acknowledgements.

Yana watched Grimm and Edwards open their doors. Water rushed in and began filling the front of the vehicle.

Edwards climbed out her side of the vehicle, and Miranda followed Grimm out his door.

Turning to Booth, she gestured upward toward the rear seats; "Your turn."

Booth climbed past her and out of the vehicle.

Yana sighed quietly to herself, then climbed out to join the others on the muddy bank.

*   *   *

Kira looked around. The soldiers had exited the second vehicle and created a protective perimeter around the team, weapons readied and pointed into the storm around them. Visibility was low in the constant downpour, the lights on the environmental suits and weapons giving the best indication of everyone's position.

"There should be two inflatable boats that we can deploy to continue across the water," said Yana as she moved toward the back of the second vehicle.

Kira grabbed the straps of her med pack, swung it onto her back, gave the straps a slight tug to make sure they were secure, and followed Yana. She knew the soldiers were doing their duty by scanning their surroundings for signs of a threat, but she felt a twinge of annoyance at the scientists for not moving to help. She didn't really expect anything from the bureaucrat.

Yana pulled out two packs and handed them to Kira before pulling out two small motors. Kira went back to the edge of the water and activated the inflatable rafts. Within seconds, the rafts inflated. Yana walked up with two buckets, each with a motor, a pump, and some tubing inside.

"We will probably need to bail out water," she said as she handed Kira a bucket. "The buckets are for in case the pumps fail or can't handle the volume."

They set about attaching the motors to the aft end of each raft.

"Three soldiers per raft," ordered Yana. "Booth, you're with me in the lead raft. Grimm, Miranda, and Edwards will follow along in the second." She turned to the remaining two soldiers; "You will stay with the vehicles. If we are not back in 3 hours, return to the landing craft and alert the ships."

The soldiers acknowledged the orders and moved first, one soldier entering each raft and moving to the front while the other two stood on either side of the raft and scanned the area around them. Two soldiers took positions near the second vehicle. Yana and Booth moved to their boat. Kira turned to see Miranda lifting her knees high with each step as she walked almost knee deep in the mud. Seeing her struggle, Kira felt a pang of regret for her quick judgements. The scientist was obviously having a difficult time in this environment.

Miranda stopped and looked at the boat.

"I'm not certain this will work," she stated.

Kira moved closer and leaned in instinctively, even though she knew the comms made it unnecessary.

"I understand this is difficult. You're not alone. We are here to help each other on this mission. It will be ok; the soldiers will protect us, and I'll be with you if you're afraid of the water."

Miranda looked at her, "I'm not struggling. The boat is not designed to hold my weight."

Kira's brow furrowed slightly in confusion; "The boats can hold the weight of several people; I'm sure you'll be fine."

"Don't worry about it," Grimm said, walking up to them.

He reached down with his right hand, grabbed Miranda's right wrist, and put her right hand on his left wrist.

"Just give me a squeeze if I start to get distracted."

Miranda looked down at his hand then up at the professor. She nodded stoically and they entered the boat.

Kira was confused by the exchange. She wasn't sure what Miranda's problem was or if Grimm's behavior was compassionate or patronizing. With a mental shrug, she entered the boat behind them.

The last soldiers on the shore joined them in the boats, and they took off.

They set up the pumps as they traveled across the water, periodically bailing out with the buckets as well.

The persistent grey of the world around them made time disappear. Kira had no sense of how much time had passed or how far they'd traveled when a large, irregular mass began to form in the darkness.

"Proceed with caution," came Yana's directive.

The boats slowly approached the object that seemed to be several meters wide and to protrude from the water about a meter. Kira's mind struggled to understand what it was she saw until Grimm spoke.

"It's those water walkers."

Now she saw it. The mound was made of the corpses of the tall, sort of hairy, tentacled aquatics. Their boat paused by the mass as Grimm reached out to examine the carcasses. Kira noticed Miranda still held Grimm's wrist as she turned to look at the mound.

Grimm picked up a piece of broken, sort of hairy flesh and held it close to his helmet.

"This looks vaguely plant-like"; he looked up at everyone. "It's almost like a plant version of an animal."

"Look: eggs," said Miranda pointing.

Everyone shifted to look at the top of the mound to see a depression in which sat several large, grey-speckled eggs.

"Everyone, move away from the—," began Yana.

One of the large, winged reptiles suddenly appeared at the top of the mound, looking down on them. The soldiers hit the power on the motors, and the boats lurched away from the nest. The creature turned, roared, and leaped after the second boat. Kira shifted away from the end of the boat as claws tore through the inflated outer ring. Water rushed downward following the creature, pulling the deflated material with it.

The soldiers at the rear disappeared under the water first, followed by Miranda and Grimm, before Kira fell in herself. She didn't see what happened to the soldier in the prow, but she assumed he fell in as well.

The downward surge of water from the creature's dive released Kira, and she swam to the surface. When her head broke free, she turned about to see who had made it.

Yana's boat was beside them, and Yana was helping the nearest soldier onto the boat while her soldiers scanned the water with their weapons for signs of the creature.

"The reptile didn't appear on the thermal scope," reported one of the soldiers.

Two of the soldiers from Kira's boat were treading water, awkwardly trying to hold their weapons and create a two-person perimeter to protect the team.

"Come back. Move toward the captain and her boat," said one of the soldiers.

Grimm was drifting way, looking for the creature.

Kira spun around. She could not see Miranda.

"Did anyone see Miranda?"

Heads swiveled, and several negative replies echoed in her ears. The doctor activated a light on her wrist and dove under the water.

Pulling herself down as best she could, she looked around. Kicking feet around her disappeared the farther she went. The water became murkier, and she reached out with her hands to feel for anything.

"Miranda!" she called, knowing full well that the comm system likely wouldn't work under water.

Eventually she found the bottom of the river but did not find a whole or even partial person. Frustrated, she surged back to the surface.

"I can't find her," she reported.

She seemed to be the last one in the water and swam over to the boat. One of the soldiers helped her on board.

"She'll be fine," came Grimm's response.

Irritation at his dismissive attitude made her whirl around looking for him. Sensing direction by sound over the comms was not possible in the suit, but eventually she spotted him perched on top of another mound on the opposite side of the boats from the mound from which they had been attacked, his form already fading to a silhouette.

"I think I've found it. Don't make any sudden moves. Just get everyone quietly into the boat and move away slowly," said Grimm.

"We're not abandoning anyone," came Yana's reply.

"The success of this mission is more important than any one person," came Booth's low reply.

Kira watched as Yana turned to look at him; "Are you able to analyze alien technology?"

Booth didn't reply, but just looked at her.

Movement and a roar drew everyone's attention to the grey form of Grimm standing slowly and stepping back as the creature rose out of the water.

Kira saw another form moving up onto the distant island. She started to open her mouth before realizing it was humanoid.

"Miranda?"

Grimm had his hand held out in the direction of the creature and both were still while Miranda smoothly exited the water and crouched behind the professor. The creature's silhouette seemed to relax and drift toward the mounds' surface. A snort could be heard through the comms, and Grimm began to approach the creature. His outstretched hand was just barely touching the snout when the peace was broken.

"What are you waiting for?" came Booth's annoyed tone.

"Stop!" shouted Yana.

Kira turned in time to see Booth raise one of the plasma rifles and fire at the creature.

The bolt of plasma tore into the shadowed creature's shoulder, and it writhed in pain and fury. Grimm turned back toward the boat with a shout.

"Idiot!" came the simultaneously condemnations of Grimm and Yana.

"Watch out," yelled Kira.

The creature lunged at Grimm. With speed greater than Kira expected from the girl who had struggled so much in the mud, Miranda was between Grimm and the creature, throwing him behind her with her left hand as she went. Her right reached out to intercept the descending jaws.

She quickly brought her left hand back in front and caught the lower jaw with her left and the upper with her right. The force of the creature's lunge drove her back, and her feet dug into the mound.

Amazement and confusion washed over Kira. She had no idea what she was seeing or how it was possible.

Before the creature could pull back, Yana's order rang out, "Fire!"

Plasma bolts filled the air between the boat and the distant island. The creature screamed in pain and its silhouette expanded. Two vast appendages surged down, and the mass of the creature rose into the air. In seconds, it was gone.

*   *   *

Booth waited impatiently for the boat to get to the two scientists and for them to board. He knew that they were integral to the mission, but delays made him look bad to his colleagues at High Command. He sneered at the pair internally when he saw that the assistant was holding onto the professor's wrist, but he made sure to not let it show on his face. It made her appear even more ill-equipped for this mission than she was already.

"How did you—" began Dr. Edwards before Grimm waved away her question.

"We can discuss it later when this is over. For now, let's just get away from the nests."

"Agreed," came the simultaneous response from Booth and Yana.

He glanced at the captain in annoyed surprise that they were in agreement but said nothing. At least this would get them moving.

The soldiers piloted the boat through the river and away from the nests as quickly as the little motor would take them. Nothing much happened in the grey haze, and Booth found himself becoming impatient and restless. He started glancing over at the soldier steering the boat, wondering if he was really going as fast as he could.

"We're here," stated Yana.

Booth looked to see a large object taking shape in the lightening shadows of the rain. The sunlight shone through the edge of the storm ring, and the desert plain began to appear on the far side of the object. It stood on a wide stone base that rose out of the water a couple meters. There was about a meter of walkway around the object as it was narrower than the stone support.

The boat gently bumped against the stone, and the crew began to climb up. Grimm helped hoist Miranda up so that she could grasp the ledge. She pulled herself up quickly, spun around, and reached down to help Grimm.

"Stay in the boat while we examine the device. The shield is probably being emitted from here, and I don't want everyone's comms getting destroyed because they got too close," said Grimm.

Yana agreed, and the two scientists began examining the device.

Booth didn't fully understand what he was looking at. The base of the artifact was a square, but the width of it decreased as it rose and arched toward the plain. It was covered in thick metal panels with disks with six holes around their circumference, similar to the probe they had first found.

Miranda gingerly reached out toward the invisible wall that connected the artifacts and presumably kept the storms off the plain. She pulled her hand back sharply.

Grimm began removing panels and setting them aside. He retrieved a device from his waist and connected it to the exposed circuitry. Miranda joined him, and they stared at the device's readout.

"Any luck deciphering the device?" asked Yana.

"Partially. It takes time to translate the alien symbols. There are still many words of which we are completely unsure," replied Miranda. "Without a point of reference or a parallel readable text, it is hard to determine."

"The devices appear to form an energy field dome that keeps the storms out. We might be able to deactivate the connection between this one and one of the ones to the side, but I can't guarantee how that will affect the storms or the shield as a whole."

"What do you mean?" asked Yana.

The scientists turned to face them; "If I'm wrong, the entire shield could collapse due to the disruption in one segment, or the storms themselves could begin to interfere as their electromagnetic disturbances pierce the boundary. Our best bet would be to deactivate it, move through, and then reactivate it. This would lessen our chances of anything potentially catastrophic."

"Will our equipment work inside the barrier once it is reactivated?" asked Booth.

"Most likely, yes. The field extends out and up to form a dome. It does not appear to permeate the plain."

"Will we be able to deactivate it from inside the shield dome on our return trip?"

Grimm paused.

"We could set a timer to deactivate the shield segment for 60 seconds every 45 minutes. That would be the shortest safe interval, according to my calculations," suggested Miranda.

"Ok," said Yana. "As soon as you give the signal, jump in and we'll drive the boat to the shore."

Grimm peeked around the edge of the device and turned back.

"There's a ramp on the other side. We'll just walk down the ramp. You drive the boat. That will be faster and easier."

"Ok," accepted Yana.

The two scientists returned to work.

"On the count of three," said Grimm.

The soldier at the motor steered the boat just past the stone base, and then they pushed away to rotate roughly into position.

"Three… two… one... go!"

The soldier squeezed the control, and the boat rocketed past the device. They burst from the wall of rain, and Booth had to squint as the bright sun blinded him. A moment later, the boat lurched to a halt as it collided with the shore.

Booth's eyes adjusted in time for him to see the two scientists casually walking down the long ramp to join them on the dry ground of the plain.

* * *

Yana led the way across the desiccated plain. She was relieved that there were no diversions or hindrances on this segment of the mission but found herself feeling suspicious of her own mental relaxation. Her head swiveled back and forth, her eyes grazing over the surface of the planet, her mind searching for anything that did not fit.

Nothing happened, except that their destination slowly grew larger in the distance.

The monotony of the trek gave her time to think. The professor had been irritatingly foolish to think he could somehow coax an alien creature about which they knew nothing with such gestures and movements. He was either foolishly hopeful or foolishly curious.

It was strange how Miranda had been able to move so quickly and hold off the creature. Through most of the trip, she had been struggling, walking almost knee deep in mud, yet at that critical time, she exhibited almost unnatural swiftness and strength. Even if the corpses of the aquatic creatures provided more stable and solid footing, what she had done didn't make sense.

A troublesome possibility flitted across her mind. She liked the young woman, respected her work. Yana shook her head; some things didn't fit. She had no definite proof, and until she did, she would make no hasty accusations.

At first the distant object was a small speck, but slowly it grew. She stared at the strange shape, trying to understand what she was seeing. Eventually it clicked into place.

Curiosity drove her to focus on the structure, so she almost didn't notice the increasing frequency in the dark, branching, irregular deposits in the ground.

"Fulgurite?" asked Grimm, standing up with a piece in his hands.

Yana glanced at him but kept going. Perhaps the aliens' shields were there to keep the lighting away?

By the time they were within roughly a hundred meters of the structure, the fulgurite was crunching consistently under foot with each step.

"Let's circle around before approaching any closer," Yana cautioned. "I don't want to walk into any surprises."

The team circled the structure. Overall, the building was composed of a central structure and an outer ring raised off the ground by a three-stepped stone dais. The main portion of the artifact was a circular building that rose to a domed ceiling. A rectangular doorway with two great metal doors was seated at one side of the stone cylinder. Around the central piece, a ring of columns about a meter from the cylinder supported a stone ring at the same height as the base of the dome, but it was not attached to it.

As they finished their cursory survey, Yana asked the team to confirm what she had observed; "I see no signs of advanced technology. This looks like an ancient stone building that easily could have been built on Terra."

"At first inspection, I would tend to agree," confirmed Everett.

"Maybe the aliens simply wanted to preserve a historical site, so they built the shield," suggested Grimm.

Yana glanced around the team and noticed everyone giving sideways looks at Booth to see his reaction.

"Did High Command's reports indicate that we would find an ancient artifact or advanced technology?" she asked him directly.

"The report did not specify what, precisely, the artifact would be, but I would not be one to doubt our orders from High Command"; he met her gaze. "Perhaps the interior is more advanced than the exterior."

"That would be fascinating," muttered the professor as he started toward the door.

Yana sighed to herself and followed. "Keep an eye out for anything suspicious. I want eyes on all sides of the structure," she ordered the soldiers.

The soldiers gave their acknowledgements and began to array themselves in a circle around the building. One of them followed the team toward the door.

Grimm and Miranda reached the door first and began examining it. Yana looked around at the smooth, pale stone walls and columns. They contrasted with the darkened, ornately molded metal doors. The two doors, when shut, formed a single image. A large tree with ten spheres in its branches formed the main pattern. Around the outer edge of the doors was a border approximately ten centimeters wide in which were inscribed strange symbols. They did not match either the alien ones they had already seen or any that Yana could remember from her history lessons many years prior.

Her gaze shifted around, and she began to notice the scorch marks that darkened the stone around the doors and may have even been at the root of the darkened color of the doors themselves.

"There does not appear to be a handle or anything to solidly grip," reported Grimm with some disappointment.

"Let's examine the rest of the outside surface. Maybe we can find another way in or a clue on how to open it," replied Yana.

The group began to wander around the building, walking on the raised platform between the ring of pillars and the central structure. Miranda, the soldier, and Booth started walking to Yana's left. Grimm started to turn away from the door and shift toward Yana's right.

Yana followed the rest of the team to the left. As she followed the curve, out of the corner of her eye she saw

Grimm move back to stand very close to the door. She turned her head at the last second and saw Grimm hold his hand between his torso and the door, palm facing, but not quite touching the metal surface.

She stopped abruptly and spun around. When she got back within range, she could see Grimm curling his fingers around the edge of the door and starting to pull it open. Apparently, the metal doors were very thick and heavy, so his progress was slow.

"How did you manage to open the door?" asked Yana approaching.

"Effort and perseverance," he said with a smile.

It was not a helpful answer, but Yana let it pass. They were almost done with the mission, and soon they would know what this was about.

The sky began to darken, and she heard shouts from the soldiers. Grimm glanced around, then continued to pull on the door. Yana looked out as a shadow grew around the artifact. She saw the nearest soldiers look, pointing their weapons at the sky before backing away to hide between the pillars.

"There's a ship above us, and it's not ours," came the report.

Miranda was standing beside the professor, looking around with a more serious expression than Yana had previously seen. Edwards and Booth had backed away and were looking up between the gap between the pillar ring and the main structure. Yana turned her head and saw the ship.

It was massive, bigger than any of the human ships, and it was still higher than the energy dome. It continued to lower until the surrounding area grew as dark as if the sun was setting. She looked ahead and wasn't sure if the energy dome itself had somehow changed to become opaque.

"Lights on. Everyone gather at the door," she ordered.

The remaining soldiers gave their acknowledgement and began to move into position.

Something moved in the air, but she couldn't tell what it was.

"Be ready; something's coming," she warned.

Large flying objects swooped in and began grabbing members of the team, pulling them away and tossing them into the darkness.

A few shots rang out, followed by startled screams, thuds, then grunts of pain. She couldn't be sure, but she thought she heard the weapons being broken.

A creature more than a foot taller than her swooped in and grabbed her by the shoulders before tossing her aside.

Yana hit the ground hard, the pain making her pause to catch her breath. Concern for the wellbeing of her team drove her to push past the pain and get up.

Ahead of her was the artifact. Everett was wrestling with a large, almost seven-foot-tall creature, while Grimm was being dragged away from the now open door by a second. A third pushed on the door and leaned its full weight into it to close it.

Yana got a good look at the creature that was dragging Grimm away from the doors. It was approximately seven feet tall and covered in feathers and scales. It had two massive wings folded down its back and a tail could be seen twitching behind it. Its legs ended in great bird-like talons. Its arms were strongly muscled and similarly clawed. Oddly, there was a second, smaller pair of arms tucked in close to the torso. The head had a long protruding snout and was covered in fine feathers. Its mouth curled open to reveal rows of sharp, pointed teeth.

The creature stopped and tossed Grimm to the ground before opening its mouth and yelling at him in some strange language. There was a loud noise, like breaking bones, and Yana saw one of the creatures crumpled on the steps of the structure as Everett dashed toward the interrogating alien. There was an anger and fear in her eyes that worried Yana.

"Everett, stop," she shouted while seeing the soldiers begin to move around her, their side arms aimed at the aliens. She held out her hands to ward them off; "Don't fire. They could have killed us, but they haven't."

The creature that had closed the door shouted something across the distance to its companion as it kneeled next to the one who had been wrestling with the young scientist.

Miranda didn't slow but changed course, running around the creature and coming to stand between it and the professor. She stared at it defiantly.

Yana walked over to stand near the scientists. She activated a control on her suit for external communications.

"We mean you no harm," she began, holding her hands out, palms forward.

The creature said something angrily and pointed a talon at the professor who was getting to his feet.

"We don't understand," Yana shook her head as she looked back.

The creature looked at her, tilting its head slightly. Maybe it could understand? It seemed like the most ephemeral of possibilities.

A strange sound came in through the suit's comms. The creature's eyes darted from Yana to something behind her. Yana turned to look at Grimm, standing with his eyes closed, head turned slightly as if listening carefully to something. He opened his mouth and uttered hesitant sounds whose patterns she did not recognize.

The creature seemed to smile and almost laugh. It said something else, and Grimm responded slowly. It didn't seem to like or agree with what Grimm said. Its expression changed, and it took a menacing step forward.

Miranda Everett reached out a hand to stop the creature's advance, her palm pressing into its chest. One of its small hands shifted, drawing Yana's attention to a device she hadn't noticed around the opposite wrist. The delicate fingers pressed a button, and the lights went out.

Yana saw Everett collapse to the ground hard in the dim light that managed to get past the alien ship. The soldiers looked down at their now powerless plasma pistols. She saw Edwards rush forward to help the fallen scientist, but the doctor was almost unable to move her.

Dreadful certainty consumed the captain. Her fears were confirmed. The young woman was not a living thing. She had harbored an illegal construct that put humanity at risk.

She looked up as more aliens descended and began seizing her crew, dragging them up toward their ship.

A sense of helplessness washed over her, as she realized that she was powerless to stop her crew from being taken by an alien species whose intentions were unknown.

Strong talons gripped her arms. She watched the prone form of the young scientist dwindle, her only consolation that her failure to protect her crew from the aliens would at least protect humanity from this artificial intelligence.

VII

Wyrm
Dynoltir, +128 TR

Pain was the only thing the young woman was aware of as she pushed to deliver the child in the inn's back room.

Before the pain, Zaria had been cursing her bad luck and questioning her decisions. Her swollen belly for the past several months had marked the reality of what many had suspected about her, but few had been willing to admit to knowing for sure in front of the other villagers. Now her nightly occupation was obvious, and her presence was marked by more judgmental glances than suspicious ones.

The village was located in a small valley deep in the mountains. As time passed and empires rose and fell, the village was sometimes a welcome way station on the path between trading partners. At other times, it was an almost forgotten place that had become resentful and suspicious of the outsiders who had otherwise abandoned it. Currently, the village was somewhere on the downward slope from the former to the latter.

Occasionally, nomads, merchants, or even soldiers passed through the village. The woman had been fascinated by the outsiders and the exotic nature of their cultures and stories. When she got older, she found they were often willing to trade what she found interesting about them in exchange for what they desired in her.

Before the pain had hit her, she had been weeping bitterly at the rejection of her parents and the villagers' disdain. Even the midwife who sat with her now seemed less than pleased at her existence.

Eventually, the pain ended. In its place came exhaustion and the screams of a tiny creature.

The midwife cleaned the baby while the woman lay back on the bed, trying to recover. After a few minutes, she walked over and handed the woman a small bundle. The woman held the bundle somewhat awkwardly at first, cradling one end near her shoulder while supporting the length of it with her arm. She looked down at the small face peeking out of one end of the bundle and squeezed it gently but firmly against her chest.

Tears began to flow down her cheeks as she looked at her precious infant child. She no longer felt anything other than never-ending love for this small life in her arms. She had never felt such affection as strongly or as instantly in her life.

*   *   *

Wyrm sat on the floor playing with a crudely carved wooden stag in a corner of a huge room. The room was filled with tables and chairs that seemed large when he was standing, but positively gigantic when he was sitting on the floor. There were people sitting in the chairs, but most were sitting far away from this particular corner.

At the sound of soft footsteps, Wyrm looked up to see his mother approaching. She wrapped her shawl tightly around her shoulders and upper chest as she approached.

"Mommy," he said, looking up at her.

His mother knelt down and gently stroked his head. "Are you having fun?"

Wyrm nodded with a smile.

"Are you being good for Auntie?" His mother glanced at the older woman sitting nearby.

Wyrm nodded and looked at the old woman. He didn't understand why, but she always seemed sad.

Wyrm's mother straightened up and turned to the old woman.

"Thank you for watching him. I need to go, um, have a conversation with someone. I won't be long."

The old woman sighed; "You don't need to do this. There are other ways."

"It's ok. Don't worry about me."

His mother knelt by him again.

"Give Mommy a hug?"

Wyrm stood up and hugged his mother around the neck.

"Mommy loves you, my good little boy," she said, squeezing him gently with her embrace.

She got up and started to walk away. Wyrm sat back down and watched her approach a man at the bar. She lowered her shawl to hang limply from her elbows as she went.

*   *   *

The hunter carefully stepped out from behind the tree, taking aim at his prey. He kept close to the tree, relying on it and the others of the forest to help shield him from view, as he waited for the deer to shift into a better position.

The deer was standing roughly facing him with its head down eating something. The undergrowth between them obscured the ground around the deer, but he assumed it was eating grass or leaves. It shifted its footing slightly and he mentally prepared himself, but it was still not in a good position.

The hunter's gaze drifted over the deer. It was quite large compared to the deer he usually found, which was exciting. A gentle breeze drifted through the trees, washing over the deer, then the hunter.

The deer's large red eyes looked up from the ground and it froze. The hunter tensed. He had never seen such eyes in a deer before. The possibility that it might be diseased or a rare breed presented itself to his mind but quickly dissolved in shock.

The deer raised its head and bared a set of viciously sharp teeth, the corners of its mouth opening wider than he'd ever seen on a deer before. That's when he noticed the blood around its mouth. The creature gave an angry growl and charged toward him. He released his arrow and it hit the deer's chest, but it did nothing to slow the creature.

The hunter spun back behind the tree and looked up. There was a branch within reach. He jumped, grabbed it, and pulled himself up in time to see the mad deer lunge and snap at the air where he had just been.

The angry creature looked up at him and roared. The hunter began to climb higher into the tree, as he wasn't sure what the creature would do. With the extra distance, he sat with his back to the trunk and relaxed momentarily, as he watched his enemy below.

The creature circled the tree a few times, then paced back and forth under where he was sitting. It sniffed and pawed at the ground, the roots, and the trunk of the tree. It stopped and looked up at him. He had never seen such hate in an animal before.

The deer walked away, and the hunter began to consider climbing down when it disappeared from sight. He decided it would be best to wait in case it returned.

A loud series of fast thuds came rushing through the brush, and the deer burst into view. Using its momentum, it launched itself up the trunk of the tree and into the branches. With dexterity and ferocity, it leaped between the branches, eager to reach him.

The hunter clumsily tried to climb around the trunk and up higher as the insane creature pursued him, but the higher he went, the more the tree swayed and the less steady he felt. Growls and scraping hooves were always a few seconds behind. With dismay, he realized he could go no further and turned to fight the creature as best he could. He drew his large hunting knife with his right hand, gripped the trunk tightly with his left, and prepared to strike.

The deer came within range and lunged at his dangling leg. He pulled his leg back and slammed his blade into the side of the deer's neck. With a roar of pain, it twisted, tearing the knife from his grip and biting hard into his wrist. The hunter screamed and was pulled from his perch. He hit the ground hard, the air forced from his lungs by the impact.

The deer dropped out of the tree and approached him, his knife still sticking out of its neck. It pulled its head back and looked at him. The head then shot forward with a growl, mouth opening unnaturally, and he felt its teeth sink into his throat. The creature eagerly drank from the gaping wound, as the hunter felt the world grow dark and numb while his life blood flowed freely into the deer's maw.

*   *   *

Wyrm stood outside his mother's room in the inn. He looked down only slightly as he stared at the door handle and waited.

The herbalist had kicked him out of his mother's room earlier that morning. His assistant, a teenage girl a little taller than Wyrm, had slipped out and returned with the tavern keeper only a few minutes ago. Now he waited.

He didn't think about much, choosing to stare mindlessly at the door handle rather than dwell on his mother's sickness and deteriorating health. He strained to ignore the broken bits of dialogue that drifted through the cracks around the door.

The door handle jerked, and Wyrm jumped back in surprise. He looked up to see the gruff old tavern keeper step out and look down at him. The expression on the man's face looked more like annoyance touched with disdain.

"She's dead. You can either leave, or you can clean the stables and sleep with the horses."

"What?" Wyrm was stunned. His throat tightened and he sniffed, barely comprehending what was being said.

"You're not my child. I have no reason to keep you for free. You can't do your mother's work, but you can clean the stables and stay there. Or don't. It really doesn't matter to me."

The old man turned and walked away.

Wyrm could feel the burning around his eyes, and the tears beginning to flow down his face. The herbalist and his apprentice left his mother's room. The apprentice looked down at him without tilting her head and made sure to avoid him. Wyrm couldn't see the herbalist's expression but did notice his mother's purse hanging from his belt as he left.

Wyrm slowly walked into the room. His mother lay lifeless on the bed. He collapsed in tears next to her, hugging her cooling form.

Some time passed, and he heard footsteps and voices approaching. His tears having subsided slightly, he wiped his face and turned toward the door.

"I don't care what you do with it, just get this filth out of my inn."

The tavern keeper stopped on the other side of the door, and two men entered wearing gloves and cloths tied around their faces so as to shield their mouths and noses. They pushed Wyrm aside and roughly began searching his mother's body.

"Nothing. The herbalist must have beat us to it."

"What are you doing?" Wyrm said in irritation.

The men ignored him and wrapped his mother in a blanket. One grabbed her shoulders and the other her feet. As soon as they began to lift her, Wyrm's grief-addled mind understood what was happening.

"Put my mother down. She's not yours. Leave her alone!" He grabbed his mother but was backhanded and fell onto the floor.

"Ha! She was everyone's."

The other man laughed, and they carried her out the door.

Wyrm shot up and ran to follow them but was caught by the collar by the tavern keeper.

"You best be running to the stables to shovel the manure out or don't bother coming back here again."

Wyrm pulled himself free and glared up at the old man. He turned, but the men were gone. He ran out into the street and looked around. He had no idea where they'd gone.

Choosing a random direction, he turned to his right and ran down the street, looking around for any signs. He turned and ran back past the inn but still could not make out anything.

Anger and pain welled up inside him. Wyrm clenched his fists and ground his teeth as tears flowed down his cheeks. No one came to check on him when he let out an anguished scream.

*   *   *

Wyrm kept his head down as he collected empty mugs from the tables in the inn. It was crowded more than normal today, and everyone was eating and drinking their fill. Wyrm was taller now but quite thin. He was usually only able to eat the leftover scraps at the end of the day. His well-trained eyes now sought only the empty cups on the tables, knowing better than to torment himself with sights of uneaten food.

"Cheers to the happy couple!"

Cheers erupted through the large room, and everyone downed more of their drinks.

"Don't touch my mug," growled one of the villagers at Wyrm as he reached for what he thought was an empty vessel.

"Sorry sir," he said, head down, hoping the man was too drunk to hit him this time.

The man spat at Wyrm and lifted his drink to his lips. Everyone else pretended to not notice the exchange and continued on about their conversations as if nothing had happened. Wyrm moved on to the next table.

The tavern keeper's daughter, Ani, had just married the miller's son, Casimir. They would soon be taking over the management of the tavern. The crowds gathered were mostly there to celebrate the union.

Wyrm continued to move back and forth through the crowds, mostly ignored by everyone. He paid little attention to the bits of conversations as he passed.

His rounds brought him closer to the bride and groom. Casimir was tall and well built. He had the faintest hints of a beard growing in. His manner was relaxed and confident. Ani was attractive with long, flowing hair that she had braided carefully for the occasion. Her demeanor was pleasant, but her posture very upright.

"Any new plans for the tavern?"

"Well, my wife wants to make some changes. She'll be in charge of it, mostly."

"So, what are your plans?"

"I mostly want to clean the place up. My father is kind of messy."

Laughter rippled around them.

Wyrm moved to the table behind them as the tavern keeper's daughter glanced around.

"He was also very lax in his morals and allowed a rather disreputable lot to take advantage of his generosity. I will not have my house turned into a brothel again. I plan to remove any vestiges of that filthy whore."

"What?" Wyrm turned suddenly and looked at the bride.

Ani turned to face him.

She looked down her nose at him; "Well, I suppose you're going to find out anyway. I don't want your whore mother's lack of morals to taint my guests."

Wyrm stepped forward, a low growl in his voice; "Don't talk about my mother that way."

Casimir stood quickly; "Lower your tone when you talk to my wife."

The room grew quiet.

"Mind your place, boy, when speaking to your betters," said one of the villagers beside him who had also risen to his feet.

Bitterness and rage drove him to speak without considering what might happen; "You're not better than me. You think your mother never sought an escape from this place?" Gesturing around the room, he said, "How many of their beds did you try before you found the one that fit the best?"

The bride's face twisted in indignation; "How dare you, you filthy whore's bastard!"

Casimir rushed Wyrm and punched him in the face. He fell back and collided with a table laden with gifts. As pain shot through him, anger rose to take its place. He had put up with the slights and arrogance for too long. His mother was taken from him because of them. They could all die for all he cared.

Wyrm screamed and lunged at the miller's son. He managed to knock the groom back a few steps but was soon doubled over in pain from a strong blow to his stomach. He stumbled back. Casimir swiftly moved in and punched him in the head, knocking him back to the floor. Several heavy kicks collided with his gut, and he curled up even more.

"Stop this nonsense," came a gruff shout.

Wyrm saw a local hunter stand between the newlyweds and his sad form on the ground.

"My brother was killed by an animal while hunting several years ago, and if that taught me anything, it's that family is important. No one wants to hear their loved ones insulted. This is a day of feasting and celebration. Let it stay that way and not be marred by unnecessary violence and bitterness."

Wyrm looked around saw a silver-plated knife on the floor next to him. He looked up and saw that everyone was looking from the old hunter to the new bride and groom. Slowly, he turned onto his hands and knees, moving closer to the knife so that he was able to slip it into his boot without being noticed as he got up.

"Fine. Just get him out of here. I don't want to see him in the tavern again," said Casimir, who then spat in Wyrm's direction.

Two villagers stepped out of the crowd and grabbed Wyrm under the arms. He struggled angrily at their touch but was dragged out of the tavern and dumped on the ground. They went back inside and slammed the door shut.

Wyrm stood and glared at the door. He could try to go back. Maybe he could use the knife.

But there were too many. The repeated blows had dissipated his anger, but he still hated them. Wyrm turned and began to walk down the street. He would leave the village. He didn't know why he had stayed this long. He must have been weak and scared.

A faint sound of wood hitting wood came from behind him, and he thought he heard the hunter's voice, but he ignored it. Wyrm didn't care what any of them had to say. He would find his own way to live in the wilds. No one would stop him or lord over him again.

*   *   *

Wyrm was no longer angry or bitter; he was just cold. He had been irritated when his fishing spot by the river began to be covered in snow, and he started searching for shelter, but too much time in the cold had drained him of the energy to be upset. Now he just trudged along in the snow, hugging himself with one hand and holding the last burning branch from his fire with the other.

It had only been a few days since he had left the village. By the first night, his anger had been replaced by a nagging fear that he might fail out in the wilderness by himself. He had never really been taught how to hunt, trap, or fish. He didn't know what berries or plants were safe to eat and which were poisonous.

By the end of the second night, he had succeeded in catching a couple fish with a spear he crudely carved with the knife he had stolen. He wasn't able to cook them until the next morning, when he finally got the fire going.

His success at catching fish and making fire had filled him with a false sense of security. The sudden dip in temperature followed by rapidly falling snow had made him realize this error, but it was too late. He cursed his lack of preparedness, bitter that he didn't know how to build a shelter. The snow would make such a task even more difficult, and he wasn't sure the knife would be enough.

Wyrm stumbled along in the snow, hoping he was heading in the direction of the mountains. Maybe he could find a rocky outcropping or cave to hide in.

Time dissolved in the haze of falling white flakes, and only his increasing discomfort let him know that any time had passed at all. Eventually, he sensed the day getting darker, and he began to curse his own existence.

"I wish I had never been born," he muttered through gritted teeth.

Through some compulsion he did not fully grasp, Wyrm changed direction slightly. The snow began to lessen as he approached the rock wall of the mountains. In front of him was a dark crack in the rock. It was just big enough for him to fit.

The crack was a tight squeeze, but it soon widened into a short passage. Wyrm held out his burning branch like a torch to see what was around him.

The area he was in formed an irregular corridor large enough for him to walk comfortably. He followed it until he reached a larger room. The light wasn't strong enough to illuminate the other side, but he could see there was something in the middle.

Wyrm carefully approached the object. He stopped several feet from it, when he could tell it was a human figure in a cross-legged seated position. The person must be dead, as he was covered in cobwebs and dust. There was an old blade on the ground in front of the body. Long since dried rivers of blood ran down from the throat, stomach, and dangling wrists across the cavern floor. His eyes traced the path until it mixed with what was now a frozen puddle of water in a depression that he had stepped over when he entered the crack in the mountain.

Just to be sure, he poked the corpse with his toe when he got within range. Nothing happened.

Wyrm walked around the rest of the cavern but found nothing of interest. He turned to look back at the corpse, debating whether to remove it before trying to make this his home.

"Please, destroy my body," came a sudden voice to his right.

Wyrm jumped, shouted, and turned to face a ghostly apparition. The figure vaguely resembled a more lifelike version of the corpse. He wasn't sure about the corpse, but the ghost definitely looked sad and tired. Oddly, he noticed pointed ears and strangely sharp teeth.

"Free me from my prison, and I can grant you your deepest desires."

Wyrm didn't know if his heart could continue beating at such a pace at the sound of the second voice. He quickly stumbled back from what was now two ghostly forms.

The new one looked almost identical to the first. The main difference was that the second looked much less worn, and a smile played at the corner of his lips every time he spoke.

"I can offer you whatever you desire. Money," the second ghost gestured, and phantom heaps of treasure filled the cave; "women," another gesture and the treasure was gone, replaced by translucent yet beautiful women pressing close against Wyrm's body; "or power!" The women vanished and Wyrm found himself coated in shimmering, ghostly armor. Phantom soldiers knelt in never ending rows on either side of a path before him. More translucent people were dragged into the empty space and slain before him. Even without seeing, he knew they were his enemies.

"Please," begged the first ghost. "If we remain, it will only mean more death and suffering. We are at a stalemate. This may be the last chance to end my suffering and protect the world from my sins."

Wyrm started to walk toward the exit. There had to be other caves out there.

"Don't walk away from your desires," said the second ghost, now at his side.

The first, sadder ghost appeared in front of him; "Stop."

Wyrm stopped in his tracks, not wanting to find out what happened if he walked through the ghost.

"Why?"

The first ghost sighed; "I know you have suffered, and I know you have cared for others. Please help me spare mothers and sons the torment that my existence will inevitably perpetuate. Cut off my head, cut out my heart, and burn them both."

"My power is concentrated in the heart and blood. If you consume them, you will gain the power to get your own revenge," whispered the second ghost behind him.

Wyrm hesitated.

"Fine."

The sorrowful ghost breathed a sigh of relief. The second ghost smiled more broadly.

With more confidence than he felt, he turned away and walked over to the seated form. He pulled out the knife and looked at it. He had no idea if this would even work. Wyrm stood in front of the figure and grabbed its hair with his left hand and began to saw through the neck with his right. Eventually, the head fell loose, and he tossed it aside. He fought back the impulse to gag and wretch.

After the head was removed, the body fell over, and Wyrm began to cut into the chest. He tried for a while to cut through the bones but failed. Eventually, he just cut into the abdomen and then reached up to pull the heart from the ribcage. He cut the vessels connecting the heart to the body and looked around.

The ghosts were gone.

Setting the heart aside, Wyrm stood and went about the task of gathering wood outside. When he returned, he used his fading torch to kindle a new fire. He tossed the head into the fire.

He walked over and picked up the heart. Wyrm stared at the heart in his blood-coated hand.

He took a bite.

Immediately he threw up. Disgust at his weakness and resentment and bitterness toward those who had wronged him gave him the strength to keep going. With each disgusting bite, he found that he was able to continue, knowing that his discomfort would lead to their greater pain.

Once the last bit of heart was consumed, he made sure to drink up as much of the blood from the corpse as he could.

His belly now full, Wyrm sat back and stared mindlessly into the fire. He felt both very warm and very cold in alternating moments. His eyelids became heavy, and he fell over, unconscious on the cave floor.

* * *

Wyrm's consciousness drifted toward a vision, a memory that was now his, whether he wanted it or not.

Wyrm sat in a boat watching an endlessly high wall of mist grow farther and farther away. The cool air swept across the waves and over the ship. Its touch made him feel both relaxed and content. His body felt healthy and strong in a way he had never known before. His clothes were nicer than any Wyrm had actually worn in his life, but the memory said he had always dressed this way.

He looked around the boat and saw a woman and two small children. They were unfamiliar, and yet he knew that this was his wife and children. All three had pointed ears, and he could sense the age of the woman more by instinct than by external detail. Somewhere in the back of his mind, strange words faded in and out; names of the family members and their species. The excitement of the children made his wife smile, and the happiness of that trio brought joy to his own heart.

The experience was familiar, but also foreign. Part of Wyrm was sure he had never felt anything like this since he was a small child, but another part of him seemed unfazed, as if this was the most normal thing in the world.

Though he could not see it, a part of him knew his face was now the more vibrant version of the sad ghost he had met in the cave.

* * *

Wyrm could sense that his body was gone, yet his mind remained, somehow, in this strange forest. Memory now demanded that he had been this way for many centuries.

Seeing the happy creatures with pointed ears leave their boat and begin to run across the beach filled Wyrm with irritation as he watched them from the tree line. These trespassers were so full of life that he could sense it even from this distance. It felt vast and never-ending. Their liveliness, joy, and eternally youthful forms filled him with a terrible ache.

He wanted that life. He wanted to be youthful, energetic, and corporeal. The fact that he was not and could not have those things made him angry. How was it fair that they were alive and he wasn't? He was older than them, wiser, and more powerful. He had seen their creation, yet here he was: formless, empty, and bitter.

Wyrm hated these creatures. How dare they flaunt what they had not earned. They did not deserve what they had.

He deserved it, and they would pay.

* * *

In the darkness, the ground scraped against Wyrm's legs and feet. Or maybe his legs and feet were scraping against the ground?

He was not sure what was happening; this felt more real and new than what he had been experiencing moments before. No old, yet foreign memories flooded his mind to explain his current situation. There was pressure around his wrists and sounds coming from somewhere, but he wasn't sure where. Maybe he was moving, or was something moving against him?

Eventually, the pressure stopped and the voices grew closer. With great effort, he struggled to open his eyes, to throw back the darkness surrounding him, but his mind and will were weak. Faint flickers appeared in front of him. A person? Maybe two people? Old?

The darkness won, and Wyrm was swallowed once more.

* * *

Wyrm was strong and eternally youthful again, but his heart was torn asunder. His arms held the lifeless body of one of his children. The child had been torn by some unknown creature's claws. He was only faintly aware of the sobs of the woman and other child from the boat that memory kept insisting were his.

* * *

Farther away, the male invader sat on a fallen tree in the forest. Wyrm watched him stare at the ground, nearly motionless. The pain and sorrow wafted off the creature, creating a pleasant aroma of suffering that made Wyrm smile in a way that reminded him of the second ghost in the cave.

Gently, Wyrm moved through the branches to stand next to the grieving father. He leaned in and whispered in his ear, "I can take away your pain."

The creature with pointed ears lifted his head slightly and continued to listen.

*   *   *

Wyrm, once again corporeal, stood in the home that memory whispered was his, though he knew he'd never seen it before. He didn't know why the woman with pointed ears was so angry with him. She kept spewing words in some language that he did not know but somehow understood.

Apparently, she was angry that he wasn't sad anymore. Why was it his problem if she allowed her grief to consume her? Was he supposed to just grieve forever? Should he always suffer?

Wyrm turned away from her to hide the irritation and disdain he was sure were becoming visible in his face.

How dare she demand that he suffer just because she could not handle her own emotions.

*   *   *

Psychological pleasure flowed through his mind as he invisibly watched the pointed eared creatures argue. It had been increasing in intensity for several days now, and Wyrm's incorporeal essence felt more vibrant as a result.

Finally, these intrusive beings with their disgusting lives were getting what they deserved. Part of him still felt the resentment toward what they unrightfully possessed, but he found that it was a quieter feeling now. It was more subdued, lying just below the surface. It was like the feeling was drowsy but not quite asleep.

The male and the female kept arguing, their rage and resentment feeding off one another in an ever-strengthening cycle. The male eventually turned away from the female. Several angrier exchanges were made, and the male walked away into the forest.

*   *   *

Wyrm's mind collided with sensations that felt new and more tangible than either the parental or incorporeal memories.

Pressure shifted along his back and sides without any discernable pattern. Sometimes he felt his body being hit by some hard surface, or maybe he was hitting the surface.

Wyrm threw his head to the side and struggled to remember how to open his eyes. Was he supposed to be able to just think about opening them? No, that didn't seem to work. How does one will something to happen?

A sudden panic that he might never be able to move under his own power erupted in his mind but was soon lost in the jostling and shifting darkness.

The jostling stopped, and after some indeterminate amount of time, there were voices. He wasn't sure what they were saying, but they were sometimes near, sometimes far.

He managed to crack open his eyes just enough to see vague figures, but soon the weight of the darkness was too much and his eyelids collapsed, taking his consciousness with them.

*   *   *

Wyrm's mind was once again in the perpetually youthful body, but immortality seemed a curse in his current state. The grief was unbearable. Everything inside of Wyrm hurt as if he had always been in pain. He could feel his face twisted in anguish as he opened his eyes and gazed down at the last of his children dead in his arms.

Screams and sobs came from a few feet away, and he looked up at his wife. The sight of her sorrow and the guilt of the knowledge of his previous resentment and rage toward her rent him even deeper. He didn't want her to suffer, either from loss or from his own cruelty.

New thoughts had begun to grow in his mind. What if she was next? He didn't think that he would have the will to live if she died too.

Perhaps he should take the spirit's offer? Maybe it could help him?

He set down the corpse and stood. His wife collapsed on top of it, and he turned and walked out the door. With shuffling footsteps, he made his way through the forest.

Wyrm opened his mouth to speak, but only a hoarse croak came out. He swallowed and cleared his throat.

"Come to me."

"Yes? How may I serve you?" came the reply from the shadows.

"Do you promise to take away this pain and give me the power to protect my wife?"

"I promise that grief will no longer consume you, and that no animal on this island will harm your wife."

He raised his head and furrowed his brow; "I accept."

* * *

Wyrm's incorporeal essence flowed into the body of the grieving father as soon as his acceptance had been uttered. The vigor he felt instantly was amazing. Never had he felt such life and energy. Wyrm looked down at his hands and flexed his fingers experimentally. It had been so long since he possessed a physical form, and this one was built to last.

The air moved across his skin. Scents flowed into his nostrils. The sounds of birds and insects hummed in his ears. He breathed deeply and enjoyed the sensations in his lungs.

This body possessed so much life. It felt endless and exhilarating. A smile uncontrollably spread across his face. Deep in his mind, the image of the second ghost's smile flitted past.

Wyrm began to run. He leaped over fallen logs and ducked under low branches. Swift, agile steps brought him high into the upper branches. His feet and legs folded beneath him, absorbing the impact as he hit the ground. Like a spring, he shot forward and laughed. It had been so long since he had been able to do this. Even the burning in his lungs from the cool night air and the feeling of exertion were enjoyable.

Eventually, his running returned to walking, which lead inevitably back to the sounds of weeping. He turned and entered the dwelling.

The weeping creature was wasting her boundless life. Old jealousies roused themselves within him. Why should she have such gifts when he had been without for so long?

The corners of his mouth began to pull back, and he felt a desire to sink his teeth into something, to consume and devour.

Wyrm rushed the grieving woman and grabbed her by the shoulders. A moment of shock in her expression registered to his mind but was immediately replaced by the sight of her throat. He tore her throat with his sharp teeth and tasted the sweet life flowing out. Greedily he drank, feeding a thirst he had not realized he possessed.

The flow faded and died, as did the woman in his arms. He let her drop to the floor as his head fell back. New life and power flowed through him, increasing the already boundless supply his host had provided. His desires now satiated, he basked in the pleasure of his feast.

*   *   *

Wyrm felt the spirit enter his body and immediately knew he had made a mistake. Bitter regret exploded within him. At least the spirit had been right about one thing: Grief was no longer consuming him.

No longer in control of his own limbs, Wyrm looked on as his body was used to kill his wife. He knew in that moment that it had not been an animal that had killed his children. It was this demon. This demonic spirit had been manipulating him this whole time.

Wyrm hated the demon, but he hated himself more for allowing himself to be misled. With rage, he attacked the parasite inside his mind and body.

*   *   *

The visions became less distinct as Wyrm's mind began to knit itself back together. The memories of the elf and the demon flowed together and gathered speed. The separation between them became less distinct.

He tried cutting and stabbing himself repeatedly but always awoke to the sadistic laughter in his head and healed wounds. When he tried to decapitate himself, his arms and hands would freeze from resistance, and he would fail.

Shame and self-loathing kept him subdued, as he walked again amid his own people. Bitterness and rage helped him overpower the fool any time he tried to communicate that he was not alone in this body.

Battles raged around him and he fought, sometimes joyously and sometimes bitterly. He never died, and he feasted frequently. Sometimes he found that he liked it more than he should. At other times, he was confused that he did not enjoy it more.

A pathetic creature, much weaker than his host, wandered into the cave one day carrying a dying torch. He was so tired of the struggle. Maybe this creature could end his nightmare. Maybe it could end his suffering but allow his revenge on this world to endure?

* * *

Wyrm awoke to the warm comfort of blankets. He appeared to be inside some sort of narrow yet long room. When he tried to move, everything hurt, and he fell back onto the cushions.

"Be careful. Don't rush anything," came a gentle voice from just out of view.

He sat up straight in surprise, winced, and looked around. A young woman roughly his own age sat off to one side near his feet. The surge of fear in his veins faded quickly, leaving him feeling sore and weak. His head swam from the sudden motion, and he fell back onto his elbows. Despite the pain, he could not let himself relax.

"Where am I?"

"You're in my grandparents' wagon."

"How did I get here?"

"My cousin found you in the woods while hunting. You were unconscious in the snow, covered in blood."

Wyrm's mind began to look backward through his memories, but a stabbing in his skull made him stop. There were very faint images but nothing distinct.

"Thank you," he said, looking around. "Who are you?"

"I'm Ashena," she said with a smile.

"Are you from another village or town? I don't recognize any of this," he gestured to the blankets and decorations inside the wagon.

"No. We're nomads. We travel around instead of living in one place."

"You live in wagons? You don't farm or hunt or build houses? How do you survive?"

The girl laughed; "We work as entertainers and artisans. We also have some livestock of our own."

He sat for a moment thinking about how his mother had wanted to travel the world and how happy she would have been to live among people who did exactly that.

"Now that you're awake, I'm going to go get my grandmother, so she can examine you."

"It's ok, I'll be fine."

Wyrm tossed the blankets aside and slowly crawled toward the door at the end of the wagon.

"That might not be such a good idea."

Wyrm pushed on the door, and it swung open.

Blindingly bright light exploded in his eyes. He stumbled back to the sounds of laughter. He squeezed his eyes shut and tried to open them a tiny bit at a time for his eyes to adjust. Eventually he could see properly, but he still felt uncomfortable. His eyeballs hurt just from the sunlight. He staggered out onto the ground and looked around.

Ashena hopped down next to him as he turned and stared at the many brightly colored wagons of the camp. People moved around the camp, engaging in tasks about which he knew nothing. The appearances of the people and their clothes, tools, and wagons were a mixture of the familiar and the foreign. The language they spoke was unknown to him, though sometimes he could recognize a word or phrase. He was filled with excitement and curiosity.

With uneven steps, he began to wander around the clearing where the wagons were gathered. He was not sure where in the forested mountains he was, but it did not really matter to him. These people were not the villagers who had so mistreated his mother. They were what she had always wanted to be: travelers.

It didn't take long for Wyrm to begin to feel exhausted. He wasn't sure why he was so tired. It had not been nearly so exhausting trekking through the forests when he left the village, and that had been a walk of several days. He stopped and leaned against a wagon wheel. The heat of the sun was painful on his skin, and he could feel himself sweating profusely.

"You should learn to do as you're told, child," came a harsh female voice.

"What?" Wyrm's head snapped up, and he glared at an old woman looking at him with a disapproving gaze. He would not be talked down to anymore.

"Ashena told you to stay in the wagon. I'm glad you're awake, but you're obviously not well enough to be wandering around out here."

Realizing who she must be, Wyrm tried to control his irritation. "It's just so hot and bright."

"You must really be sick," she commented dryly. "It's actually quite cool outside. Ashena, take him back to the wagon."

"Yes, Grandmother. Come along, let's get you back inside."

Wyrm hesitated. He didn't like being told what to do or treated as if he couldn't make decisions for himself.

"It's ok, Grandmother will have you better in no time. She's kept you alive this long, so we should trust her judgement."

He looked at Ashena. Her expression was kind and patient. It was very strange to him. He had so rarely seen anything like it growing up in the village. With a sigh and a nod, he pushed off the wagon wheel and followed her.

When they got back to the wagon, he crawled up on the platform below the door and sat down.

"At least let me sit here awhile. It feels like forever since I've had fresh air."

"Ok," she said pleasantly. She disappeared into the wagon and returned with balls of yarn and a partially completed blanket. It occurred to Wyrm that this must have been what she was working on while he was asleep.

"Would you mind telling me more about your people?" he asked, feeling strangely shy.

"Sure," she said brightly as she looked down and began knitting again.

*　　*　　*

Wyrm could not stay asleep and eventually gave up. He sat up quietly and looked around. Ashena and her grandparents were asleep in beds that folded down from the sides of the wagon on either wall. As quietly as he could, he crawled across the floor and snuck out the back door.

The cool air washed over him as he slowly closed the door. It felt amazing. It made him feel so alive and well. Wyrm wandered around the camp, enjoying the darkness and the new sights. There were close to twenty wagons, and they formed a rough circle inside the clearing. In the circle were the remnants of campfires and logs used as chairs and benches. The livestock were penned in by several of the wagons spaced closer together. A makeshift fence formed the other half of their enclosure.

Wyrm's meandering brought him into the woods and eventually to a stream. He knelt and scooped water with both hands and brought it to his lips. It tasted different than he remembered water tasting, as if it was somehow unappealing or dissatisfying now. He opened his hands and let the rest of the water fall away.

"Be careful wandering around in the dark. You never know what animals may be hunting at night, and most humans are not so trustworthy when it comes to activities outside their norm."

Wyrm's head snapped around, and he saw an elderly man standing off to one side watching him. Who was this person to tell him what to do?

"Who—"

"I'm Ashena's grandfather," the old man explained.

Earlier that day, Wyrm had fallen asleep to escape his sunlight-induced headache in the afternoon and had not met the old man when he returned to the wagon.

Standing up and turning, he replied, "Thank you to you and your wife for taking care of me. I really appreciate it."

The old man nodded in acknowledgement; "Do you remember what happened to you before we found you?"

Wyrm looked away, trying to remember.

"I vaguely remember a cave, and then I feel like I dreamed some weird things, but that's about it."

The old man nodded again.

"I'm going to back to sleep. Enjoy the night. Don't get yourself killed."

The old man turned and disappeared amid the trees. Wyrm wandered around for a while, but, with nothing particular to do, he returned to the wagon.

* * *

Wyrm trudged through the forest, dragging a small cart behind him filled with firewood as he headed back to the travelers' camp. Over the past few days, Ashena's grandparents had observed that he was more energetic at night and given him a list of chores to complete while everyone slept. At first, he was annoyed at being given orders, but after a while, he calmed down to the point where now he didn't really mind at all. They were overall quite kind to him, and the night was quite inviting. It felt like his senses were adjusting to the darkness, bringing to his attention what he was never able to sense before.

He unloaded the cart as quietly as he could into a pile just outside the ring of wagons.

"Are you hungry?" asked Ashena from behind him.

Wyrm turned to look at her; "Oddly enough, I'm not really hungry."

"Well, I haven't seen you eat since you woke up, and you definitely couldn't keep anything down while you were unconscious. If you don't eat, you'll get weak, or Grandmother and Grandfather will get suspicious of you."

He smiled; "Ok," he said and followed her to where she had setup a little table near a small fire.

"I checked the traps this morning and found this," she smiled as she held up a large rabbit.

Wyrm complimented her catch and watched as she butchered it. The smell hit him as soon as it was cut open. He had never been aware of this sort of scent in the past, and the sight of the raw flesh made his mouth water.

Ashena finished skinning and gutting the rabbit before impaling it on a stick and setting it over the fire. She then went about preparing some porridge.

"Oh, and I found these nuts last night. Here, try one."

She handed him some nuts, and he ate them quickly. The taste was confusingly unpleasant. He had eaten nuts before, and they had never evoked such a response in him. It wasn't so disgusting that he couldn't eat them, though, and he forced them down.

"You don't like nuts?"

Ashena was watching him intently.

"It's not that. I mean, thank you for the nuts, but they just taste different than I remember."

"So, you're saying I poisoned them?" She narrowed her eyes at him.

"No. That's not what I meant," he stammered.

Ashena let out a laugh and held her sides.

"Relax, I'm just teasing."

A little embarrassed, Wyrm laughed more cautiously.

Ashena turned back to her cooking. Wyrm felt compelled to stay but also felt awkward just standing, watching her work.

"I'm going to finish fetching the water," he stated.

"Ok. It will take a few minutes for the food to be ready anyway."

She smiled at him, and he returned the smile before retrieving the first of the water buckets and heading to the nearest stream. He enjoyed his interactions with Ashena, but he was never sure how to act. In the village, people either ordered him about, ignored him, or insulted him.

Wyrm pondered this as he made his many trips to fill all of the camp's buckets. When his task was complete, he returned to Ashena's side.

"Welcome back," she said pleasantly. "Here, try some of the porridge and some of the rabbit." She handed him a wide, shallow dish with a piece of meat on one side and a spoon sticking into the porridge.

Wyrm took a bite of the porridge and almost gagged. It was extremely unpleasant.

"Oh, so I'm that terrible at cooking, am I?" Ashena glared at him, her hands on her hips.

"No, it's just me. Here, I'll try some of the rabbit." He quickly took a bite of the meat. It was very tasty, more so than he had remembered meat being, but it still felt like it was lacking something. It felt like the meat was close to some craving he didn't know he possessed and could not identify. "Wow, that's good," he said and devoured the rest of it in a flash.

"Ha," she laughed, "so I'm only half a bad cook."

Wyrm started to respond, but she cut him off.

"Relax, you were really out of it for several days. Maybe this is just a side effect of whatever made you sick."

"Maybe," he said, then paused. "Do you think I could have more of the rabbit?"

She smiled and handed him more meat, which he snatched from her hands and devoured with more enthusiasm than he intended.

Ashena laughed pleasantly as she watched him eat.

*   *   *

The wagon rocked slightly as the horses pulled it down the road and through the forest during the early morning hours. Wyrm and Ashena sat on the platform on the back of the wagon with their feet hanging over the edge, watching the other wagons behind them. It had been several weeks since he had woken up, and they were moving camp.

"So where are we going exactly?"

"One of my cousins scouted a village nearby. We're going to stop there to resupply. We'll do a few performances and maybe make some money at the same time. Usually, we do some trading as well"; she shrugged, "or we could just get run out of town. You never know."

"Why would people do that?" he asked in irritation.

"It's hard to say, really. Grandfather says sometimes it's the over-exaggeration of an otherwise reasonable self-preservation instinct to mistrust outsiders. Grandmother says sometimes people just need someone to hate, so they don't hate themselves. Other times, they don't really say anything."

"If they attack you unprovoked, you should hurt them back," he said, turning to face her, anger beginning to contort his expression.

Ashena looked up at him, a mixture of concern and kindness on her face. He turned and stared at the receding ground so that he wasn't inadvertently glaring at her.

"If we attack them, then we are only proving their suspicions to be correct, and it will just bring more trouble on us. If we treat them with kindness and leave, then some might see that they were wrong, and there will be less trouble when the next group of travelers arrives."

"I don't think people are that forgiving."

"Some are and some aren't. It's not fair to treat everyone as being irredeemable based on the actions of a few. If we only hate and never forgive or show kindness, then we will only end up destroying each other."

"Maybe they deserve it," he said in a low tone.

Ashena gently touched his arm. His head snapped up to look at her. The contact made him suspicious, but seeing it was her and her smile made his anger dissipate.

*   *   *

"I don't know about this," Wyrm muttered as they setup outside the village where he had grown up. It had not occurred to him that they would wind up here until he saw the buildings as they came into sight.

The wagons had stopped in a clearing just north of the village. The road they had ridden down ran north and south. The clearing was on the west side of the road and was bounded on the north by trees, the west by fields, and the south by the village itself. The wagons were positioned with the back ends of the wagons facing the clearing so that anyone could easily and quickly leave and get back on the road.

"What's wrong?" asked Ashena.

"I grew up here, and these are not kind people."

"Well, they didn't run off Grandfather when he spoke with them yesterday, so maybe it won't be so bad."

Wyrm grunted and helped the others set up tents. When the time came for the performances to start, he made a point of staying near the wagons and out of sight. He didn't want to interact with the villagers or deal with their mutual hatred. The sounds of singing and music drifted from the tents, and curiosity overcame his misgivings.

He walked over to the back side of the tents and watched quietly through the small gaps in the sheets of fabric that formed the walls. The captivating performances ran until the sun had set, and he stayed until they were all finished. The sounds of the exiting villagers brought him to his senses, and he hurried to disappear into the shadows so as to avoid them.

Mistrust of the villagers prompted him to stand near the trees and watch the milling crowds as they left slowly. Travelers exited the tents and moved toward the wagons. Wyrm scanned the crowds for Ashena. He saw her exit a tent with a couple of her friends and watched as they started to head into the village. He wasn't sure why they would be doing that, so he decided to follow them.

The road ran south, entered the village, and was intersected by another road running east to west. The travelers and villagers headed to the west when they reached the intersection. He watched Ashena and her friends approach the tavern where he had grown up. A sense of anger and betrayal shot through him, and he raised the hood of his cloak as he approached. No one paid him any attention, and he was able to slip inside and take a seat in a corner. He watched as villagers and travelers milled about, talking, eating, and drinking. After several minutes, he realized that nothing sinister was happening, and he began to feel foolish and embarrassed. When a server approached the table, he kept his head down, grunted, and left.

Wyrm walked away from the tavern as quickly as he could, eager to return to camp and pretend that none of this had happened. In his eagerness to leave, he turned sharply down an alley between two buildings and ran face first into someone.

Taking a step back, Wyrm looked up and started to apologize.

"Oh, if it isn't the whore's son," said the son of a local farmer that Wyrm had seen many times at the tavern. "Are you here to gawk at the travelers? Or maybe you came to beg for your old room again?" he asked with a laugh.

Wyrm glared at the boy who was a few inches taller than him. "Shut your mouth and get out of my way," he growled.

The farmer sobered up for a brief moment and looked Wyrm dead in the eyes. "Make me, whore's son. Or are you too tired from servicing the travelers?"

Wyrm roared and lunged at the young man. The smile disappeared from the farmer's face immediately, and they exchanged blows. A meaty fist impacted Wyrm's face, and he fell over. As he looked up at the arrogant villager, his mind swam with thoughts of violence. He imagined breaking bones and tearing flesh. The thought of agonized screams filled him with a new desire. His eyes focused on the throat of his opponent.

With sudden speed, Wyrm launched himself off the ground and grappled the farmer, pushing him farther into the dark alley. The young man tripped, and Wyrm fell on top of him. The farmer punched him in the face and pushed him off to one side. Wyrm felt his back collide with a rock, and pain shot through him. He twisted on the ground and grabbed the rock before standing and turning back to the farmer.

These villagers had mistreated his mother, abused him his whole life, and now they were trying to kill him in some dark alley. He didn't deserve to die. They did. They could all die for all he cared.

Wyrm lunged at the farmer who was beginning to stand and slammed the rock into the side of his opponent's head. The young man fell over, blood pouring from the wound.

Wyrm looked down in victory. One villager was defeated, but it wasn't enough. He wouldn't be satisfied until they were all dead at his feet. The farmer's head moved, and Wyrm's gaze shifted to the blood pooling around it. Suddenly he realized he could smell the blood. It was amazing, unlike any scent he had yet encountered. He licked his teeth, imaging how good it must taste if it smelled this pleasant.

He dropped to his knees and licked up some of the blood. It was even better than he had imagined. Eagerly, he began to lap up the rest until he started to taste dirt. Spitting out the dirt, he looked over at the bulging veins in the farmer's neck. Wyrm opened his mouth and clamped his teeth into his tormentor's throat. For a brief instant he wondered what he was doing, but then he felt his teeth sink and tear into the flesh. Warm, sweet blood flowed into his mouth, and he drank deeply. It was as if he had been dying of thirst and never realized it until this moment. The world disappeared as he drank until there was nothing left.

Wyrm's head swam with the pleasure of the kill, and he staggered to his feet. The night air was cool, and he could feel every slight twist and turn in the breeze. Scents from the nearby buildings blossomed images of people, livestock, and pets in his mind, but not as vague groups. He was distinctly able to sense each individual creature. He could hear human footsteps, whispered words, and scurrying claws. Wyrm stopped and looked around. Every detail of the alley was visible to him now. He had to look up at the stars in the night sky to make sure that he had not somehow slept until the sun had risen.

The newness of his senses overwhelmed him, and he meandered through the alley, across fields and into the woods, fascinated by everything around him.

*   *   *

Birds chirped in the air around him, and Wyrm slowly drifted back to consciousness. He was lying curled up in a bush somewhere in the forest. Confused, he looked around, but no one was nearby.

Why had he woken up in a bush? Why didn't he go back to camp last night?

Images from the night before surged through his mind. He remembered the fight, the kill, and the blood.

Wyrm turned over and tried to vomit, but nothing came up. The muscles in his torso contracted and convulsed, futilely attempting to remove whatever he had consumed the night before.

In the morning light with his body trying to wretch, he was no longer angry. There was neither pleasure nor joy. There was only horror and regret.

Why had he killed the farmer? Even worse, why did he drink the farmer's blood? How could he have enjoyed it so much? What was wrong with him? All this just because of a few insults? He had ended a life in horrific fashion, just because of some angry words?

Wyrm sat up and choked back tears as he thought about returning to the camp. If Ashena found out, she would hate him. How could she tolerate such a perverse murderer?

His mind shifted to Ashena's grandmother and grandfather. If anyone found out what he had done, they might trace it back to camp and take it out on the travelers. They had been so kind and helped him so much, and yet now he risked bringing down the wrath of the village on them.

Wyrm looked down at his blood-soaked hands and clothes. He wiped at his mouth and felt the dried blood there. Quickly, he looked around to make sure no one was there to see him. He sighed with relief when he didn't see anyone.

Staggering slightly, Wyrm rose to his feet and moved deeper into the woods. He knew there was a small stream nearby. If he could get there undetected, he might be able to clean up.

Wyrm started to walk toward the stream and found himself running almost immediately. The speed of movement was exhilarating, and he didn't feel any sense of exertion or fatigue. In a few moments, he reached the stream. With more speed than he realized he was capable of, he stripped and dove into the water. He scrubbed and washed himself until he was clean. Then, he waded back to shore and began the same process for his clothes. Only once everything was clean and stretched out on a large rock in direct sunlight did he relax.

The sun was warm, bright, and quite irritating now that he wasn't so distracted by the fear of being caught covered in blood. It occurred to him that it didn't feel as painful to his skin and eyes as it usually did, though it annoyed him mentally more than normal.

Time passed and his clothes soon were dry enough to wear again without looking suspicious. He wasn't sure what he would tell everyone at the camp and tried to push the worry away, out of his awareness.

Wyrm trekked back to camp. When he arrived, he moved as quickly as he could to avoid anyone and get back to the wagon without being noticed.

"Where have you been? Rather late in the day for you to be up walking around."

Wyrm stiffened and turned slowly to face Ashena's grandfather.

"I, uh, celebrated a little too hard last night," he lowered his gaze. "It was not a pleasant sight, so I spent the morning cleaning myself up after I woke up."

"Hmm"; the grandfather narrowed his eyes at Wyrm. "Learn restraint or you'll spend every morning cleaning yourself up." The old man gestured to the camp; "Do it now or do it later, just make sure your chores are done before tomorrow morning." The old man walked away without further comment.

Wyrm sighed in relief and climbed back into the wagon. Despite how he had felt earlier, the sunlight was starting to get to him, and he felt drained. The headache was coming back as well. Wyrm curled up and fell asleep.

*   *   *

Wyrm stretched like a cat in the darkness and snuck out of the wagon. The night was almost as clear to him as day, even though it was the new moon, and the sky was heavily clouded.

His steps were faster and required less effort that he remembered as he moved through the camp to retrieve the cart for the firewood. Even the cart felt unusually light as he began to move it. He gripped it tightly and lifted it over his head. To his surprise, he could barely feel the cart's weight.

The night's chores proceeded much faster than usual. When he swung the axe, the wood split clean through regardless of whether he was chopping through a trunk or dividing a section into smaller pieces. The weight of the full water buckets was negligible, and he carried them back with ease.

His chores done early, Wyrm was left to sit alone in the dark on the end of the wagon with his thoughts, which inevitably returned to the previous night's events. As soon as he thought about the farmer, guilt and anxiety rushed into him. He was worried that someone would find out but also too scared to ask. If he asked questions and something had happened, then others might suspect he had something to do with it. When the idea of checking to see if the body had been discovered flitted across his mind, he rejected it instantly. If he was caught near the scene of the murder, it might draw suspicion. No matter what, he did not want to get caught.

"Good morning. Done already?"

Wyrm jumped slightly and turned to see Ashena slipping out of the wagon. He had been so absorbed in his thoughts that he had not even noticed the door opening.

"Yeah," he muttered and shifted his gaze. He could not bring himself to look at her.

Ashena paused and looked at Wyrm for a while, then hopped down next to the wagon.

"Then come for a walk with me," she offered.

Wyrm nodded and hopped down next to her. He kept his gaze on the ground as they meandered through the camp and out near the tree line.

"Are you feeling better?"

"Yes."

"Grandfather said you were out celebrating last night. Is that true?"

Wyrm hesitated, "I had to clean myself up yesterday morning."

Ashena remained silent as they continued to walk.

"I know what happened."

Wyrm's steps faltered, and he stammered, "What?"

"I thought I saw you in the tavern and then leave from there, so I followed you. You turned down an alley, but when I got there, I saw the dead man. I know you said they were abusive to you in the village, so I'm sure it was self-defense."

"I—I'm sorry," Wyrm choked. "I'm not really sure why I did it. I'm sorry I brought trouble on the travelers. I can leave so that they don't come after you."

Ashena turned to him. "That's not what I said."

Wyrm looked at her somewhat confused.

"I took care of it. No one will find the body. No one will track it back to us. I just want you to know that you're not alone."

Wyrm didn't know what to say. He just stared at her. How had she hidden the body? Why would she even do that?

He opened his mouth; "Why?"

"I know you, and I don't want anything to happen to you. I want you to stay with us, to stay with me. You will, won't you?"

Wyrm nodded dumbly. This whole experience made no sense to him.

Ashena hugged him tight. He returned the embrace, still slightly confused.

* * *

Two days had passed, and Wyrm's vigor when performing his nightly chores had decreased drastically. He wasn't sure if he was weaker than before the events in the alley or if the sudden drain, compared to how he felt two days ago, made the difference more noticeable. Exhausted, he plopped down on the ground next to the wagon and leaned against one of the wheels.

"Are you ok?" asked Ashena a few minutes later.

"Yes, I'm just tired tonight."

"Too tired to help me cook before Grandfather and Grandmother get up?"

"Never," he smiled and joined her as she set up her little table next to a small fire.

They went about their usual tasks, but when she retrieved a rabbit, he noticed that it didn't smell quite as good as it had before. When it was done, he tasted a small piece. It tasted good but was somehow disappointing and unsatisfying.

A small noise from Ashena's direction caught his attention, but as he turned a familiar scent greeted his nostrils. It was blood.

Ashena was wrapping a piece of cloth around a small cut on her hand.

"What happened? Are you ok?"

"Oh, it's nothing. I reached for the knife without looking and accidentally cut myself."

Wyrm was suddenly aware of the sound of Ashena's heartbeat. He licked his teeth, imagining sinking them into her flesh. His eyes focused on her neck. Her back was turned. She would not see it coming. He could grab her with one hand, cover her mouth with the other so no one would hear her scream, and sink his teeth into her soft throat. The blood would flow.

Wyrm took a step forward and froze. He shook his head and turned. As fast as he could, he ran. Guilt and fear gave him speed and stamina until the sun began to rise. As the light found its way through the trees to his skin, he felt sick.

Wyrm hid in the woods all that day and well into the night. He did not want to hurt Ashena, but he was now certain why he was feeling weaker and what he needed to do to feel strong and invincible again. More than just an intellectual awareness was the growing thirst he had not realized he possessed. Now that he had smelled blood, it was as if a new desire had been aroused within him. It consumed his thoughts and fought with his feelings for Ashena.

The next night Wyrm wandered back. The thirst was driving him crazy. His insistence on denying it had only made it louder. Every sound, every smell made him think about consuming blood again.

Before he realized it, he was at the tree line. The villagers were leaving the performance tents again. Someone strayed over to the fields. Wyrm followed.

He didn't recognize the man, but he did recognize the unpleasant scent of urine as he approached. He glanced in the direction of the tents and dwindling crowds. No one was nearby. The night was dark, and the crops were tall. No one could see them.

Wyrm rushed his prey. His right arm circled around the man's upper arms and torso, pinning them in place. His left hand wrapped around the man's mouth, stifling a scream as he wrenched the head back. Wyrm's teeth almost ached in desire and were quickly satiated as they sank into the neck.

Sweet, warm blood flowed into his mouth. Greedily, he consumed everything. The man went limp in his arms, but Wyrm didn't stop until there was nothing left. With a satisfied sigh, he let the corpse drop to the ground.

The night was alive again. He could sense everything around him in exquisite detail. His fingers curled and uncurled. His muscles flexed and relaxed. Every part of him felt strong and so incredibly alive. Gone was the thirst. His mind was clear and satiated, basking in the new life flowing through him.

Looking down, he pondered the corpse. It would not do for the villagers to find it. Casually, he bent down and grabbed it by the ankle. Wyrm dragged the body easily into the forest. Eventually he found a large rock and shoved it aside. He dumped the body where the rock had been and moved it back over the corpse to hide it.

Wyrm cleaned himself and his clothes in a stream, then sat next to a small fire he had built to dry his clothes and pondered the world around him. At first, he was surprised to realize that he didn't really feel any guilt about the kill. It had satisfied his desires, and no one was likely to know.

The second thought that came to him was that only a monster would feel nothing when taking a human life. A new kind of guilt dampened his mood as he realized that he should feel bad for killing a defenseless person, but yet he did not. What was wrong with him? How could Ashena love him now?

Wyrm curled up and waited for his clothes to dry.

*   *   *

Wyrm stood in the darkness outside the tavern and listened to the conversations inside. He was waiting, not sure if or who to strike. The thirst needed to be quenched again.

"How are your chickens doing? Have you been able to keep the predators out?"

"Did you see the travelers' performance tonight? It was amazing."

"I started teaching my son the craft, and he's a natural!"

"I can't wait until those filthy travelers are gone."

"Are you ok? You don't look well."

"I haven't seen my son in a few days, but I keep having these horrible nightmares."

"What do you mean?"

"It's like there's something wrong with him. I barely sleep. I feel like he's draining my life."

Wyrm turned slightly to stare at the wall.

"My sister says she's been having strange nightmares about her husband, and she's wasting away."

"Where's your sister's husband?"

"Don't know. He's been missing for a couple nights now."

"Where was he last seen?"

"She said he told her he was going to go to the tavern."

"I saw him at the travelers' tents a couple nights ago."

"What if those filthy nomads did something to his son and your sister's husband?"

"What if they ran off with some traveler?"

"Maybe they're all sick, and hallucinations are the first sign?"

A few chairs shifted quickly in the tavern.

"Meh, my son is not so foolish. Something bad has happened; I can feel it in my bones. I'm going to stay up to see if he comes home. If he doesn't, I'll go looking in the morning."

A chair scraped across the floor, and someone exited the tavern.

Wyrm watched an older man exit the tavern and head down the street. He recognized the man as the father of his first victim.

What if Ashena had failed to properly dispose of the body? What if the farmer hadn't died? What if she had lied?

A new sense of worry crept into Wyrm, and he began to follow the old man. The old man headed east along the road, then turned north at the main intersection. A small side rode veered off to the east, and the old man followed it. Eventually, they reached a set of fields with a house set back from the road. Wyrm followed the man and watched him enter the house.

Quietly, he moved closer and peered in through the cracks near the doors and windows. The old man was the only person in the house.

Maybe the old man was just crazy?

But what if he wasn't?

Wyrm found a place to sit high in a tree where he could lean his back against the trunk and watch.

Hours went by, and Wyrm was getting restless. Maybe he should just drink the man and be done with it.

A sound of something moving through the crops caught his attention. It had been a couple nights since he last fed, and his senses were somewhat diminished, but he could still see a dark figure approaching. Wyrm held perfectly still, instinctively focusing on his prey and inhibiting any actions that might give away his presence.

The figure approached the house. When it reached the shafts of light slipping out of the cracks, it was clear. The figure was the farmer's son, his first blood meal. Wyrm was confused. How could he still be alive? He knew that he had drained the young man until his heart had stopped. But here he was, moving.

If he was somehow still alive, would he come after Wyrm, try to turn Wyrm in, or even go after Ashena?

Wyrm watched in anxious fascination as the supposedly dead farmer snuck in through the window.

"Son?"

The figure moved closer.

"What's wrong? Speak to me!"

The figure grasped the old farmer and lunged. In shock, Wyrm realized that his supposed victim was actually feeding on the old man. It was just like he himself had done.

Wyrm dropped out of the tree and approached to get a better look. As he neared the window, the figure turned.

The young man's eyes were animalistic and became enraged as they looked at Wyrm. His teeth were sharper than normal, and the wound in his neck had healed. Blood covered his face.

The creature growled at Wyrm and leaped through the window at him. Surprised, Wyrm struggled with the creature and fell over. It kept snapping its jaws at him, trying to bite his neck. With great effort, he shoved the creature off him and regained his footing.

Irritation at the aggression of this creature replaced his concerns about it being able to reveal his misdeeds. When the creature lunged again, Wyrm's instincts kicked in. He shifted to his right as the creature moved past him and snatched the figure by the hair with his right hand. Twisting back toward his right, he pulled the creature back. The throat now open and exposed, Wyrm lunged and sank his teeth into the creature.

The blood was tasty, but weak, as if it lacked something that his previous victims had held in abundance. Wyrm kept drinking as the creature struggled. He could not sense the heartbeat weakening as before.

A yell followed by several stabbing pains made him realize that the old man was not dead. Wyrm dropped the son and rounded on the father. A pitchfork protruded from his side, and he angrily tore it free. Before he could attack the old man, the creature was on him again. Wyrm managed to grasp the creature's throat with his left hand. Angrily, he shoved his right fist down its throat. The creature's teeth cut deep grooves in his flesh, but Wyrm didn't care. This thing would die no matter how much pain it cost him. His fingertips exploded into the chest cavity and wrapped around a fist-sized, pulsating organ. Wyrm's fingers curled around the object, and he pulled back with all his might. The teeth shredded his forearm and hand even more, but his fist burst free, holding the creature's heart. The creature dropped to the ground, lifeless.

Wyrm tore at the heart with his teeth, thirst and anger mixing together as he rent the organ into tiny pieces. When it was drained and done, he tossed it aside.

A sorrowful cry reminded him that the old man was still alive. Wyrm turned and stalked toward his new prey.

"Why? Why did you kill my son?!"

Wyrm fell on the old man and began to drink. With his dying strength, the old man pulled free a knife and started stabbing Wyrm. He ignored the pain and fed that much harder, even as he felt the blade pierce his chest and internal organs in several places.

Eventually, the old man's flow of blood weakened, and he dropped to the ground. Wyrm felt the surge of life as before, but it was tempered by the pain of his new wounds.

Holding himself in a vain attempt to keep his blood from leaking out, Wyrm staggered north into the forest. His breathing was ragged, and his strength was slowly draining out of him.

The pain and blood loss became too much, and Wyrm collapsed as his conscious mind disappeared.

* * *

Everything was on fire. The pain was so great that Wyrm was only faintly surprised that he was still alive. Instinct held his eyes shut.

He had to get out of this blazing torment. Frantically, he clawed at the ground. His fingers dug into the earth, tearing it into ever smaller pieces. Each time his hands disappeared into the dirt, there was a small decrease in the pain, as they were shielded from the horrid light that both illuminated the world and blinded him.

Soon he could feel a hole in front of him, and he dove into it. The hole wasn't deep enough to shade him, so he lay on his back, scraping at the sides. Eventually, enough dirt fell down on top of him that he was free from the bright pain.

With relief, Wyrm's mind let go and fell back into darkness.

* * *

The darkness scratched against his eyes as he tried to open them. Wyrm had never felt weight to darkness before.

As he struggled to move, he realized that he was covered in dirt. The events of the previous morning flooded into his mind.

The layer of dirt had only been thick enough to block out the sun, and he was soon free of the earth.

He wasn't quite sure how, but he felt different. His mind replayed the most recent events in an attempt to understand what might have changed.

The strange monster version of his first victim had been a surprise. He wasn't sure how that had even occurred. Then he had fed on the old man, but the old man had stabbed him several times in the chest.

A sudden concern made Wyrm grope his own body, feeling for wounds. His clothes were soaked with dry blood, but he could detect no holes in him. For the first time, he was glad he'd eaten that heart in the cave.

Wyrm absentmindedly began to stroll back toward the village and the travelers' camp, pondering the old man and the monster. For a brief moment, it occurred to him that he didn't feel bad about killing either one. He didn't even feel guilty for not feeling guilty. Somehow, it didn't seem to matter to him anymore.

Wyrm reached the edge of the village and paused. He was thirsty, and no one in this village had ever really helped him. A smile crept across his face.

He would just start with the first house and drink as much as he could.

Wyrm entered the first house on his left. Inside there was a man, a woman, and two children. The children were quiet and provided neither fight nor enough blood to satisfy him. He stood at the foot of the bed, watching the adults sleep.

Patiently, he walked around to the husband's side of the bed. He looked from the man to the woman and back again. With speed that surprised him, he attacked the man and began to drink. The husband flailed around and tried to push Wyrm away but was unsuccessful. This aroused the wife, and she turned and screamed. Wyrm released the man and grabbed the wife before she could get away. He dragged her back over to the bed and fed on her until her pulse grew weak. He then dropped her next to her dying husband.

Wiping his mouth with a sleeve, he walked out of the house and looked around. He felt fuller than he had in a while, but he could drink some more. The next house wasn't far.

Wyrm crossed the street and entered the next house. An old man was hobbling his way over to the window, presumably to see what caused the scream earlier. When he saw Wyrm, the old man gave a shout and backed up but was not fast enough to evade capture. The man gave everything he had to Wyrm's thirst.

Finally feeling as if he may have eaten too much, Wyrm collapsed in a chair near the window. He leaned against the windowsill and noticed that his chest was not rising and falling. He shrugged to himself and stared out the window in a daze.

Sometime later, his half-closed eyes caught movement, and he watched as the two children from across the street scurried out of the windows of their house. They each went different directions, and Wyrm watched in fascination as they entered homes nearby.

*   *   *

The sun set, and darkness rose to replace it. Instinctively, Wyrm drifted back to consciousness with the setting sun. As the light faded from the land, he grew more energetic and awake. Above him were the floorboards of a home he had invaded the previous night. They had been easy to pry up, and he had made his bed in the small space between the floor and the dirt.

With ease, Wyrm pushed the boards up and pulled himself into the house. The corpses were long since gone. They had reanimated a few hours after death and wandered off, just like all the others these past few nights. Wyrm neither knew nor cared where they had gone. It was a new night, and he would soon be feasting on new prey. He washed himself with the buckets of water that had been gathered the day before.

The village seemed unusually quiet. The sun had only been set for a brief time. There should still be people wandering to and from the tavern, but there was no one. Even most of the houses seemed quiet. A faint glow to the north caught his attention.

Curious, Wyrm followed the light until he reached the field where the travelers had set up camp. The wagons were on fire.

Ashena's face flashed before his mind, and he ran to the gathered crowd that stood near the burning remains. As soon as he approached them, he realized that the crowd was made up of the villagers, not the travelers. Angry shouts rippled through the crowd.

"My wife is dying!"
"My children are dead!"
"This sickness didn't start until you arrived!"
"What have you done to us?"

Wyrm pulled his hood up over his head as he pushed his way through the crowd, hoping very strongly that no one would recognize him. There were too many of them, and he did not want to be stabbed again. He wasn't sure how much he could take and still survive.

When he reached the front rows of the crowd, he saw what they were yelling at.

The travelers were bound and on their knees. Several villagers held axes, pitchforks, knives, and clubs. They had surrounded the travelers.

The miller's son, Casimir, stepped out in front of everyone. He turned to address the masses.

"People! Please, listen! We all know that the disappearances and sickness started a few days after this trash arrived in our village. Before that, we were healthy and strong. But this is no normal disease. This is a cruel illness that strikes the survivors with horrible nightmares of twisted visions of the dead. Such cruelty must be an intentional act of sorcery."

The tavern keeper's daughter, Ani, stepped next to him and gestured to the travelers; "We welcomed them, and they repaid our kindness with evil. Whatever dark magic they have used to curse us can only be destroyed by fire! Prepare the stakes!"

Several villagers stepped out carrying wooden poles that had been sharpened on one end. They proceeded to dig holes, then they drove the stakes into the ground with hammers. Other villagers carried firewood and dumped it at the base of the poles. Casimir walked over to the burning wagons and lit a branch from the blaze.

A calm yet stern voice rang out from the travelers. It was Ashena's grandfather. He stood and turned toward Casimir and Ani.

"We did not bring any diseases upon your people. Neither have we cursed anyone. Even some of our own have fallen ill this morning."

"See their wickedness? They are even willing to sacrifice their own to harm us."

"At least let the young women and children go," intoned Ashena's grandmother, standing to join her husband.

A sense of dread came over Wyrm. These were the people who had helped nurse him back to health, yet they were about to die because of what he had become. He took a hesitating step forward, then stopped.

A sudden fear gripped him. Thoughts of being overwhelmed by the mob and dragged into the fire filled his mind. The sunlight alone had been an unbearable pain beyond anything he had yet experienced. How much more excruciating would the flames themselves be?

"You heard their pleas, yet it is our families who lie dead and dying. What is your judgement?" shouted Casimir.

"Burn them," yelled the mob.

The travelers were dragged to their feet and tied to the stakes. Several were tied to each stake, and Wyrm looked, trying to discover the fate of Ashena.

He found her as she was being tied to a pole. Her eyes locked on his and she cried out.

"Please! Tell them it wasn't us. We would never do anything to hurt them!"

Wyrm started to open his mouth but froze.

The torches were being lowered.

He needed to do something.

Cold thoughts began to seep into the edges of his mind. He must survive. It was a primal instinct that could not be ignored. Even if he managed to rescue Ashena and escape the entire village attacking him at once, she would eventually come to resent him. If it was not for the loss of her family, it would be for his newfound nature and thirst. She would reject him, and he would be alone once more. In the end, her survival would not matter.

The flames leaped up around the travelers, and they began to scream. Tears streamed down Ashena's face, and she mouthed something that Wyrm refused to translate into words.

It was too late. There was nothing to be done. His mind focused on the cold, determined to pretend there was nothing else.

He stood and watched.

Eventually the screams stopped. The crowds dispersed and everyone wandered back to the village.

He waited until the flames died down. Wyrm approached the charred, burnt corpses. He reached out and gently stroked Ashena's face, but it fell away, breaking into hideous pieces.

The ice inside him cracked. Numb and refusing to think, Wyrm staggered back toward the village and kept walking until he had passed it entirely.

He wasn't sure what to do or why anything mattered.

If he had acted sooner, maybe she would be alive. A terrible pain tore through his heart and mind.

But if he had moved, then he could have been killed by the mob. A coldness passed through him, quenching the pain slightly.

Wyrm collapsed to his knees and screamed, clawing at his head in a frustration that he didn't know how to end.

The events replayed over and over in his head: Ashena being dragged to the stake. Casimir lighting the pyre.

Casimir was to blame. He had turned the villagers against the travelers in much the same way his wife had turned them against Wyrm. That whole family was to blame... the daughter, the husband, and the father. None of them had cared about his mother. They had all mistreated him. And now they had destroyed the only people who had ever shown him kindness. They were to blame for Ashena's death.

And the villagers had been complicit in all of it.

Anger and hatred replaced his grief and guilt. He felt only purpose and focus. There was no need to think about the situation any longer, no need to dwell on what had happened. All that mattered now was his revenge.

The village would die, and the tavern keeper's family would die too.

*   *   *

The next several nights passed in a haze as he made his way around the perimeter of the village. Doors opened before him. His teeth sank into sleeping, screaming, and fleeing throats. Blood filled his belly, but the euphoria of new life was not as potent as it once was.

Wyrm walked from empty house to empty house before reaching the tavern. Inside, he could hear the hushed voices, shuffling feet, and stifled whimpers. Parents tried to coax their children to sleep. Adults whispered in fear. Eyes peered out of the cracks in the now boarded-up windows.

Now they knew it wasn't a plague.

As the night progressed, the villagers that he had recently killed began to meander toward the tavern. By midnight, the building was surrounded by the gaunt, pale forms of men, women, and children, all eager for the lifeblood hiding within.

A smile crept across Wyrm's face. He was pleased at the progress of his revenge. Most of the village was now undead. Tonight he would have satisfaction.

Wyrm made his way to a back window of the tavern. He tore his way in and climbed inside.

The sound of the crashing boards brought two of the villagers rushing into the room. Wyrm was on them in a flash, tearing open the first man's throat with his teeth and ripping the other's with his claws. He dropped them both without draining either one. He needed to stay empty and alert for what came next.

As he walked into the front main room of the tavern, all eyes turned to look. Gasps of recognition and horror rippled across the survivors as they recognized who he was and the blood dripping from his mouth and fingers.

"What are you doing here?" demanded Casimir stepping forward, conspicuously keeping himself between Wyrm and Ani.

The sound of Casimir's voice reawakened Wyrm's hatred. He rushed the miller's son, grabbed him by the throat and lifted him off the ground, his claws digging into the man's flesh.

Ani screamed and backed away. Two men ran to stop him. Wyrm threw Casimir into a wall and turned on them. Swiftly, he ripped out their throats with his teeth and dropped their bleeding forms on the ground.

Screams erupted throughout the room.

"Why?" pleaded Ani as she tried to help her husband stand.

Wyrm turned to glare at them; "I will make you pay, but first you will see everyone around you die."

He turned, dashed to the front, barricaded entrance to the tavern, and tore away the horizontal beam used to lock it shut. Within moments, the undead outside began to drift in.

Screams and gasps erupted at the sight. Those few remaining turned to flee farther back into the tavern, only to find their way blocked by the undead who had followed Wyrm in through the window.

"No," gasped a villager.

"Please," begged a woman.

"Father," cried a child.

"My daughter," whimpered a man.

Wyrm walked calmly back to Casimir and Ani as the undead villagers fell on their living counterparts. He grabbed the objects of his hatred and held them by the back of the neck, one in each hand, and forced them to watch as the last of the villagers were devoured.

"Let us go," raged Casimir in vain while Ani merely wept.

The last of the undead villagers from outside entered the tavern and looked in their direction.

"You will die now," Wyrm whispered in Ani's ear before tossing her forward.

Ani tried to scramble back, but the undead villagers lunged and attacked her.

Casimir roared and tried to break free; "Don't touch her!"

Wyrm twisted the man's arm behind his back and pulled his head close.

"Watch her die as I had to watch Ashena die," he growled in the man's ear.

Ani's screams faded and her body went limp.

"I'll kill you," roared Casimir.

The man's defiance and anger fed into Wyrm's own hatred and rage. He gripped the man's head and crushed his skull.

Wyrm tossed the corpse at the eager undead who quickly began to feed.

He walked to the door of the tavern, closed it, and replaced the horizontal beam. He knocked over several candles by the door so that the fire began to spread to the surrounding wood. Wyrm walked to the back rooms, grabbing another candle as he went. When he left the main room, he tossed the candle on the ground, igniting the hallway.

* * *

Standing back, he watched the tavern burn. Smoke rose into the night sky, and ash began to drift down around him. He had killed everyone who had ever wronged him, but now that they were dead, there was nothing for him to focus on. With no focal point for his rage and hatred, his mind kept replaying the deaths of the travelers, and a nagging voice kept whispering that it was his fault. He should have stopped it. He should have rescued Ashena.

His mind rushed backward through the series of events, his hatred now aimed at himself as the pain of watching Ashena die tore through him. The travelers were killed because of a supposed plague, which was the result of him feeding on the villagers and unknowingly creating the undead. If the travelers hadn't had compassion on him in the woods, then they never would have suffered because of him. If he hadn't entered that cave and eaten that heart, then he never would have had such a thirst or become a monster.

And if the villagers had not mistreated him, he wouldn't have left. If they hadn't mistreated his mother, then he wouldn't have been left alone to their torments.

The events cycled through his mind relentlessly, shifting his rage between himself and the village. He tried to focus on the village, but some horrid part of him kept pointing out his own willful inaction at the pivotal moment of Ashena's death.

If he had just stepped forward and stopped them, Ashena would still be alive.

Tears poured down his face, his throat constricted, and his mouth twisted in grief.

Everyone was dead, but it didn't matter.

Wyrm watched the tavern burn, unaware and uncaring if any escaped. Snow began to mix with the ash. By the time the flames began to die, he didn't have the energy to grieve.

Numb, he turned and wandered out of the village and into the wilderness. Any time his mind began to stir, it brought back memories of Ashena and the travelers' deaths. The pain was too much. Nothing could replace it.

Wyrm turned away from his rational mind. There was only sensation and instinct as he wandered deeper into the forest through the falling snow.

VIII

Desert Flames
Niwltir, +103 ER

The mist wall towered over the endless desert, stretching from the shifting sands to the cloudless night sky. No matter how high the two owls flew, they never saw the upper edge of the mist wall. If the space above was infinite, so too must be the heights of the wall itself.

The lead owl was slightly larger, with streaks of white in its dark feathers around its head. Their bodies were shades of brown on top and a pale grey underneath. Their eyes were a red-orange color, the edge of the irises rimmed with flame like swirls of a misty grey hue.

The two owls were mostly able to glide on the currents as they continued along next to the mist wall. Their journey had started several years prior, as an expedition to explore and examine the boundaries of the otherwise endless desert. During the day, they would rest, and during the night, they would fly, scanning the ground by the light of the moon and stars. Through this time, they had only discovered sand, rocks, and the occasional hidden spring; nothing that was out of the ordinary.

Keen eyes scanned the sands and caught sight of something different. A strange dark object appeared partially buried by the desert. At first, the lead owl was not sure what it saw. Its eyes focused, and eventually patterns emerged. There was some kind of wooden vessel below, though it was unlike any it had yet seen.

The lead owl turned and began a spiraling descent toward the ground. The slightly smaller one followed suit.

This gave them time to continue examining the strange object. The shape reminded it of a ship, but with an enclosed upper deck and no sails. In some ways it resembled a large, broken seed.

As the owls neared the sands, grey flames licked around the edges of their forms. The feathers receded and shifted. The legs extended, the torso lengthened, and the wings grew and hung down at their sides. Two robed, hooded figures stepped out of the swirling flames and walked across the sands.

They paused, examining the object before approaching. There were no signs of damage beyond what the wind and sand had begun. Estimating based on what was still exposed, most of the bottom half of the vessel had been buried.

The lead figure was taller and broader than the second. It approached the vessel and walked around it. The second figure followed, but from a greater distance, watching carefully what would happen next. Climbing on top of the object, the larger one found a circular hatch. The figure bent down, opened the hatch, and climbed inside.

The interior was dark with few furnishings. Flames leapt around the figure's hand, creating a light in the darkened vessel. Another hatch nearby lead to another deck below. There were only two or three rooms per level and only three easily accessible levels.

The former great owl searched the vessel and found an unconscious person in the front end of the ship. Their skin was dry and parched. Their hair was long and white, and their ears were pointed. The hooded figure knelt and reached out toward the stranger.

*   *   *

Cyfeiriad slowly became aware of the still, cold, dry air around him. He sensed something near him and opened his eyes. A bright, flickering grey flame made his eyes squint before they adjusted enough to make out a figure kneeling over him. The figure removed its head coverings to reveal the face of an older man with greying hair and beard. His eyes were hard, but not cruel, and there was sternness to his expression. There was an interesting, almost flamelike pattern around the outer edges of the man's irises, the tips of the flames reaching in toward the pupil.

Get up and live, or stay here and die.

Cyfeiriad blinked in surprise. The words, or at least the concepts, had entered his mind, voiced by someone other than himself.

The old stranger stood and turned away. He watched the flame extinguish before the stranger climbed the ladder up out of the ship.

With a sigh, Cyfeiriad's eyes gazed up at the wooden beams, and his mind reached backward in time to remind himself how he had arrived at his current location and state.

Images of the burning mountain of the high elves flashed before him. Memories of pain and regret stabbed his heart. He sailed into the mist and sat there in the still, timeless void. His thoughts had ceased, and he became a statue in self-imposed exile, sitting on the floor of the ship.

Now he was lying on his back in a very cold, dry place. His emotions were spent. He didn't feel the pain and guilt like before, but he didn't really feel a desire for anything else either.

A cold, distant part of his mind stirred. It was a strange mixture of emotionless logic, coolness, and animal instinct.

He would get up, and he would follow these strangers. He would not lay here and die.

Cyfeiriad sat up and climbed out of the ship. He paused on top of the vessel. Outside the ship was an apparently endless desert. A gentle breeze moved over him, bringing with it traces of a formerly more familiar sense of happiness.

The old stranger was walking away from the ship, but Cyfeiriad could see a smaller robed figure still watching. Eventually, it too turned and began to walk away.

Carefully, the elf climbed down onto the sand and followed the strangers.

*   *   *

The trek along the mist wall boundary was extremely unpleasant for Cyfeiriad. His body was sore, fatigued, and severely dehydrated. He felt as if he had been baked inside the ship for several days. There was no way to know how long he had been walking or how much farther there was to go. Despite feeling like he had been drained by incredible heat, the night was frigid. The shifting of the sand with every step made him feel like he was taking twice as many steps as he needed to, which only tired him faster. The air and everything he could see was dry, as if water was a foreign concept. The wind was cold and harsh, bereft of the scents of sea or vegetation that he was used to. He wrapped his arms around his chest as he staggered onward.

Trying in vain to swallow, he looked around at the endless sands to his left. It was a baren place, and the cold wind was biting into his face and fingers, though he noticed his body was beginning to feel relatively normal and warm from the heat of exertion. He looked ahead at the leading robed figures. They seemed unfazed by the environment.

Fatigue, soreness, and dehydration gnawed at his mind. How could he survive in such an arid wasteland? Would there be any water? Would he just die out here?

The distant part of his mind that he had never fully noticed before that day began to speak. He had two options. He could stop, which meant that he would never find water, shelter, or food. If he stopped moving, the cold of the night would consume him, and the heat of the day would destroy him. This would mean certain death.

Conversely, he could keep going. If the strangers could survive out here, then it was likely he could too.

Cyfeiriad kept walking, then turned his head slightly.

Alternatively, he could just walk back into the mist. He knew how it worked. He knew how to travel back. The sea elf laughed at how long it had taken him to think of that. He must be more exhausted than he realized.

But where would he go? His homeland was destroyed. His people would not want him around, since he had failed to arrive in time to save everyone.

But there were other lands out there. He knew this from experience. He turned and looked at the strangers ahead. He was curious to know more about them, and staying in this desert was a reasonable exile. If things deteriorated to the point where he thought he might die, he could always escape into the mist and find a new land to which he could banish himself.

Determinedly, Cyfeiriad continued to trudge through the sand after the strangers. Eventually, faint rays of light began to peak around the edges of distant dunes. The figures picked up their pace when a large outcropping of rock appeared in the distance. When they arrived just outside the rock formation, they stopped and turned to face just to the left, away from the mist wall.

Cyfeiriad walked up behind them and waited. They did not acknowledge his presence, but the smaller one stepped forward and held up its hand.

The sand before them began to rise, pulled by invisible forces into tall, intricate shapes. The sea elf's eyes went wide, watching the sand take on the form of a delicately crafted house with several rooms. Suddenly, flames leaped from the figure's hand and swirled around the structure, first hardening it to glass, then blackening the glass until it was opaque.

The stranger lowered its hand and walked into the structure, followed by the taller one. As Cyfeiriad approached, he noticed that the glass was thick and solid. He marveled at the small palace that moments before had not existed.

The old stranger inspected the smaller figure's work and nodded. Both of them walked back outside and into the crevice between the rocks. Cyfeiriad followed them, not sure what was going on. After a few bends in the crevice, the path opened to reveal a small, sheltered clearing, in the middle of which was a small pool of water and a few plants.

On sight of the water, thirst became the only thing in Cyfeiriad's mind. He took two hurried steps forward, but halted and allowed the strangers to approach it first. They both knelt and removed the coverings from their faces before reaching out and creating small glass vessels for themselves in the same way the dwelling outside had been made. They filled the vessels and began to drink. Cyfeiriad watched for a moment, then approached the water and knelt. He reached out with his hands and scooped up water greedily. Water had never tasted so good or felt so refreshing on even the few inches that touched his hands.

Sensing something, he looked up to see the strangers watching him. The old male reached out to create another drinking vessel, and Cyfeiriad finally saw clearly in the brief glow of the flames that the second figure was a young female with a vague resemblance to the old one. She had long black hair and the same red-orange eyes with mist grey flame-like swirls. The old one handed the vessel to Cyfeiriad, and he took it with a respectful nod.

The three sat and drank until they were full, then the strangers filled the vessels one more time. The old male and young female stood and walked back the way they had come. Cyfeiriad hurriedly filled his cup and followed after them. They entered the glass dwelling and sat down.

Cyfeiriad sat a little way off, watching and listening as the two conversed. He had no idea what the strange sounds they uttered meant. The older one had a generally stern expression, but Cyfeiriad still didn't sense any hostility in it. Despite this, he got the feeling that the stern older male quickly would judge his failures should they be exposed. The young female's expression was also stoic but noticeably kinder. Neither addressed him, and he wasn't sure what to do. He leaned his back into a corner of the room, pulled up his knees, and wrapped his arms around his legs. Eventually, the day's journey got the better of him, and he succumbed to fatigue.

A gentle touch on his shoulder jerked Cyfeiriad back to reality, and he blinked up at the face of the young female. She had a slight smile on her lips. The sea elf carefully sat up and looked around. The light was beginning to fade from the land. The already dipping temperatures felt good to his day-warmed body.

"Good evening," he said.

The young woman looked at him for a moment before saying something he did not understand. Cyfeiriad looked at her quizzically. She glanced in the direction of the open doorway, then looked back at him.

She repeated the sounds. *Good evening.*

He blinked. It was as if he heard two voices at once. One was the clear sound of her strange language in his ears and the other was understood, but hard to define in his mind. It wasn't quite words. It was more like the basic concepts behind the words, images, sounds, and various feelings, both corporeal and incorporeal, so that his mind was able to instantly translate them to his own language.

"How? Can you understand me or are you reading my thoughts?"

The young woman repeated the sounds, then came, *Repeat, good evening.*

He blinked and did his best to replicate the combination of sounds that she made. The young woman nodded and smiled.

Cyfeiriad pointed to himself; "Cyfeiriad."

She pointed at him and repeated, "Cyfeiriad." Then she pointed at herself and said, "Libuat Alnaar."

"Libuat Alnaar," he repeated.

She smiled again.

* * *

Libuat Alnaar followed her father over the sands with their guest moving close beside her. He was now dressed in robes similar to ones she and her father wore. They had met another group of nomads several days after their initial encounter who had provided them with an extra set of clothes. It had been seventy-three days since the elf had joined their journey.

The jinniya glanced at the interloper. His eyes were more focused and his expression more determined than when they had found him. He no longer had the distant, lost gaze in his eyes and followed beside them instead of lagging behind. She had watched his strength return and his coordination grow as he was able to eat, drink, and acclimate to the desert. He no longer hugged himself or seemed to be tensing against the cold at night, instead relaxing into it and allowing himself to naturally warm up and acclimate to it as he walked.

The elf had even learned the Jinn language, or at least the better part of it. She knew that it would have taken longer had she not projected the meanings directly into his mind while teaching him the sounds. Her father had said that the newcomer needed to learn the hard way, but she reasoned this was an appropriate compromise between his intention to train the elf and their need to communicate and gather information.

Masidus slowed his pace at the top of a dune and looked around. Libuat Alnaar came to stand beside him, and the newcomer took his usual position a few paces back. He no longer watched them exclusively or expectantly, instead he scanned the area himself, though she was not sure if he knew enough yet to understand what he saw.

Looking ahead, Libuat Alnaar took note that they were now facing almost exactly north, the mist wall still to their right. This meant that they had traveled roughly three quarters of the perimeter of the desert. When they reached the point where the mist wall was to their right and they faced due west, then they would be near where they had started.

There was a faint brightening of the upper reaches of the mist wall, indicating the impending sunrise. She was not sure how the sun moved through or if it moved above the mists. When they had transformed into birds, they had been unable to reach an upper edge. It was either infinite or too high for them to climb. The mechanics of how their desert world interacted with the mist wall were a point of curiosity that she intended to explore in the future.

At a nod from her father, she stepped forward and formed the sand into a temporary glass palace. Masidus entered and moved back to his rooms. The elf moved up beside her.

"Why do you make the glass house, and he does not?" Cyfeiriad asked, examining the intricate details of the structure.

"Practice. My father is several centuries older than me."

She scanned the results of her work, marking the swirling scorch marks that turned the glass almost completely opaque.

"How do you do it?"

Libuat Alnaar paused, rewatching her memories of her years of training, looking for a simplified way to explain it all.

"I use my mind. My will extends beyond my body, and I form the sand into the shape I want. Then I send my own flames out to turn the sand into glass."

"How did you learn to move the sand with your mind? The structure is so intricate and detailed, and the sand flows almost like water."

"We observe and analyze the ten thousand details. When learning to move objects, we practice focusing, observe the state of our mind, and analyze the differences between when we succeed and when we fail. As far as the intricate structure of the building, the process is similar. We grow up studying the patterns of nature and the designs of machines. We learn to pay attention to details and to use reason to piece things together."

Libuat Alnaar paused, not sure if that was the best way to explain it.

Cyfeiriad's gaze drifted to the ground as if lost in thought.

"Come over here," she said and walked a little way along the crest of the dune.

"Which way are we facing?" Libuat Alnaar quizzed him.

The elf looked at the fading stars. They had discussed the constellations early in his lessons. Cyfeiriad had revealed that his people had similarly named their constellations after things found in nature. Even if the sun's rays weren't there to give away the answer, he would still be able to deduce the directions by the stars.

"We must be heading directly north now."

"Good. From which direction comes the wind?"

Cyfeiriad's eyes shifted from the sky and gained a faraway look indicating that he was focused inwardly instead of outwardly. Libuat Alnaar gently grazed his mind and sensed him focusing on the sensations of the air moving around him, brushing his skin, and moving his robes.

"It is coming from the east," came his reply.

"How do you know?"

"I can feel it."

Libuat Alnaar pointed into the distance; "Can you tell me the direction of the wind a couple miles from us?"

"I would assume it to be roughly the same, but I'm not sure."

"Look at the ridge line of the dunes. What do you see?"

Cyfeiriad looked out over the dunes; "Sand dunes, lots of sand dunes."

"In which way do the crests of the dunes run?"

Cyfeiriad paused. Libuat Alnaar saw images of waves of water, more water than she had ever seen, overlaid on the dunes as understanding blossomed in his mind. She sensed his embarrassment at only just realizing the similarity now.

"The wind blows the sands from east to west, forming dunes with ridges that end up running north to south. I don't know why I didn't notice it sooner." He turned to look at her; "But what does this have to do with using your mind to shape the sand?"

"It's a lesson in observation and reason. The desert is a harsh environment. Our ability to shapeshift greatly improves our chances of survival, but there is still danger. Observation and reason are the tools that help us thrive, and they can be applied in a variety of ways to a variety of endeavors."

Libuat Alnaar turned and walked back toward the glass building. She did not hear Cyfeiriad's footsteps behind her, so she turned and looked.

The elf was standing, staring at the ground in front of him. Her eyes shifted to the sands at his feet. Nothing moved in a way contrary to the direction of the subtle breeze.

* * *

"We have completed the circuit."

The old jinni's words caught Cyfeiriad by surprise. He rarely spoke, especially in a way that even remotely resembled addressing or including the elf in the conversation. This time, he was looking directly at Cyfeiriad while they sat in the glass structure, just before daybreak.

"What do you mean?" he asked tentatively. The usual silence of the old jinni made it difficult to guess how he might react to anything the elf did, which made Cyfeiriad tend to assume that any misstep would be treated harshly.

"We have been scouting the perimeter of our land to discover the cause of the disappearance of several of our people. You are the only anomaly that we have encountered on our mission."

Cyfeiriad looked nervously from Masidus to Libuat Alnaar. She looked at the ground, not offering any support. The elf turned to face the old jinni again.

"How did you come to be here?"

"I'm not exactly sure. I remember sailing into the mist and just sitting there indefinitely. I guess I fell asleep at some point. I don't know how I would have made it out in that state."

"Does that mean that you are able to navigate the mist when you are conscious?"

"Yes."

"Are all of the elves capable of this feat?"

"No, at least not that I know of. I was one of two assigned to find a way through the mist. I don't know if the other was successful."

"Have the elves ever met the jinn before?"

"Not that I know of."

"Have the elves also had people go missing?"

"I never heard of anything like that, but we are generally solitary and spread out. It is not uncommon to go years or even decades without interaction."

"Why were you sent to learn the secret of the mist?"

"We were told that the Enemy had returned."

The old jinni paused, a grave look passing over his face. Cyfeiriad sensed recognition in his reaction.

"Why did you sail back into the mist?"

Cyfeiriad hung his head; "Because I failed."

"How?"

"I didn't get back in time. Everything was on fire. The Elders were all dead."

"Did you know exactly when the attack would come?"

"No."

"Did any of your actions that resulted in your delay directly lead you off of the Narrow Path?"

The elf paused and replayed the events in his mind; "Not that I can tell."

"But you arrived just as the survivors were nearing the mist wall, correct?"

"Yes."

"Then either you arrived exactly in time to help them, or you could not have known when the attack would occur, or you should pray for forgiveness and accept it. Whichever possibility is true, there is nothing to be gained by catatonic penance, and it will not change anything that has already transpired."

Cyfeiriad mulled this over in his mind.

*   *   *

The journey back to the place the jinn called home was mostly uneventful. They continued to travel by night and rest by day, but now they were heading south. At first, he meditated on how Masidus had analyzed his past failures. He was unsure if he could accept the first two fully but was unable to argue with the third. His immense feelings of self-loathing and regret had diminished in the unknown years in the mist and been worn away by the exertion of his initial desert travels. The result was that he was more inclined now to view himself and the events more dispassionately than before. This made it easier to eventually accept what the old jinni had said. Eventually, his mind drifted to other topics to pass the time while they walked.

When next they came across an outcropping of rock, Cyfeiriad made a point to gather a few small stones. He reasoned that a solid, easily grasped object would be easier to practice on than shifting sand.

During the nightly treks, the elf began to ponder his own mind and how it interacted with his body. He tried incorporating the ideas that Libuat Alnaar had mentioned. He observed that there was a difference between thinking about doing something and doing it. Imagining his hand moving was different than it actually moving. Instead of images of movement, the willing of it was more a blank space in his mind. He wondered if there was a way to apply this void to things outside himself.

Before they slept and just after they rose, while there was still light from the sun, Cyfeiriad began to practice. He would stare at one of the rocks, either in his palm or on the ground in front of him. He would then try to analyze how his mind felt while trying to focus on moving the rock. This led to the quick realization that thinking about how he was thinking while trying to focus, instead of just focusing, quickly destroyed any concentration that may have existed.

Frustration and a sense of futility soon began to fester at the corners of his mind. He was only able to keep his emotions at bay by reminding himself that he had seen levitation work for the jinniya and tapping into the same emotionless determination that had kept him going when marching through the desert. The frustration also led to a certain tension when he tried to concentrate that he suspected only hindered his progress, as he had noted a certain amount of relaxation of the mind when willing himself to do tasks utilizing the members of his own body. It was similar to how he would relax and intuitively navigate instead of tensing and focusing on his fears of failure.

Despite all the jinn had taught him, he still had no sense of how much time passed as they journeyed through the desert. Enough time passed that he was beginning to wonder when or if they would ever arrive, when mountains appeared in the distance.

* * *

Cyfeiriad stared at the small rock hovering a few inches over his upturned palms as he walked. The moon was just bright enough that he could see the stone. His initial success had occurred a few days after the mountains came into sight. It had taken the past several weeks to finally be able to walk and levitate the stone at the same time. It took nearly all his concentration to keep the stone afloat, and the added distraction of walking made being relaxed and focused that much more difficult. It was like his mind had to be in two places at once, but not actually in either.

The rock dropped into his palms as he released his concentration. He sighed and looked around, hoping he hadn't wandered away from the jinn again. With relief he noticed them several yards ahead. He quickened his pace to catch up with them.

As he looked beyond them, he could see the mountains and a city between them and the mountains. It had been growing larger and nearer each day.

When the sun began to rise, they did not stop. They kept going until they reached the outer walls of the city. The walls were fifty feet high and made of stone. Intricately intertwined geometrical designs decorated the ramparts above and the arches around the gates. When they entered the city, Cyfeiriad could not help but to look around in awe.

The buildings were tall and gleaming with metal, stone, and glass in greater quantities than he had ever seen. Stalls and businesses lined the irregular streets. Crowds moved back and forth through the streets. Many carried various devices that Cyfeiriad had never seen before and could not identify.

"Amazing," the elf murmured, looking around in awe before he turned and saw that Masidus and Libuat Alnaar had raised their hoods.

Unsure what was wrong, he raised his as well. The two jinn were moving slowly, looking around, examining everything carefully. Cyfeiriad also began to observe more closely.

The jinn moving past them in the street walked slowly and joylessly. They were mostly quiet, their shoulders and backs slumped forward. Most kept their heads tilted down, eyes on the ground. While the clothes were different than what he was used to in his elvish homeland, he noticed the telltale signs of wear. Seams were faded and worn, and the edges of material were beginning to fray. Most of the shops and stalls had been closed, and those that were open did nothing to attract attention. Transactions were carried out quietly and succinctly.

Stay close and stay quiet, came a mental message from Masidus as they picked up the pace.

After a few twists and turns through the streets, they arrived at a store front. The signs on the building indicated that they sold books. Masidus knocked, and they waited. After a few moments, another, older looking jinni opened the door and looked up at Masidus. A look of recognition flashed over his face.

He looked back and forth quickly, then ushered them inside; "Enter quickly, Hariq Qadim."

Once inside, the older looking jinni locked the door and lead them to an inner room, where he closed the door again. He offered them something to eat and drink, but Masidus refused politely. They all took seats on cushions on the floor.

Cyfeiriad observed that the older looking jinni's eyes were a similar red-orange to Masidus and Libuat Alnaar, but with pale blue flame-like swirls. While Masidus was taller than Cyfeiriad and built more powerfully, this apparently older jinni was thinner and shorter than Cyfeiriad. Despite appearances, Cyfeiriad sensed that Masidus was actually the older of the two jinni, causing him to wonder why a shapeshifter would choose to age so noticeably.

Masidus and Libuat Alnaar removed their hoods and Cyfeiriad followed suit.

"Welcome back My King, Princess," the older looking jinni said, nodding to the two jinn in turn.

He looked at Cyfeiriad and his eyes narrowed slightly, but he did not say anything.

"It is good to see you, Hatif," said Masidus.

"Thank you for inviting us in. Is everything ok with you? How is your family?" asked Libuat Alnaar.

Cyfeiriad saw Hatif's eyes shift back over to him again before looking back to Masidus.

"Is it safe to speak around this foreigner?"

"He has not given us any reason to distrust him. What has happened?"

"A few years after you two left on your journey, the sand covering the sphinx gate exploded. When we went to investigate, we found that it had been activated. Visitors appeared in the sphinx gate. They sought an audience with the queen, Taeziat Jamra. After that first meeting, an announcement was made. The outsiders would open the sphinx gate to their own realm, and we would begin to trade ideas and resources. They presented several fascinating new devices to Queen Taeziat Jamra and offered to allow our most gifted scientists and engineers the opportunity to study in their lands.

"Several of the younger jinn went eagerly through the portal in the coming months," Hatif paused and sighed. "My son was among them. I have not seen him in more than ten years."

"I'm sorry for your loss," said Masidus gravely. "Has anyone gone to the other realm to find the missing youths?"

"None who have gone through ever returned, other than the visitors themselves. We began sending mined aether crystals through the gate as well. At first it was freely given and voluntarily mined, but within a year, the queen took control of the mines and decreed that everyone must do their share to mine the aether. In the mines, some of the mountain jinn have been placed in charge. They direct the workers but do not dig themselves. It was also around this time that the jinn began to be selected to serve as guards in the palace."

The king looked at Hatif, his brows furrowed in a stern expression.

"Why does the palace need guards? Has someone attacked the city or the palace itself?" asked Libuat Alnaar.

"There has been no large-scale violence, but I don't know how long that will last. The people are growing weary of being forced to work the mines and seeing their friends and family disappear. Every year the requirements are harsher, and the people's trust diminishes. The uncharacteristic decrees from the palace have raised suspicions, but anyone who voices doubts about the queen's true identity disappears."

"What about the council of Elders?" asked Libuat Alnaar.

"When the visitors came, those Elders who were in the city at the time joined the audience with the visitors. After the initial meeting, the queen announced that they had left to visit the visitors' homeland as a special envoy. No one I have spoken with saw them leave. As Elders have returned from the desert, they have gone to the palace, but none have been seen leaving again."

"What are these visitors like?" asked Masidus.

"They called themselves goblins and seem to come in two varieties. The first kind that made the initial contact with us are only slightly shorter than we are. They have green skin and black hair. The other kind has skin that is mottled greens and purples. They have long, pointed ears, and stand roughly chest height. All of them smile and say kind words, but there are subtle changes in their expressions and the movements of their eyes that betray contempt. The shorter ones are less skilled at hiding such expressions."

"Does anyone know how to operate the sphinx gate to get to the outsiders' realm?"

"No. The goblins never align the rings for an outbound portal. They only open it from their realm. However, they do follow a very regular schedule so that we can provide them with a steady supply of aether."

"Do you know when Taeziat Jamra next plans to appear before the people?" asked Masidus.

"The next address should be in two days. You can stay here as long as you like. I only ask one thing: Please help me find out what happened to my son."

"We will do what we can," replied the king solemnly.

*　　*　　*

Their second day in the city was spent inside Hatif's shop. Masidus spent long hours with him, going over the fine details of the events through the years he had been gone.

Libuat Alnaar and Cyfeiriad perused the various books in the shop. She pointed out her favorites and which ones would be most useful for him to learn about the jinn realm. As they discussed books on the jinn society and history, Cyfeiriad asked some questions to better understand them.

"Can you tell me more about the sphinx gate?"

"It is a set of rings forming a disc surrounded by three sphinxes and four gryphons. Do you have anything like this in your homeland?" She looked quickly over the shelves and pulled out a book. Turning to the desired page, she showed Cyfeiriad a diagram of the sphinx gate.

Cyfeiriad examined the drawing; "Not that I have seen. There is a set of circular ruins that might have once been what you describe, since the Elders referred to it as a gate. If there were statues, they were broken beyond what I could recognize. The Elders said that the Enemy broke the gate in fury in the first days. Were you able to use it to visit other places?"

Cyfeiriad wandered past the shelves, scanning the titles, while Libuat Alnaar did the same farther down.

"No," she said, closing the book and replacing it on the shelf. "The gate was buried in the hope that it would make further visits by the Enemy impossible. Large stones were laid across the rings, and a structure was built around it. Then, the whole thing was covered in sand."

"Have the jinn ever had visitors from other realms before?"

"The only times we have seen outsiders were during the visitation of the Enemy in the first days and the warning we received almost two hundred years ago. After the warning, we developed some small weapons and safehouses, while the Elders mostly dispersed into the desert to keep watch. The Enemy had not been exceptionally violent in the first days, and nothing happened for about eighty years after the warning, so we began to relax. It was not until close to a century after the warning that we realized that many of the Elders were missing. Several expeditions failed to discover answers, so my father and I eventually decided to survey the perimeter of our realm ourselves."

"How do you know I'm not in league with the Enemy?"

Libuat Alnaar turned and faced him; "My father is an Elder. He was there when the Enemy visited our people. He knows the appearance of the Enemy, both his physical form and his mind. You do not have the Enemy's eyes, and your mind lacks the proud complexity and power of the Enemy."

Cyfeiriad was somewhat taken aback by this statement. He wasn't sure if it was a compliment, an insult, or merely a description of a powerful and arrogant adversary.

* * *

Masidus, Libuat Alnaar, Hatif, and Cyfeiriad stood in the crowd, hoods covering their heads, waiting outside the palace for the Taeziat Jamra's address to her people. Most of the jinn around them waited in silence. None showed signs of excitement or happiness.

A musical fanfare drew everyone's attention to a balcony high above. Libuat Alnaar watched closely as guards took positions at the corners, their posture stiff and upright as they held their weapons at their sides. The weapons, long poles with double edged blades at the top, were similar to instruments used for hunting larger animals. It was unusual to see anything presented as a show of force next to the queen of the jinn. Taeziat Jamra stepped out between them and stood at the wall of the balcony. Libuat Alnaar scanned the face of her mother, noting the similarities in appearance between the two of them before moving on to her mother's unique features. Her face showed some signs of age and slight streaks of grey in her hair, but her movements were sure and strong. Gone were the simple but expertly made garments she had seen her mother wear while growing up. Now she glittered with metals and gems crafted into intricate shapes and patterns. She looked out over the crowd and raised her arms wide to greet them.

The guards raised their weapons and struck the ground with ends of the poles. At this sound, the crowd kneeled, heads bowed before their ruler. Hatif knelt beside them. Libuat Alnaar and her father quickly followed suit, but she had to jerk quickly on Cyfeiriad's sleeve to get him to drop to one knee, as he had been staring transfixed at the sight of the queen.

"My loyal subjects, thank you for gathering here today. We have accomplished much in our great work to bring the forces of the aether under our rightful dominion. Through this, we strengthen our ties with the benevolent visitors as well as the power and security of our own kingdom. As thanks to the generosity of the goblins and as reward for our labors, I have proclaimed a feast to be held in one week's time. It shall be a time to celebrate our tireless efforts to bring strength and security to the kingdom."

Libuat Alnaar watched her mother closely, head tilted down, eyes angled up, as her speech continued. Only Taeziat Jamra's eyes turned down to gaze at the crowd from time to time. Her head did not move. She frequently raised her fist, tensed her muscles, and added emphasis to her tone of voice when speaking of strength and power. It was her mother in voice and appearance, but not in tone and mannerism.

"Go forth, do your duty, obeying my emissaries as they obey me."

The queen turned and walked back into the palace. Once she was out of sight, the guards stamped their weapons on the ground, and everyone rose. The crowd began to disperse slowly.

Libuat Alnaar pondered what she had just observed. Her mother had always been kind, speaking directly to the people, not at them. Even though her father and mother held the titles of king and queen, they had not regularly commanded the jinn. Typically, the djinn went about their business with little interference from the royal family. If decisions that would affect the whole of the society or disputes between jinn arose, then the king and queen would convene the council, act as mediators, break tie votes, and generally go about ensuring that the final decisions were carried out.

Libuat Alnaar turned to her father, the question already on her lips.

The old jinni looked at his daughter, a grave expression on his face. "It's not her," he responded, before she could utter the words, his own tone low and menacing.

The king turned to Hatif; "Take us to the mines. We must see what is being done to our people before we reveal ourselves."

*   *   *

The mines were deep in the mountains to the south of the oasis and the main portion of the city. Hatif lead the way, and they were able to go unnoticed in the normal stream of jinn going to and from the mines. They kept their hoods up and their heads down as they went.

"Why don't you three just change into birds and spy out the mines in disguise? Wouldn't that be easier and faster than walking there in these forms?" Cyfeiriad asked quietly.

Libuat Alnaar turned her hooded head slightly in his direction; "We are jinn, a people of shapeshifters. To you and the animals in the wilderness, we are hidden when we change, but to each other, it is always obvious. Jinn cannot hide from other jinn by changing shape." She smiled slightly; "If we could, our parents would have lost us long ago."

Cyfeiriad mulled this over. It made sense, and he realized he had not thought about how shapeshifters would be able to interact with each other if changing their forms made them truly unrecognizable.

When they reached the mines, they noticed jinn standing near the entrances, holding weapons. Their eyes were the usual red-orange, but with flame-like swirls of yellow-brown, giving an overall amber tone to their irises. Carts and tools had been lined up outside. At first glance, the carts were generally large, open-topped boxes with wheels. Closer inspection revealed mechanisms attached to the wheels and controlled by a set of switches along the top of one end. The mechanisms included bright gems, similar to what he'd seen in the various devices throughout the city and in Hatif's home. The tools had similar designs involving gems, wires, and gears. Following Hatif's lead, they each took a cart and a device that featured a large, thin, circular disk. Hammers and picks lay inside the cart. Activating the switches, they were able to drive and steer their carts after Hatif inside the mountain.

The rough-hewn stone surfaces of the first section of the tunnels had been secured with metal supports where necessary. Cyfeiriad reasoned that they must not have many trees in the desert to waste them in the tunnels. The farther they moved, the more precisely cut the walls seemed to be. The tunnels eventually led to a large open chamber that was filled with multicolored lights.

Cyfeiriad paused involuntarily in awe at the sight of a long thin ribbon of rippling colors stretching from one end of the cavern to the other. At either end of this ribbon, jinn labored away, digging into the rock wall to further uncover more of it. Along the length of the ribbon, others worked at cutting out large chunks of multi-colored crystal, tossing the smaller pieces into the carts. Hatif led them to a spot, and they went to work. The elf watched the others activate their devices. The thin discs spun quickly and silently, then were lowered through the glistening mist surrounding the crystals. They cut where they could when the crystals protruded out, sometimes using hammers to break a chunk free if they couldn't cut clean through. Where the mass of crystal became more solid and uniform, the picks were used to break it up into chunks.

As he looked around, he saw a space where a jinni had just finished mining, and the crystals had been harvested down to the floor. In their place stood a swirling mist of colors that rose slowly into the air like steam. Near this ribbon of color, small crystals could be seen forming as the mist swirled together.

"What is this?" asked Cyfeiriad in a hushed tone.

"This is the aether vein. Several were discovered centuries ago in the deep mountain caves. The aether leaks out and crystalizes around the vein. We harvest the crystals and use them in our technology," explained Libuat Alnaar from his left.

"I've never seen anything like this," he said, picking up a gently glowing red-orange rock.

"That is crystalized fire aether. If you apply sufficient pressure or electrical current, it will convert from its current form into flame," explained Hatif from his right.

The elf paused and looked around. Masidus was working quietly on the other side of Libuat Alnaar, but Cyfeiriad could see him looking around intently as he did.

Hours went by as they mined the crystalized aether. The mountain jinn supervisors, the ones with the yellow-brown traces in their eyes who carried weapons, as Cyfeiriad soon learned, wandered in and out of the chamber. They would survey the work, sometimes inspecting someone's progress. If someone tried to leave without a full cart, they were told to return to work until it was full. This was usually conveyed in threatening tones, rough handling, and brandished weapons.

At one point, one of the mountain jinn raised a whip and beat an older jinni until his blood ran out on the cave floor. The elf turned, but Libuat Alnaar grabbed his arm. When he looked at her, she shook her head slightly. He suppressed his anger and realized that they were there to gather information. If they acted too swiftly, their presence would be reported to the false queen. The elf looked over at Masidus and saw his knuckles turning white as he gripped his tools.

The work was long and difficult. Cyfeiriad could feel himself sweating from the exertion. He also noticed that this cave was not as cool as the ones he had explored in his homeland. He wasn't sure if it was the desert heat seeping in, the warmth of the many working bodies, or a side effect of the aether vein that kept things warmer.

Eventually, they filled their carts and Hatif lead them out of the mines. They followed a well-paved path that wound down through the mountains and to the east. The path ended in a large depression between the mountains and some of the larger hills nearby. In the center of the area stood the sphinx gate.

Again, Cyfeiriad had to hide his astonishment as they approached. Four large stone gryphons stood menacingly, facing out from a central raised stone platform. On the platform itself stood three even taller stone sphinxes gazing inward with closed eyes. Most marvelous of all was the giant swirling sphere of energy that stood in the center of the disc.

As they approached, half a dozen strange creatures stepped forward. One held up his hand, palm out, as a sign for them to stop. The creatures were roughly chest height, with long pointed ears and skin that was green mottled with shades of dark red or purple. Overall, their frames were slender and wiry, their movements quick despite the heavy armor plates they wore. Their eyes darted over the small group, expressions twitching toward disdain before being forced back into open, inviting faces.

"Welcome, beloved allies," greeted the lead figure.

Hatif stepped back from his cart, and the others followed suit. The goblin looked over the full carts and nodded.

"Thank you for your generosity," it said, "we will take it from here. May our peoples grow strong together."

Cyfeiriad and the others watched in silence as the creatures steered the carts into the swirling multi-colored sphere of energy. When the last goblin had passed through, it collapsed. Cyfeiriad blinked at the sudden loss of shifting lights. They approached the platform and examined the fifteen metal rings inscribed with strange symbols that encircled the six foot in diameter central disc.

"These have not changed position since the last time we experimented with the gate," stated Masidus. "The goblins don't want us to know how to reach their realm."

"Do they always exit in the same direction, toward the road?" asked Cyfeiriad.

"Yes," replied Hatif with a slight smile.

"We will wait on the other side and enter the gate when it next opens," said Masidus.

*   *   *

"When we, um, reach the other land, let me scout ahead," Cyfeiriad suggested to Masidus, keeping his gaze on the darkened gate from their new vantage point in a depression on the opposite side from the road.

"Why?"

"I explored and made maps in my homeland. Navigating unknown territory is something I am very good at."

Cyfeiriad looked up to meet the silent jinni's gaze.

"You and your daughter have taught me much, and I want to be able to help you in return."

"That is reasonable. You will scout ahead."

The sun was beginning to set when the gate opened again.

"This should be the last shipment of the day," whispered Hatif.

Goblins exited the gate on the far side, though they could not all be seen as the sphere of swirling colors partially blocked their line of sight.

After several minutes, the sounds of wheels crunching on sand could be heard just around the bend. The goblins who had been milling about turned and moved toward the drop-off point for the carts.

Before the final shipment came into view, Masidus gestured, and the three jinn and one elf moved swiftly and silently into the portal.

*   *   *

The sky was on fire and the clouds were black smoke. The wind was weak and acrid. The desolate land around the gate contained only a few strange, sickly plants, showing a combination of purple and green shades.

Cyfeiriad paused in horror for a split second before moving swiftly away from the gate. The rest followed suit, staying crouched to avoid detection. The land sloped down into what was likely a dried riverbed or lake; it was hard to tell at this point. When they were low enough to stay hidden, they turned, lay flat on the ground, and slowly crawled until they could just see over the edge.

The elf could just make out movement on the other side of the gate but could not tell what it was. The land seemed to slope away on the other side of the gate, and he could not see what lay beyond. Several long minutes passed before there was a change in the movement, and the gate closed.

The goblins were steering the carts away from the gate and away from the hidden spies. They quickly disappeared down the opposite slope.

They waited until the sounds of the creatures and the carts had faded beyond hearing. Masidus tapped Cyfeiriad's shoulder, and the elf slipped silently over the rim and approached the gate.

He looked down at the fifteen rings of the gate and noted the symbols on a scrap of parchment. Keeping his head on a swivel, he moved through the statues to the far side and crouched as he approached the downward slope.

Below, the land was filled with an endless sea of buildings. They were rectangular and utilitarian, lacking in any apparent ornamentation. Strange objects that looked like large, oddly shaped carts moved through the streets, being neither pulled nor pushed by any of the goblins or beasts of burden. The creatures were at the bottom of the hill, loading the carts into one of these larger wheeled vehicles. There were very few goblins walking about the streets.

The elf's gaze drifted out over the strange city, until he spied a large mountain that ascended into the clouds.

He turned to get the others, then looked back. It wasn't a mountain. It was a large, stepped pyramid bigger than any artificial structure he had yet seen. Every so often, the pyramid's slope would cut in with a horizontal landing and then continue as a slightly smaller pyramid before eventually disappearing amid the dark clouds of smoke.

Cyfeiriad returned to the others and informed them of what he had seen. They followed him back up over the rim but then moved to the right until they came to a shallow ditch that they could use for cover as they descended toward the city.

When they reached the buildings, Cyfeiriad realized that they were roughly three stories tall. They appeared to be made of large blocks of a cold, grey stone-like material. High above he could see a set of windows. He turned in time to see the jinn transforming into birds and flying up to the windows. The elf looked around and walked away from the wall a few paces. He turned back, took a deep breath, and ran at the wall. At the last second, he focused his mind down and away from him, just as he had focused on the rock, and launched himself up toward the wall. His feet touched the rough surface for two steps, and he flung his arms up and forward. The elf's fingers caught the edge of the wall where the windows were recessed, and he pulled himself up. The ledge was just big enough for him to sit sideways. His fingers tightly clutched the edges of the slightly open windows.

Cyfeiriad looked at the birds on either side of him and realized the jinn were staring at him. He smiled and turned toward the building's interior.

Below them were machines unlike any the elf had seen before. They were taking aether crystals and incorporating them into an endless stream of identical objects. Moving through the machines, as if inspecting them, were more of the goblins they had seen earlier.

The birds flew down from the ledge and Cyfeiriad hopped down. The jinn retook their bipedal forms as they landed.

"Why don't you just stay as birds and explore that way?"

"There is very little life here. I have not seen or heard any birds since we arrived. They might notice the sudden emergence of such rare animals," replied Masidus.

The elf nodded and they moved on.

Many of the buildings they examined were similar to the first. Others were filled with rows of tall shelves filled with various devices and supplies that he could not identify.

Several streets in, they came across a building in which they found something other than the goblins. The robes of these figures were tattered, and the goblins seemed to be supervising them. The robed figures also appeared to have some sort of metal collar etched with aether crystal around their necks.

Those in the tattered robes were working on a large object; its construction was incomplete, with appendages resembling the folded wings of a diving bird of prey. It had intricate patterns of finely etched aether crystal inlaid throughout. There was a definite greater concentration of red-orange aether crystal at one end of a series of cylindrical structures that were built into the wings.

One of the robed figures stumbled and dropped a large intricate piece of crystal, and it shattered on the hard ground. The figure cried out as one of the blotched creatures gleefully leaped forward and lashed him harshly with a serrated whip.

"Son," whispered Hatif.

Hatif whirled off the ledge and down toward the open doors of the building. Masidus and Libuat Alnaar quickly followed after him as Cyfeiriad hopped down.

As he ran to the doorway, he could hear strange, harsh words being spoken and Hatif shouting.

"Don't touch my son!"

Harsh chattering resounded through the building.

"Dad?"

Masidus and Libuat Alnaar transformed into bipedal form as they rounded into the doorway.

The elf entered in time to see the old jinni rushing the goblins. The blotched creatures reacted quickly, raising their bladed whips and lashing out toward the oncoming jinn.

Masidus reached out his hand, and one of the goblins flew through the air into his waiting grip. Libuat Alnaar transformed instantly into a lioness and attacked. Masidus clenched his fist around his prey's throat and crushed its windpipe. It fell to the ground in a heap. Libuat Alnaar's teeth and claws began to tear into the backs of two of the goblins that had managed to overpower Hatif. Masidus strode farther into the room, reached out with both hands, and pulled two of the blotched creatures to him. He slammed their skulls together with a sickening crunch before casting them to either side.

One of the goblins rushed Cyfeiriad, and he barely dodged the bladed whip. Going on instinct, he ran deeper into the large room, hoping to use the contents as obstacles to escape his pursuer. The elf was able to deftly move over, around, and through the various carts, shelves, and ladders in the building, until he had started to come back to the main entrance. Intuitively, he dove toward the ground and rolled back up to his feet just in time to hear the whip crack behind him. He dashed down an aisle between two rows of shelves and turned sharply to his right. The creature's footsteps followed close behind, then stopped in a gurgle and a crunch. Cyfeiriad looked back to see the lioness holding the crushed skull in her jaws. Masidus stepped forward and looked at the sea elf.

"Do you never hunt or fight in your homeland?"

"I've hunted big fish and reptiles," he looked down at the floor, "but I usually just ran away from the truly large ones."

"I fear that may not suffice in the days to come," the king replied solemnly.

I'm not even sure how to fight, he thought to himself.

Libuat Alnaar transformed back to her normal shape and approached Hatif, kneeling to examine his wounds.

"Are you able to stand?"

"Give me a minute, I think I can shift myself back together."

Cyfeiriad watched as the pale blue flames licked over the old jinni's body in thin sparks and ribbons. When they faded away, his wounds were healed.

Masidus approached the cowering prisoners; "Do not fear. We are here to help. Are there others of our kind here?"

The prisoners looked at each other, then one stepped forward.

"There used to be more, but they were taken several months ago. We have not seen them since, and we suspect they are dead. We have heard screaming from some of the buildings"; he hung his head, "I don't want to know what they were doing in there."

"Have you seen Taeziat Jamra here?" asked Libuat Alnaar.

The young jinni bowed his head again; "No, we have not."

Hatif held out his arms and stepped toward the speaking prisoner. Tears streamed down his face as they embraced.

"Son!"

"Father!"

"We need to leave. We can take the rest of you back to our homeland," stated the king.

The others nodded, and Masidus turned back to the elf.

"Lead the way, scout."

Cyfeiriad nodded and moved to the doorway. He looked both ways. No one was coming.

"Stay close and move fast," he whispered back to the jinn.

Swiftly and silently, the sea elf moved through the maze of streets, alleys, and buildings. He made it back to the ditch that they had used for cover, and they quickly ascended the slope. When they reached the top, they continued along the hilltop until they reached the dried riverbed. They used this as cover and made their way to the place closest to the gate. Cyfeiriad peered over the rim and surveyed the area. No one was nearby.

He moved quickly toward the gate, the others close behind. When they reached the gate, Libuat Alnaar moved past him and held out her hand. The rings on the platform began to spin, and the portal opened.

Cyfeiriad lead everyone through to the jinn's realm.

* * *

Libuat Alnaar stood in Hatif's shop with the elf, her father, Hatif, and the rescued jinn. They had snuck back during the dark of night.

"What is this collar around your neck?" asked Hatif, examining the device around his son's neck.

"It prevents us from shapeshifting and dampens our concentration," replied one of the jinniya.

Masidus stepped forward, gripped the ring with both hands and snapped it in two. He did the same for the rest of the freed jinn.

"Tell us what happened in the other realm," he said, sitting down and gesturing for everyone else to follow.

Everyone sat down, and Libuat Alnaar observed the tired and pained expressions on the young jinn as they alternatingly looked at each other or the floor.

"When we first arrived, we were taken to a facility and given several tests by the taller goblins to measure our knowledge and skills," began one of the jinni.

"The desolation of the landscape gave me a bad feeling, but there had been no directly threatening behavior up to that point, so I didn't say anything or attempt to leave," commented one of the jinniya.

"After the tests, they sorted us into groups based on our abilities. They put the collars on us, and we were placed in cells at the end of the day."

"That's when I knew for sure that they meant to cause harm. These weren't small, barren rooms, they were cages from which we were not able to leave."

"As the days followed, we were dragged from the cells and taken to other facilities."

"They showed me pictures of all sorts of animals and objects to see what I could shift into. If I argued or refused, I was beaten."

"They gave me broken devices and evaluated how well and quickly I could fix them."

"Some of the others reported being cut open or having limbs amputated and then being told to shift themselves back together."

"They couldn't keep up forever and eventually never returned."

"Some days you could hear screams from the buildings you passed."

"In the end, we were selected to work on a project, creating an aether-powered flying craft. That is what you saw in that building."

There was a long pause as everyone pondered the information.

"So, what do we do next?" asked the elf to Libuat Alnaar's right.

"We need to go back with more jinn, make them pay," said Hatif harshly.

"We should spy out their land more, learn what their true motives are," suggested Libuat Alnaar. "Mother is being held there somewhere."

Everyone turned to look at her father. He gazed downward; his brow furrowed in thought.

"I cannot allow the false queen to continue oppressing my people. We must free them first, then we can turn our attention to the goblins' realm. On the day of the feast, I will force the imposter to reveal her true nature for all to see."

"We want to help too," said a young jinniya, rubbing her neck in remembrance of the goblins' collar.

The other freed prisoners echoed her sentiments.

"Return to your families under cover of night. Let them know that they should only reveal your return to those they most trust. If dissenters are being made to disappear, then some among us have been compromised. We must be cautious, while still organizing support for what comes next. Once the false queen is removed, we must take control of the gate area. We don't know the sequence to reach the goblins' realm, so we need to maintain the illusion that she is still in charge for us to continue to gain access to their realm. The people will not want to continue mining once she is removed, so we need to make as many understand as possible."

The freed jinn nodded in agreement.

"The mountain jinn who more directly serve her will either rush to her aid, attempt to flee at the next scheduled arrival of the goblins, or hide in the desert. Are we prepared to kill our own people?" asked Libuat Alnaar, looking at her father.

A somber expression passed over him; "We must avoid the deaths of our own people as much as possible." He looked around the room. "Make it clear that no jinn kills another. We must not let them turn us against each other."

The other jinn and the elf nodded.

Libuat Alnaar swallowed her concerns. She understood her father's priorities and thought of the risk that the goblins could be alerted. Then they would lose their chance at finding her mother altogether. The thought of never seeing her again and that she might be dead or tortured caused her heart to ache. Gazing at the faces of her people who had just returned from captivity and torture, she nodded inwardly. It would not be right to seek her own desires if it meant that more of her people would suffer.

"There won't be any shipments on the day of the feast, but we must still be prepared to prevent anyone from fleeing to the gate," began Masidus.

"I would suggest that those of you with skilled hunters in your families organize to create a perimeter around the gate area," offered Libuat Alnaar.

Masidus looked at her and nodded.

Libuat Alnaar turned to the elf who was watching them, listening to the plans.

"Cyfeiriad will accompany us to the palace. His abilities have improved greatly since he arrived, and his presence may add some confusion to our enemy. The false queen will not be expecting an elf to be present in our realm," said Libuat Alnaar.

Masidus turned toward the elf; "This will not be a time for evasion. The false queen must not be allowed to escape back to the gate under any circumstances."

Libuat Alnaar could sense the uncertainty in the elf begin to solidify into a decision.

"I will go with you to the palace," his eyes narrowed; "I will not flee nor allow others to do so."

Libuat Alnaar hoped he would hold true to the determination he felt in the moment of safety while danger was merely imaginary.

* * *

Cyfeiriad followed behind Masidus and Libuat Alnaar as they approached the palace gates. As they neared the guards, the king removed his hood. The elf and Libuat Alnaar kept their hoods up and allowed him to proceed. The mountain jinn guards looked at each other nervously but still moved weakly to block the entrance.

"Step aside," commanded the king.

The guards quickly lowered their weapons and opened the way for them to pass.

Inside the palace walls, servants scurried out of the courtyard as the two jinn and the elf made their way to the throne room. The two jinn proceeded without hesitation, but Cyfeiriad had to refrain from looking around in awe at the stone, metal, and glass constructs of the palace. Water flowed through the palace, bringing life to countless plants and turning the palace into a garden.

Masidus pushed open the large double doors to the throne room, and they heard the false queen on the other side.

"Who dares disturb us," she questioned imperiously.

Her expression shifted quickly when she saw Masidus's face. The false queen rose from the throne when she saw them enter. A bright smile spread across her face, and she rushed to meet them. She was slightly taller than Libuat Alnaar but not quite as tall as Cyfeiriad. her eyes were a metallic gold with streaks of red bordered by green.

"My husband! It is so good to see you. You have been gone too long. How are you? How is Libuat Alnaar?"

"Where is my wife?" asked king coldly, holding out a hand to prevent the imposter's embrace.

"What do you mean? I'm right here."

"Do you think I really would not know my own wife after nine hundred years of marriage? Do you really think that I could not recognize her in any form?"

Masidus stepped toward her menacingly, and the false queen took a step back. A strange expression passed over her face, as if strained by mental effort. The imposter's expression darkened, her brows furrowed, and she glared up at Masidus.

"Don't test me, little jinn," she growled in a low voice. "I rule here, and you will bow like the rest of them."

Masidus winced and jerked his head back. Cyfeiriad wasn't sure, but sensed that the older jinni had attempted to mentally probe the false jinniya.

"Obviously, the king has lost his reason. Guards, take this filth from my presence," she commanded with a wave of her hand as she turned her back on them and began to walk away.

Mountain jinn approached from their positions on either side of the door and either side of the throne. Cyfeiriad and Libuat Alnaar each stepped out to one side of Masidus, preparing to deal with the interference.

"Stop," commanded the king, as he grabbed the false queen's arm.

"Don't you dare touch me," roared the false jinniya, her eyes flashing.

"Where is my wife!"

Masidus's form expanded, and he reached out with a giant fist and seized the false queen as his head and shoulder burst through the palace ceiling. Libuat Alnaar, Cyfeiriad, and the guards ran for the outer parts of the throne room as stone and glass shattered and rained down.

Cyfeiriad looked up in time to see the sky darken and a massive bolt of lightning strike the enraged monarch. A figure fell to the ground and landed on its feet.

Libuat Alnaar gasped somewhere to his left. He could hear the guards dropping their weapons and fleeing, but the elf didn't turn to look. Instead of the mature, yet strong jinniya stood a woman as tall as Masidus. She had long black hair pulled back and held by a gleaming metal band. Her wrists and ankles were adorned with wide, bejeweled golden bands. Her form was beautiful and strong, her exposed skin and demeanor displaying both a desire for admiration and a casual dismissal of environmental threats.

She took a step forward, and Cyfeiriad saw Masidus lying on the ground, once again his normal size.

"Know your place, little spark," said the woman in a menacing tone.

Masidus looked up at her as she approached and began to sit up.

The woman lunged and planted her foot firmly on his chest, slamming him back into the ground.

A large lioness bounded out of the shadows of the broken palace and attacked the stranger, knocking her back from the fallen jinni.

Cyfeiriad rushed out while the fight ensued and helped Masidus to his feet.

"Are you all right?"

"No retreat," said the king as he looked up at the battling titans.

The imposter managed to pull the lioness off, its teeth leaving huge gashes in the woman's neck and shoulder. She threw the lioness into a wall.

Masidus leaped across the distance and grabbed the woman from behind. She reached up over her shoulder, grabbed him, and brought him up, over, and down into the stone floor with a sickening crunch. The stranger raised her foot to stomp on his head, and Cyfeiriad thrust his right palm forward. The woman flew back and crashed into a pillar.

The stranger's eyes narrowed as she looked at the shocked elf. He hadn't been sure it would work, and now her wrath was aimed at him.

"How did you not burn with the rest of the scurrying little rats on that mountain," she said, getting up and stalking toward him.

Cyfeiriad looked around frantically for something to use and spotted a fallen spear that one of the guards had dropped. He reached out with his left hand, and it flew into his waiting grip. The elf spun back toward the woman and thrust the spear at her center of mass.

The woman's hand caught the shaft, and she snapped it with a twist of her wrist. She swung the broken piece of spear into the side of the elf's head. He fell, his vision blurred, and all he knew was pain. Blood ran down the side of his face.

He scrambled away and fought to regain control, before stumbling back onto his feet.

The woman was on him instantly, and he instinctively held out his hands and pushed with his mind. The imposter's body froze as if stopped by an unseen force.

The woman laughed. Cyfeiriad felt his knees buckle as the force from her downward moving arm drove him to the ground, though his mind still kept it from making contact. He could feel the force of her will increasing exponentially against his mind.

A massive serpent coiled around the woman, pinning her left arm to her side and sinking its fangs into her right shoulder. The woman screamed, and Cyfeiriad felt the force lift away from him. He watched as poison traced veins across the woman's upper body. She staggered back and fell, then grabbed the serpent's head.

Masidus ran over and grabbed the impostor's right arm and managed to pull it away from the serpent's head, holding the wrist tightly with his arms and pushing down and away with his legs, feet firmly planted against the snake's encoiled body.

"Now," shouted the king.

Cyfeiriad ran toward the struggling figures. He reached out toward the broken spear tip which flew into his grasp as he felt the air around them begin to move and the sky begin to darken above them once again.

The elf looked at the visage contorted in rage and brought the spear's point down through her forehead, pushing until he felt the metal tip collide with the stone.

The anger left her features, and the sky began to lighten. Her body went limp, and Masidus released his grip. The serpent uncoiled and tongues of fire licked over it until it was once again in the form of Libuat Alnaar.

The three of them stood looking down at the creature's strange golden eyes streaked with red and green.

Masidus sighed heavily; "The Enemy has indeed returned."

* * *

Libuat Alnaar surveyed the area around the sphinx gate from her vantage point high above. Her keen hawk eyes spotted the sentries spaced around the gate. It was not yet time for the next shipment.

Movement just to the east caught her attention. She circled around and examined a slope on the opposite side of a hill to the gate itself. A small animal was trying to dig its way into the sand.

Tilting her wings, she circled into position and dove. Before the animal had a chance to react, her talons had latched onto it, and she was taking it high into the air.

The creature began to struggle, and yellow-brown flames leaped over its body that quickly grew too heavy for her to carry. She dropped it, and the flames poured over it again, this time ending in the form of a bird. Libuat Alnaar turned in pursuit, crying out as she did.

The sentries below took notice. Within seconds, an arrow had pierced the fleeing bird's wing, dragging it back down to the ground.

Libuat Alnaar and the nearest sentry descended swiftly on their prey. Flames licked over her body while she transformed back into bipedal form as she landed.

"Please, just let me go," begged the mountain jinni, holding his injured arm, too distracted to try to shift it back together.

"I cannot allow you to warn our enemies," she said coldly, before reaching out with her mind and forcing him unconscious.

* * *

Cyfeiriad stepped out of the mist into the icy, frozen wasteland he had accidentally found when searching for a refuge for the elves. This time he was prepared, dressed in several layers of robes from the jinn. The moon shone brightly, its light reflected off the snow, illuminating the night. He wrapped a scarf tightly around his nose and mouth, then turned back to face the mist.

A jinniya dressed similarly stepped out of the mist. She was soon followed by several more jinn. They looked around at the ice-covered peaks before turning to the elf.

He counted them, making sure everyone was present.

"Good work, time to head home," he said, though his voice was immediately drowned out by the harsh winds.

Cyfeiriad took a step toward the mist wall. No one moved.

Home.

The group turned and followed him into the mist.

They stepped out into the cool desert night and went their separate ways.

A messenger handed him a note when he arrived back at the camp, an underground complex built to blend in with the dunes. He moved through the labyrinth with ease, arriving in a large hangar that housed a ship. It somewhat resembled the angular craft that the captive jinn had been building for the goblins, except its wings were broad and open. It was like a great metal bird with intricate patterns etched in its surfaces, inlaid with aether crystal.

"My father has agreed that we should explore the other realms as we continue our current operations to prepare for the possibility of war with the goblins," said Libuat Alnaar as she approached.

Cyfeiriad turned to look at her.

"There may be more enemies than we know or more allies than we expect. Either way, the more we learn of the wider world, the better off we are."

"That sounds like a good idea," commented the elf.

They both turned toward the craft, and she asked, "do you want to learn how to fly?"

Appendix I

The Aether

Aether is an elemental form of energy that forms the basis of the world tree. It is the substance from which the world tree is made.

The aether in Niwltir is known to leak in through various rifts. The jinn were the first species in Niwltir to discover such a rift and begin to study and experiment on the aether.

As the aether enters Niwltir, it mostly forms large crystalline structures with some of it dissipating into the surrounding environment. The end result is what frequently looks like a multicolored channel of crystal with whisps of plasma or mist drifting off of it.

The crystallized aether can be harvested, shaped, and used in various technologies that are unique to the inhabitants of Niwltir. Electrical current is used to destabilize the crystal in a controlled fashion, so it converts from a solid crystal into a manifestation of its particular element. Pressure can also be used to convert the aether crystal into its physical manifestation, but it is a cruder method not suited to precision that comes with the risk of fracturing the crystal.

The aether comes in several varieties, each representative of a different element. The four most easily identified are fire, water, wind, and earth. When a current is passed through a fire crystal, flames leap forth. When a current passed through a water crystal, water flows out. As the crystals are converted into their physical substances, they diminish in size. The jinn made use of these properties to devise many technologies more advanced than their counterparts.

These initial four are recognizable by the color of the plasma and crystals. Fire aether is red-orange, water aether is pale blue, earth aether is yellow-brown, and air aether is a misty grey. Very rare traces of other colors have been seen in the wafting plasmas, but no such crystals have yet been discovered by the jinn to allow for experimentation.

Did you like the book?

Recommend it to a friend.

Did you hate the book?

Recommend it to an enemy.

Best of all, don't tell them how you felt about it first.

Thoughts, comments, theories, or questions?

emrys@thewanderersnotebook.com

Made in United States
Orlando, FL
13 April 2024